# SOUTHERN CROSS

By the same author

*Hidden City*
*The Serpentine Wall*

# SOUTHERN CROSS

## Jim DeBrosse

ST. MARTIN'S PRESS • NEW YORK

*Production Editor: David Stanford Burr*

Library of Congress Cataloging-in-Publication Data

DeBrosse, Jim.
    Southern cross / Jim DeBrosse.
        p.  cm.
    ISBN 0-312-11070-7
    1. Decker, Rick (Fictitious character)—Fiction.    2. Missing persons—Caribbean Area—Fiction.   3. Journalists—Ohio—Cincinnati—Fiction.    I. Title.
PS3554.E1768S68    1994
813'.54—dc20                              94-6609
                                          CIP

First Edition: October 1994

10  9  8  7  6  5  4  3  2  1

For Madeleine and Patrick,
who slept so soundly while their father wrote.

*Every journalist who is not too stupid or too full of himself to notice what is going on knows that what he does is morally indefensible. He is a kind of confidence man, preying on people's vanity, ignorance, or loneliness, gaining their trust and betraying them without remorse.*

—Janet Malcolm

*My only obligation from the beginning was to the truth.*

—Joe McGinniss

# SOUTHERN CROSS

# Prologue

The phone rang at five till eight that Saturday morning. Decker groaned. With his head still anchored to his pillow, he reached out from his bed, stabbed the receiver, and settled it against his ear.

*"Kuh-noo! Kuh-noo! Kuh-noo!—"*

He pressed the mouthpiece against his cheek: "Damn you, Riley." He hung up, closed his eyes, and hoped for peace, but it was not to be. The phone rang again.

Decker grabbed it and snapped, "Alec!"

*"Kuh-noo! Kuh-noo!—"*

"Now?"

*"Kuh-noo! Kuh-noo!—"*

Decker tugged the blinds and knew he couldn't refuse: it was a sunny, delicious day. Janet was still in bed, sleeping off a sixteen-hour shift in the ER, but Decker went ahead and said why not. (*Why not?* He could still hear the blasé tone of his voice in those ominous words.) He hung up and Janet rolled over to his side of the bed and moaned a little. He found her mouth and kissed her slowly awake. Then, under a steady breeze fingering the curtains by the bed, they made a dreamy, effortless love and, still entwined, drifted off to sleep again.

They woke at noon, surprised to find the sun still waiting for them after so many weeks of rain and chill, and rushed to meet the Rileys at one.

Then there was the long drive out of Cincinnati in Alec's Jeep, he and Alec yukking it up with ancient stories about their high school exploits while Janet and Edie talked of more sober things quietly in the back.

Alec pulled off the road west of Lebanon, just short of the I-71 overpass, and showed off the Jeep's stuff by easing it down the steep embankment and across the mud flats to a wide patch of gravel below the bridge. They all agreed it was the ideal spot for putting in.

It wasn't until he hopped out of the Jeep that Decker heard the mean, steady hiss of the water—a sound that for weeks, months after would fill his anxious moments like endless white noise.

He studied the river for a moment. It was fast and high but glassy smooth, moving downstream in a continuous sheet about a hundred feet wide. Debris bobbed here and there in the swifter currents, and in spots along the banks the water roiled through dense jams of logs and litter. No one else was on the river.

"Are you guys sure this is a good idea?" Janet said.

"Piece o' cake," Alec answered, already unstrapping the canoes—two brand-new fiberglass beauties on a trailer behind the Jeep. "We've done worse, haven't we, Rick?"

"Are there life preservers?" Janet asked.

Edie spoke up. "Why, of course. Alec and I never go without them. I wouldn't allow it."

Decker shot Janet a look that said she was ruining the fun. She folded her arms and looked away.

Decker felt he and Alec had good reason to be confident. They were competent canoeists, and they had done this stretch of the Little Miami many times before. Just the same, at Janet's insistence, he donned a lifejacket.

Decker took the steering position in the rear of the canoe and Janet knelt in front, her heart-shaped bottom perched in readiness on her heels. Alec shoved them off the gravel, and the instant the canoe was buoyant, the river whisked them away with startling force. Decker's stomach sank a little: He paddled fast and hard to line them up with the current, feeling the river's muscle, fighting it, just below the smooth surface.

It was better once they hit midstream. The river was strong, but it was free of white water, and in most places, Decker knew, it rarely rose above the waist. Only the occasional log jam had to be avoided, and Janet was religious about warning him ahead of time.

Eventually Alec and Edie, an agile team, pulled out in front and led the way. Edie was good at spotting snags just below the surface, Alec at dodging them with a few deft strokes. Decker labored to follow in his course.

After rounding a long, loose bend through an open pasture and past a couple of befuddled cows, front legs planted in the stream, they reached a stretch where the river turned wide and slow and the trees grew thick on either side. Decker relaxed and let the river do the work, dipping his paddle every now and then to stay the course. Janet, too, let down her guard a little and sat with her paddle on her knees. In silence they marveled at the passing trees, nebulous in their fresh burst of April green. Birds called out from everywhere.

They heard giggling. Ahead, Alec and Edie were veering left toward shore.

"Go on," Alec said as Decker and Janet drifted by. "We're making a quick pit stop. We'll catch up later."

"A pit stop. R-i-i-i-ght," Janet teased, and Edie giggled like a schoolgirl.

Decker and Janet continued, lulled by the slow drift of water and the sun on their faces and the hushed twittering sounds of spring. They said nothing, harmonizing in their solitude. Suddenly, Janet pointed high to her right. A blue heron broke from a treetop, flapped its enormous wings once, twice, and glided in a half circle across the river. It disappeared into another treetop, the whole tree swaying pendulously under its weight. It was an awesome and eerie sight, a throwback to the days of dinosaurs and oversized living things. To utter a word would have broken the spell.

They were still voiceless a minute later when the canoe jolted and the fiberglass bottom began to pop and scrape.

Decker stabbed the water with his paddle, desperate to keep the canoe from rotating, but there was nothing he could do. They jammed sideways against the snag, listing toward the rushing current as the full might of the river bore down. Janet screamed but held on. Decker jabbed the tip of his paddle against the snag. He saw it—a thick, slimy log an inch or two below the surface—just before they tumbled in.

Decker's breathing ceased on impact: The river's icy fist plunged inside his chest, gripped his lungs, crushed his wildly beating heart. He surfaced in time to see the canoe flip bottom up and start downstream. He was thinking, oh shit, there goes Alec's brand-new canoe, when the current spun him around, slammed the back of his head against the log, and took him under.

He couldn't believe the angry force of the river. It was alive in its vengeance, clutching at his legs, his feet, yanking him down like a bully in a swimming pool. He kicked and flailed, the water rushing over his mouth and nose. He could taste river bottom deep in his throat.

Then came the self-defining moment—no more than five seconds, really. Less time than it takes to button a shirt on a lazy morning.

He turned and there was Janet, clinging to the log. In a panic, he lunged at her, grabbed for her lifejacket, for her neck, anything to break the river's pull. Janet lost her grip and they both went under, the water closing over like a collapsing wall.

Decker couldn't see, could only feel the black, angry swirl of water all around. His skull glanced against something hard and slick and he went deeper, Alice into the rabbit hole, helpless against a gauntlet of scrapes and blows as his body passed through the tangle.

Here the tape playing in his memory goes blank. Nothing recorded, nothing to play back. It seems as if the river, having found the challenge laughable, simply spewed him upward. What he remembered next was his head breaking above water, his greedy mouth stealing breath after breath.

He didn't think once about Janet until he looked back and saw the length of the river: empty and black as death.

He cried out her name. The birds mocked him from the trees.

He thrashed his way upstream, only to lose the few feet he had gained when he dived under and tried to see through the ooze.

He surfaced and called out her name again, to the sun, the clouds, the trees. His only answer was the mean, steady hiss of the river.

He clawed at the water in rage, turning in every direction to see, until he heard a deep frantic gasp, a scream in reverse. Not far from where he had emerged seconds before, he saw her head, tilted backward, mouth agape.

Decker swam after her, inching diagonally across the current as she whisked toward him downstream. When they intersected, he tried to take her arm, but she pulled away shrieking, "Don't touch me! Don't touch me!"

She was in pain, surely. Her face was gouged: four parallel cuts, from ear to mouth, red stripes on shock-white skin. He couldn't imagine what beast had left those marks until she turned and swam toward shore, and he felt the answer squeeze at his heart as though he'd plunged a second time into the icy river.

The marks were his—the red badge of his cowardice.

# 1

"Ah drop yoh by de comin' gap, okay, mon?" the driver said.

"Fine," Decker said, although he wasn't sure what the driver had said at all. Did they truly speak English in the Virgin Islands?

Decker sat back and took a deep breath. He could smell the sea close by, the dark brooding vastness of it, as the cab slowed to a stop within the lighted circle of a streetlamp. It was a sticky night in August, almost eleven, and the narrow, harborfront streets of Road Town, Tortola, lay choked and still under a heavy fog.

Next to the streetlamp was a metal stand-up sign, the kind gas stations use to advertise cheap beer and cigarettes. It said: Cruise Passengers, Pier One Straight Ahead.

Decker elbowed his partner, Rebo Johnson, whose head was flopped over the back of the seat.

"Huh?"

"We're here."

"You're kidding." Rebo stretched and yawned and looked at his watch. "Only took us—what?—sixteen hours."

They'd left Cincinnati at seven that Sunday morning, missed their connection in Miami, and spent six hours knocking around the Miami airport waiting for another flight to San Juan that wasn't filled. Then in San Juan, they'd lucked out and caught the last puddle jumper to Beef Island, the pilot landing, it seemed, by sheer instinct in the darkness and fog. That experience was topped only by the taxi ride from Beef Island to Tortola, the driver blaring his horn around the narrow, hairpin mountain roads to warn any hapless oncomers. Amazingly, Rebo had slept through the worst of it, while Decker, tensed and washed out, felt like somebody's knuckles around a roller-coaster bar.

The driver reached now through a curtain of hanging plastic beads, palm open. Decker slipped a ten into his hand and told him to keep it. The tip was more than twenty-five percent, but what the hell, Decker thought, it would probably feed his family for a week. The driver said nothing.

Decker and Rebo stepped outside and behind the cab, waiting for the driver to retrieve their bags. Instead, he popped the trunk from his seat and pointed, the ten spot still in his hand.

"How do you like that?" Rebo said. "A fine way to treat one of the brothers."

Rebo, Decker knew, was being facetious. He didn't trade on skin color; he didn't need to. He was six-four, 220 pounds, and he was arguably the best spot news photographer in the Midwest.

They got their own bags, but Rebo suggested they leave the trunk open: "I believe he could use the exercise."

"Good night," the driver said softly through his open window. "Mash de lid, please."

Decker moved closer. "Mash the lid?"

"Like dis." The driver raised his hands, brought them down again.

"Oh, close the trunk."

"Yes, mon. Mash de lid, okay?"

Decker could hardly refuse when it took him so long to understand. He mashed the lid gently, and the taxi sped away in a clank of gears and a cloud of smoke, leaving Decker and Rebo alone in the middle of nowhere.

"So this is the friendly Caribbean," Rebo said.

"We need a phone," Decker said, his mind shifting into work mode. He stuffed his hand in his pocket for change.

"Why?"

"Farlidge said we should check in." The truth was, Decker wanted assurance he hadn't been cut off from civilization. A good reporter always knew the location of the nearest phone. Phones were the umbilical cord of the profession.

"To tell Farlidge what?" Rebo said. "We finally got our asses down here? Let's get on this damn boat and phone in when we've got a story."

"All right, forget it."

Decker picked up his green duffel bag and slung the strap over his left shoulder. "Just what I've always wanted—an all-expenses-paid vacation in the Virgin Islands."

"Now *that's* the proper attitude."

On Friday, when word got around, Decker and Rebo had been the envy of the Cincinnati *Eagle* newsroom: They were being sent to the Caribbean on assignment, although no one but Farlidge and a few top editors had been privy to the details. Their mission: to investigate the disappearance of Justin Grammer, the twenty-two-year-old scion of one of Cincinnati's oldest and wealthiest families, whose early fortune in hog slaughtering had been sanitized generations ago into blue chip stocks and gold-plated securities.

Grammer had vanished five days earlier while cruising on the *Southern Cross*, a windjammer party ship plying the waters from Tortola to Antigua. Before that, Justin had been just one more struggling off-off-Broadway actor in New York, waiting, no doubt, for his family trust fund to kick in.

The AP story out of St. Thomas had been lean, to put it mildly: four graphs on the who, what, where, when, but none of the far more interesting how or why. Felix Grammer, Justin's father and patron of nearly every Cincinnati cultural institution from the ballet to the bug collection at the zoo, had refused comment, other than to announce through his lawyers that "the matter was in the hands of the British Virgin Islands police and the American consulate."

Since then, all three local TV news stations had dispatched reporters and camera crews down to the islands, but none had been permitted to board the ship or interview the passengers. The crews had sent back live stand-ups on the islands' sparkling beaches, drank themselves silly for a day or two, then packed up and headed home.

On Friday, two days after the AP story appeared, Farlidge had hatched the idea of booking last-second reservations for Decker and Rebo on the *Southern Cross*. Passage cost $3,000 each—a figure that galled Decker because he had been turned down for a fraction of that sum to finance a computer search of the county's tax assessment records, hoping to match lowered appraisals with generous donations to the local GOP. Who cared about old-fashioned graft? Papers like the *Eagle* were taking their cue from the TV tabloids: Hard-hitting celebrity journalism (a.k.a. "dirt") is what readers really wanted.

Decker had refused the assignment at first (it was an ethical, not to mention logistical, nightmare) despite Farlidge's thinly veiled threats of a transfer to the copy desk. Farlidge could fire him for all Decker cared. Now that he and Janet had split—permanently, it seemed—so had his last and only ties to Cincinnati. In the end, though, he had accepted, and he wasn't sure why, except that he had never seen the Caribbean.

Rebo refused help with his four pieces of luggage, most of it bulky camera equipment, including a "Road Warrior" portable film-developer and a brand-new digital scanner for transmitting his photos, via phone lines, back to the *Eagle*. Both pieces had their own black nylon carrying cases. His precious cameras and lenses were locked in a separate, foam-padded metal suit-case. Fully loaded, Rebo was a walking, state-of-the-art photo lab.

They started up the wooden pier.

"You're sure they're coming to meet us?" Rebo said.

"The agent said they'll send a launch."

"Even in this soup?"

"We can always find a motel." They had passed a string of cinderblock establishments in a rainbow of grimy pastels on their way to the pier.

"Ha," Rebo grunted. He had a way of compacting all the world's absurdity into that one small sound. "I didn't bring enough Raid to check into one of those places."

At the end of the pier, they dumped their bags in the trapped yellow light of a second streetlamp and peered into the harbor's foggy gloom. The outlines of a few ghost ships—big sailboats, really—were bobbing in the haze. There was no breeze to speak of; the warm, moist sea air seemed to bathe the lungs in brine. For the first time in months, Decker hadn't the least craving for a cigarette.

"Listen," he said.

"What?"

"Hear it?" Somewhere across the harbor a steel drum band was playing a painfully slow, off-key rendition of "Yesterday."

Rebo grunted again. "Bad steel music. I guess we're in the tropics after all."

Decker sat with his feet dangling over the end of the pier, studying the yellowish green flatness of the water in the pier's aureole of light, wondering how in God's name had he come to be here at this place, at this moment in time. Still, it beat sitting alone in his messy apartment and sucking down beers in front of the tube. If he kept himself busy now, he could go for hours at a stretch without thinking of Janet.

He reached for his duffel bag and pulled out a small notebook from a side pocket. Taped inside the cover was a color photo of Justin Grammer, a candid shot razored from a Yale freshman yearbook. (Farlidge had called on one of his Yuppie pals in the local Yale Club to supply the book.) He was a dreamy-looking kid, thin and delicate, left shoulder leaning against a massive old tree trunk in front of a white picket fence—somewhere, no doubt, on the family's Indian Hill estate. The youth had one hand stuffed in his front jeans pocket, the other flexed above his right temple, tucking a strand of his long dark hair behind an ear. The eyes were deep brown, haunted but somehow defiant, staring dead-on into the camera. In a nutshell, he looked bright, sensitive, persecuted, like the endless St. Sebastian portraits Decker had seen one summer in the Louvre—all that melancholy young flesh pierced by arrows.

Decker had been able to dig up very little on Justin's background before their departure from Cincinnati. He checked the *Eagle* clips and found his name mentioned in a couple of items—runner-up in the state doubles championship as a high school junior, one of the city's twelve National Merit finalists his senior year, and a sad-funny photo of a politely restrained Justin squiring some overweight society chick during a debutante bash at the Omni Netherland.

Decker had also chatted with the *Eagle's* society editor, Fawn Ellen Sutton, who made some quick calls to her sources, but none had seen Justin back in town since he'd left for Yale five years before. "Rumor has it he's been persona non grata around the Grammer household for several years now," Fawn Ellen had said. "His father, of course, is not pleased with his choice of career."

It appeared to be a classic case of young suicide—a too-perfect kid with a daddy he couldn't please. Still, twenty-two was a little old to be grappling with daddy problems.

"Are you looking at that damn picture again?" Rebo said. Decker shut his notebook. "It doesn't hurt to memorize."

"Hell, that shot's more than four years old. He could have a buzz cut by now and a couple of rings through his nose."

"I doubt it."

"Shows how much you know about college kids."

Rebo had certainly changed his own appearance in the last year, dating back to his marriage to a public health nurse he'd met while doing a photo spread on child victims of lead poisoning. He'd traded his dreadlocks for a close, natural cut and a pair of Malcolm X glasses. Decker teased him about looking like a funeral director.

Rebo stood his brushed metal suitcase on end and squatted on it, proof of its advertised indestructibility.

"Maybe we should build a distress fire," he said.

"They *have* to know we're here," Decker said. "Maybe there's a spotter."

Anyone could see they were Yankee turistos waiting for a cruise ship. Decker in a short-sleeve Oxford shirt and Docker pants, his summer uniform; Rebo in jeans and a red-green-gold Hawaiian shirt that had screamed for his attention from a duty-free shop in the San Juan airport.

Somewhere through the fog, the steel band savaged another tune, either "The 49th Street Bridge Song" or "I Can See Clearly Now." Decker had almost made up his mind on the latter when another sound came drifting their way—the chuffing and clacking of a small diesel engine. They both listened. In a while they could see a searchlight, a blind man's cane, sweeping back and forth across the water. The light touched the pier once, twice, and found them.

A bright feminine voice cut through the gloom like a silver beacon: "Hello there!"

Decker shouted back: "Are you from the *Southern Cross?*"

"You bet!"

The launch materialized about ten yards from the pier. A black deckhand with a flashlight was standing at the bow, a second was sitting at the tiller. Standing between them was the Great White Huntress herself, a tall, striking brunette, looking cool and crisp in blinding naval whites. As the boat tied up, she hopped onto the pier and greeted them with the first big smile they'd seen since arriving in the Caribbean.

"Welcome to the British Virgin Islands, Mr. Denker and Mr. Johnson." She put out her hand to Decker first.

"Actually, it's Decker. Rick Decker." It was nice to touch her hand. She had soft olive skin and warm brown eyes that seemed to like everything about you all at once. Her hair was loosely pinned back, and strands of it curled like tendrils down her neck. Somehow, she managed to look professional, instead of schoolgirlish, in white culottes and knee socks.

"I'm sorry, Mr. Decker. My name's Mary Beth. I'm the purser aboard the *Southern Cross*. Have you two been waiting long?"

"Not long at all," Decker answered cheerily. Rebo rolled his eyes.

"We always figure someone will arrive this late, air connections what they are these days."

The deckhands went about their work quietly and efficiently, unsmiling but not unpleasant, either. The one in the bow took their bags and, under Rebo's watchful eyes, set them carefully in the bottom of the launch. The tillerman helped Decker, and a disdainful Rebo, down into the softly rocking boat. Mary Beth followed and they were on their way.

"I understand you're both from Cincinnati." She was trying to make amends, it seemed, for having botched Decker's name. "I have a cousin up there who works for the airlines. Delta, I think."

"They have a hub there."

"Really?" she said, as if this was exciting news, then quite innocently asked, "What do you gentlemen do?"

Decker cringed as Rebo beat him to the lie. "We're in communications. I shoot the pictures, he does the words."

"How exciting! Well, you'll have plenty of opportunities to take pictures here."

As the launch chugged through the endless fog, Decker reviewed for the hundredth time the *Eagle*'s rules for going undercover—no other way to get the information (true); no offense committed greater than the one being investigated (that depended on what had happened to Justin Grammer); and no one placed in danger (not yet anyway). It was a question of situation ethics, although no one—least of all his editors—knew the situation.

The man at the tiller seemed to reckon his course by the tinkling sound of the steel band. Decker could see only a narrow skirt of black water all around. Occasionally, when the launch drew close enough, the smeary cabin lights of a sailboat slipped by. The *Southern Cross* seemed nowhere in sight until they broke into a clearing at the far end of the harbor and suddenly, looming before them like a cliff, was the ship's dark hull.

It was a sleek vessel, a three-masted schooner that reminded Decker (who knew little about sailing vessels) of the old Yankee clippers. The nostalgic effect was mitigated by the floodlights in the rigging and the din of passengers partying on deck. Several came to the rails and hooted and waved. Mary Beth waved back.

"You're just in time for the limbo contest," she told Decker. He attempted a smile.

Once on board, they followed Mary Beth through an open bulkhead to the ship's saloon—all dim and cozy inside, and stuffy from the heat. The decor was a kind of *Treasure Island*

Gothic: bench-and-table nooks of thickly varnished wood and well-worn leather; a low, curved ceiling hung with storm lanterns, and cathedral windows of fake stained glass. It was a kid's fantasy of life at sea: All they needed were some phony gold doubloons, which Decker discovered later was the currency at the bar.

At the back of the saloon, they followed Mary Beth down a spiral staircase to the cabin deck, where the *Treasure Island* motif continued with varnished walls and faded prints of tall ships and old navigation charts. The cabin hallway was narrow and the air cool and damp with a hint of brine in it. Decker could hear an overworked air conditioner somewhere down the hall.

Mary Beth led them to the last door on the left. Cabin number 2. She knocked first, then pushed the door open and let them in.

"Our cabins are never locked, in case of fire," she said. "However, we do our best to respect privacy."

The room was cramped but neat and, to Decker's disappointment, lacked a porthole. A double wooden bunk was built into the hull on their left. On the right was an alcove with a chest of drawers, a mirror, and a hanger rod. Just in front of it was a tiny, all-in-one bathroom: sink, toilet, shower head in the ceiling. If you cared to, you could sit on the toilet and take a shower. All in all, the cabin reminded Decker of a prison cell.

"Don't worry," Mary Beth said, as if reading his thoughts. "You won't be spending much time in here."

A deckhand arrived with the rest of their bags. Mary Beth squeezed past him to the door. "Come on up when you're ready, gentlemen. We wouldn't want you to miss the limbo contest. And don't worry about clothes." She eyed Decker's pants. "We're very informal aboard the *Southern Cross*. Most of us spend the week in our bathing suits."

She flashed them one last enveloping smile and vanished.

"You want lower or upper?" Rebo asked, stowing his camera equipment under the bunk.

"Doesn't matter," Decker said.

"I'll take the lower then. I used to fall out of bed as a kid."

"That explains a lot."

"Shut up."

Decker didn't have much to unpack—mostly T-shirts, shorts, and underwear, along with four reporter's notebooks, a handful of pens, and his laptop. Optimistically, he'd also brought along his snorkeling mask and fins, hoping he might have time to relax. He took out his clothing and shave kit and placed them on an empty shelf in the alcove. He decided to leave the rest out of sight in his duffel bag, which he stowed under the bunk next to Rebo's gear. He had one good shirt that needed hanging—a cotton madras Janet had bought him during a medical convention in Miami. Two years ago? Three? In all, they had lasted four years together before things ended with a whimper, not a bang.

Janet had carried the scratches from their canoe trip for nearly a month, during which time he could hardly bring himself to look at her. She tried to reason with him: It had been his survival instinct kicking in. She, or anyone, would have behaved the same way under the same circumstances. But Decker's pride resisted and, in time, he began secretly to blame her for his shame: It was she who had made him utterly dependent, the Earth Mother who had taken care of all his needs. In a crisis, what else could he do but throw himself at her?

They no longer talked about the incident after the cuts had healed, but the psychic scars only went deeper, at least for Decker. They stopped making love. Janet suggested counseling. Decker refused.

There followed a long stretch in which they both buried themselves in their jobs, and finally an argument one morning over some stupid little thing—he hadn't folded the laundry when he'd promised to. He would always remember the mundane setting: her digging through a laundry basket in the bedroom, him shaving in the bathroom, careful not to nick the underside of his nose, when she said very calmly, very matter-of-factly: "I don't want to live with you anymore."

When he returned from work that evening, her things were gone and the house seemed to hum in all its sudden, inexplicably empty spaces. There had been no tears, no fights, not even a note. Only later, when she told him she was now "seeing" her residency supervisor, did he feel depressed, panicky, angry, jealous, as though he were being held under water. Many nights, lying alone and disheveled on his sofa, he willed himself to sleep by imagining he was dead, obliterated, neutralized—that he had, in fact, drowned that Saturday afternoon in April.

"I don't know about you, but I'm doing as the Romans do."

Rebo slipped out of his jeans and pulled on a pair of lime green swim trunks with a blue whale print. They made a smashing ensemble with his red Hawaiian shirt.

"You look like a refugee from a Christmas luau," Decker said.

"Shut up, I'm undercover. What say we check out the action on deck?"

"I'll be up. Give me ten minutes."

Decker took a quick shower in tepid water (the only kind, he soon discovered, available on the *Southern Cross*), slipped on a pair of tan Bermuda shorts and exchanged his Rockports for some flipflops. He took a quick look in the mirror next to the sink. He had put on some weight since Janet had left—maybe ten, fifteen pounds. But then he'd always been too thin, anyway. At thirty-six, he looked closer to his actual age now—no more posing as a skinny teenage punk. He liked it that way. He got more respect; kids called him "sir."

He wondered what shirt to wear and, thinking what the hell, decided on the madras. Janet had always had good taste, although maybe not in men.

The main deck was bigger, and more ornate, than Decker had expected: a hundred feet of varnished teak surrounded by spindled mahogany railings and built-in benches. The bar was less impressive, almost utilitarian—a rectangle of beaded wood plunked down behind the foremast. Obviously not part of the original equipment.

The five-piece steel band was set up at midship, just in front of the jacuzzi, while a line of twenty or so dancers snaked around the mid-deck, waiting to go under the limbo pole. The band, at last, had found its stride, switching from half-hearted American oldies to island music, pouring its Caribbean soul into the night.

At the bar, the rum punch specials were moving like sodas in a cafeteria. The bartenders mixed big pitchers of the stuff—a potent blend of local rum, pineapple, and passion fruit—then set up rows of plastic tumblers and splashed the mixture down one row and up another as though watering crops.

Decker found Rebo at the end of the bar, sipping a margarita and watching the action on the dance floor. He was barefoot.

"You look mighty relaxed," Decker said.

He hoisted his drink. "Looks are deceiving. I'm scouting the scene."

"I guess I'd better get down to work, too."

He ordered a Heineken and surveyed the deck. There were about fifty passengers in all—an intimate number by cruise standards. Young couples. Retired couples. A few families with adolescent kids. But mostly it seemed to be singles, twenty-something and thirty-something professionals, determined to have a good time. They were the ones guzzling the rum punches in their bathing suits and clogging the dance floor.

He turned to Rebo. "Justin's recent demise hasn't affected the party mood, I see."

"I don't blame 'em. They paid enough for their fun."

The officers circulated freely among the crowd in their bright formal whites and bare feet, the official windjammer uniform. They were a young, tanned, Anglo-Saxon lot and, as Decker learned later, recruited from the best English naval schools. Everyone except Mary Beth, that is, who had been a private nurse in Miami. She mostly hovered near the captain, a short, troll-like figure with a dark beard and long red nose.

"I feel naked," Rebo said. "I'm getting my cameras."

"Be discreet. Don't bring your telephoto lens."

"You stick to the words. Leave the pictures to me."

The instant Rebo left, someone sidled into his place.

"Hi, Lyle Hughes." He grinned and pumped Decker's hand like a long-lost friend's. "I'm in the insurance business."

"No kidding?"

Lyle belly-laughed. "Don't worry. I'm not here to sell. Just used to saying that, I guess."

"Never hurts to advertise, huh?"

"You got it."

Lyle looked more like a burnt-out golf pro. He was taller, paunchier and a few years older than Decker, maybe forty, with a dark, even tan and sun-streaked hair. His blue eyes were glazed with an excess of booze. He spoke with a smooth Carolina drawl.

"You just get in?" Lyle asked.

Decker told him about the missed connection in Miami.

"Well, forget all that shit. It's time to get down and par-TAY. There's some dynamite-looking babes on board."

"I've met Mary Beth."

"There's a hell of a lot better than Mary Beth. Besides, she's diddling the captain."

"Diddling?"

"Yeah, how do you think she got her job? Hell, all she does is smile and write down names."

"That's still more than Vanna White does."

Lyle showed his appreciation with another belly laugh. "Hey, you're pretty funny, you know that. How long you sign up for?"

"A week."

"Just a week? Most of us signed up for two. Let me tell ya, it gets better every day. Where'd they bunk you?"

"Cabin two."

"No shit." Lyle grinned, holding back something.

"Why, what's the matter?"

"Nothing, except the guy who was in that cabin last week just up and disappeared."

"Really?"

"I personally think he took off for one of the islands and decided not to come back. Glad he did, too. One snotty little sonuvabitch. And weird, too. Took a Bible with him all the time, and never wore anything except blue clothes."

"You're kidding?"

"God's truth. He had this thing about blue. Said it gave him positive energy or something."

"Any ideas where he might have gone?"

"Who gives a shit?"

Lyle finished off his drink and signaled the bartender for another—a double Chivas on the rocks. It looked more like a triple. Lyle slapped down a handful of "doubloons" and lifted his cup.

"To getting laid," Lyle said. Decker took a sip on his beer

and watched Lyle chug, his Adam's apple bobbing like a trapped animal underneath the thick tanned skin. He wanted to ask Lyle more about Justin, but he didn't want to seem too eager.

"That guy who disappeared, did he have a roommate?"

Lyle rolled his eyes. "Only the best-looking piece o' ass on board."

"Who?"

"Take a look around the dance floor. See anybody you recognize?"

Decker took a glance. "No."

"Oh, Gawd almighty, look. She's about to go under the limbo pole." Lyle leaned close to Decker and unleashed a noxious gust of scotch vapors. "The one with the sarong thingie around her legs. That's Danielle Evans herself."

She was wearing a knitted bikini top—two triangular bits of orange cloth, each straining to handle its designated area of coverage. The "sarong thingie" was a delicate wraparound of flowered silk. It split the length of her left thigh as she spread her legs and began to fold herself under the limbo pole—pelvis bobbing, shoulders twitching—all in perfect rhythm to the beat. The pole seemed impossibly low, maybe two feet above deck, but Danielle had no problem. She was young, no more than twenty-two, and as lithe and sleek as an Olympic gymnast.

She shimmied under the pole to her chin and paused there a moment, balancing the weight of her body on her insteps. Then, with the crowd urging her on, she tossed her head back, slipped under, and snapped her body straight again—all in a single motion and with such force you could almost hear her spine twang. The deck exploded in applause.

"Sweet Mother of Jesus," Lyle said, shaking his head. There was a tone of pure reverence in his liquored voice.

"I'm sorry to ask this," Decker said, "but who is she?"

"Oh come on. You've never heard of Danielle Evans?"

Decker shook his head.

"She's the famous model, does all the Maybelline ads."

"Oh sure. *That* Danielle Evans." Decker was a celebrity illiterate. He decided he should pick up *People* magazine more often.

"I'll tell ya, that woman is so fine she could make a man crawl over broken glass just to lick her snatch. Know what I'm sayin'?"

"You have a way with words, Lyle."

Danielle embodied all the current modeling clichés: a healthy, glowing blonde with long, straight hair and pouty bee-stung lips. Her eyes seemed perpetually half-closed, as though she were terribly bored or—viewed more wishfully—about to open her mouth for a kiss. She was the center of attention, all right, but she paid a heavy price for it: every pose, every move, every facial expression seemed calculated to advertise Danielle Evans, Maybelline Girl.

Decker wondered why a top fashion model would book a windjammer cruise with a bunch of losers like Lyle. Why not lease a private yacht? Isn't that what the rich and famous did? Then again, nothing about her situation was very typical, not when your roommate is Little Boy Blue and he suddenly disappears.

On Danielle's heels in the limbo contest came a tiny brunette, at least a head shorter than Danielle, but not so limber. Still, she gave it her perky best and was doing quite well until her chin reached the bar. That's when she lost her balance and dropped with a soft thud to her sweet little bottom. To polite applause, she picked herself up, flushing now with embarrassment. Danielle bounced over and folded her in a hug.

"That's her friend Ellen," Lyle said, and added from the corner of his mouth, "Jewish."

"Really? You mean they're allowed on these cruises?"

Lyle missed the fast ball. In fact, he never got the bat off his shoulder. Decker would have excused himself, only Lyle was loose and supplying too much good information.

"You said Danielle was rooming with this guy who disappeared," Decker said. "Where's she rooming now?"

"They moved her in with Ellen," he said. "She was scared, I guess."

"Scared of what?"

"Hell, who knows. There's all kinds of crazy shit going down on this ship."

"Crazy? Like what?"

"I don't know. These nigger deckhands are up and around all night, for one thing. Gives me the creeps."

"Did I hear somebody call my name?"

Lyle snapped his head around so fast Decker could hear the vertebrae crack. Standing behind Lyle was Rebo, all six feet four inches of him. He had a camera hanging from each broad shoulder.

"Lyle, I'd like you to meet my roomie, Rebo Johnson."

Lyle collected himself enough to shake hands, then quickly excused himself.

"Who's the colonel?" Rebo asked. "He's got a nasty mouth."

"And a big one. He gave us lots to go on." Decker told him about Justin and Danielle, then pointed her out in the crowd.

Rebo blinked and popped his eyes wide. "My, my, this assignment gets more rewarding by the minute. Excuse me while I slip away and snap a few shots of our principal subject here. Very discreetly, of course."

The steel band wrapped up the night with "Yesterday," and, to drunken applause, started packing up. The night seemed to be winding down until a raspy, drunk male voice somewhere on the dance floor shouted, "Hit the damn tape, Maurice!" and, a few seconds later, "Twist and Shout" bumped like a shock wave from the two big speakers on the foremast.

The dance floor flooded with frantic young bodies in motion, stripped down to their bathing suits, perfumed and sweaty in the Caribbean heat. The real party had begun.

Decker pulled a long chug to finish off his Heineken and thought, Ah, sweet wasted energy of youth. He decided to go off to bed.

He scanned the deck for Rebo and was surprised to spot him in the middle of the action, twisting with Danielle. He seemed to be humoring her, barely moving his big feet and shoulders, while Danielle gyrated around him with total abandon, all parts of her bobbing, twitching, jiggling. She was one drink shy of sloppy drunk but still on her feet, her well-conditioned body to thank for that. Ellen was dancing nearby, alone and painfully conscious, it seemed, of every movement of her pale limbs. After a closer look, Decker realized she hadn't much youth to abandon; she was a good ten years older than Danielle. You could see it in the weariness of her eyes.

Decker spotted another interesting couple—a lanky teenage girl in a black maillot and pink shorts dancing with Kevin, the ship's first mate. The girl's hair was dyed black and buzzed over the ears. She held her hands behind her head as she danced, pelvis undulating—fifteen aching to be thirty. Kevin's age was harder to peg; anywhere from nineteen to twenty-nine. He was an overgrown schoolboy, tall, blonde, almost as lanky as his partner. The prom-night gleam in his eye was unmistakable: He expected to get lucky that night.

Danielle raised her arm and beckoned Decker to join in. "Come on! Don't be a geek!"

He hadn't heard "geek" since college, but he was old enough now, and secure enough, to know it was a pretty fair description of what he was. He smiled and waved her off when another young woman in a black one-piece suit danced out of the crowd, bare shoulders shimmying, hips rocking, and grabbed him by the hand.

"Come on," she teased. "Join the fun."

She was blonde, about Janet's age and height, but without the softened edges. She seemed more blunt, more sophisticated somehow. Perhaps it was the trendy haircut: straight and combed to one side, then chopped thickly along the clean line of her jaw. She had blue eyes like Janet, too, only different— icier, more intense.

"Come on, you can do it. I know you can."

Something playful in her voice caused him to twist low to the floor, surfer-style, and she gasped and gave him a mock startled look from the corners of her eyes. Somehow he found his old college mixer form and he yanked her by the hand and they spun off together, a couple of gyros bumping and twirling around each other. Her blunt cut spun out whenever she twirled. When she smiled, the blue eyes narrowed and sparked and seemed to pulse with a life all their own.

A second or two before the music died, he stopped and stood there, suddenly conscious of dancing with a stranger.

"Very impressive," she said, "—for a geek."

"Thank you, if that's a compliment."

"Only to a geek." She smiled. Her bluntness was cushioned by the merest trace of a soft Southern accent.

She offered her hand and looked him square in the eye. "I'm Leslie Stanton. Who are you?"

There was time for chitchat while someone fiddled with the sound system. Leslie asked what he did. "Communications," he answered, and quickly asked her the same. A beat later, the big speakers rattled with the first few chords of "Jumpin' Jack Flash." The dance crowd shrieked.

"I teach phys ed," Leslie shouted over a thumping bass.

"You what?"

"I teach physical education."

"Really?"

"You were expecting someone in comfortable shoes?"

Just when Decker thought the evening could hold no more surprises, he caught something from the corner of his eye: Danielle was staring at him. He turned his head and she looked away. He was mystified. Decker fancied himself many things, but never the cause of feminine rivalry.

When the rock music segued into the bluesy intimacy of "Unchained Melody," most of the dancers stopped cold, uncertain how to handle the awkward transition with their partners. Danielle had no trouble making up her mind: She threw herself at Rebo. Decker could see the sweat breaking out on his colleague's face as Danielle draped her long, cool arms around his shoulders and laid her head against his chest.

"May I have this dance?" There was Leslie, ice blue eyes smiling up at his.

Why not? he thought. He reached for her waist and thought of Janet as his hand fit snugly in the soft curved niche just above her hip, resting easy, as though his hand belonged there. He shuffled off into his all-purpose two-step and Leslie followed with uncanny anticipation, so smooth and assertive that, by almost imperceptible degrees, she began to lead and he to follow.

Decker supposed she could throw a baseball the way a man would, too, putting plenty of arm and shoulder into it; he could respect that. But at the same time it didn't cancel the things that were feminine and inviting about her—the glossy smoothness of her tanned skin, the strong, clean curve of her jaw.

The Righteous Brothers were still ooh-ing and ahhh-ing over the big speakers, being so righteous, when Decker spotted trouble coming in the form of Lyle Hughes. He charged onto the dance floor, arms swinging loose at his sides. He slapped Rebo's shoulder, impatient to cut in. Rebo stepped aside, only to have Danielle shoot Lyle a look that would have burned holes in a rubber life raft. Lyle froze, startled into momentary sobriety, his arms still positioned in the air. A tense second later, it was all over. Lyle shook his head, turned, and walked away.

Leslie had seen it, too. "Poor baby," she said, but she was smiling when she said it.

"Poor jerk," Decker said.

"True," she said, giving Decker's hand a little squeeze, "but unrequited lust is such a terrible waste. Don't you agree?"

Decker stopped in midstep. His whole day had been a long ride on a runaway train, and now that it had finally slowed down, he was ready to jump off.

"Thanks for the dance," he said.

"Thank *you,*" she said in her best honeyed accent. "I'm the one who asked."

Decker decided to have a peaceful moment by himself before turning in. He walked away from the unquiet loneliness and lights of the dance floor and up the sloping foredeck. He passed the open forecastle hatch—the banter of the deckhands pulsing in waves from their steamy quarters—and stepped carefully through the clutter of an honest sailing vessel: cleats, tacks, rusty anchor chain, the neatly coiled piles of hemp that left a dusty bite in the air, like hay pollen in a barn.

He stood alone in the dark by the railing. The fog had lifted in every direction and the night air was crystalline. He stared upward through the rigging at the bright sprinkle of stars and then around to the necklace of lights surrounding the bay. Turning and looking out to open sea, he felt on first glance that piercing melancholy sweetness that only the sea can give—of utter loneliness and yet oneness with something vast and mysterious and overpowering.

But as he soon discovered, he was far from alone: Giant island bats (he thought they were swallows at first) were flapping around the hull, skimming the water for small fish lured into the ship's peripheral light. A dip and a splash and the bat would rise with a shiny treat wriggling in its teeth.

Decker shivered and looked beyond the bay again. Sky and sea were fused in a single blackness and the only way to distinguish the two was to watch where the shower of stars drowned and disappeared. Far to his left, just short of the horizon, was a bright cluster of four stars, a diamond shape obliquely inverted, like a flaming kite out of control. He was surprised that he could identify it almost immediately, having never seen the constellation before: the Southern Cross, plunging headlong toward the sea.

He lifted his face to the breeze and thought for a moment of Janet—the other Janet—the one of good times he tried always to keep separate in his memory, the one he wanted beside him now, just the two of them, staring into the night. There were still times when nothing he experienced seemed quite real without her, as if his own taste and judgment, even his senses, had to be validated by the assent of her voice or her touch.

He killed the mood himself, drowning it in fatalism. If he had lost her, he told himself, it was because he had never deserved her in the first place. It was no use. He had to let it go. He had to move on.

He took a last deep breath of sea air and walked away.

When he opened the cabin door, he found Rebo sitting on the bottom bunk. He was hunched in worry over the photo scanner in his lap, his wounded baby. The room was a mess—drawers dumped, bunks stripped, the floor cluttered with clothing and the scattered contents of their bags.

"Oh man," Decker said, fear and anger hollowing out his stomach.

Rebo rattled the scanner like a box full of broken toys. He looked hurt, dumbfounded.

"We can get it fixed, can't we?" Decker said.

"No way. The CPU's been yanked out of the damn thing."

Decker stepped around the room, kicking scattered items in disgust. "Is anything missing?"

"Oh, just your laptop. And my backup cameras. The portable developer is a piece of shit now, too."

"Jesus, Rebo, *why?*"

"I'll tell you why—because we've been found out, that's why."

"You think it was the crew?"

"The crew would have kicked our asses off the ship and been done with it. Somebody's trying to put a scare in us."

"But they had to be looking for something."

"They could look all they want without bustin' up our shit."

"Should we pull out?"

Decker looked steadily at his partner, the almost cocky calm of his eyes, the hard set of his jaw. Like a couple of junior high kids, they had a way of egging each other on, daring each other to new heights—or in this case, perhaps a new low.

Rebo cracked a thin smile. "Hell, no. I'm havin' too much fun."

Decker kicked a loose can of shaving cream, soccer-style, with his instep. It landed softly in Rebo's open suitcase. Decker turned and smiled. "Me, too, pal."

# 2

At 6:30 A.M., the only sound on the deck of the *Southern Cross* was the soft padding of bare feet as the crew went about its work, silently, efficiently, the peace of the islands showing in their strong black faces. They unfurled the sails, coiled the lines, and prepared the anchor for weighing, while Kevin, the young and lanky first mate, moved here and there among them, quietly dispensing orders and pitching in where needed. He looked bleary-eyed but contented, entirely in his element. Chances were, he'd gotten lucky with his Madonna wannabe the night before.

"Where we headed this morning?" a passenger asked.

"Virgin Gorda," Kevin answered.

"The Baths?"

"Yes, then off to Spanish Town for the night."

At that hour, the mighty Caribbean sun was a pale orange wafer pinned above the misty hills of Tortola, the harbor water a peaceful expanse of leaden gray. To the east, though, along the horizon, big clouds were beginning to break and clear, pinking around the edges, and from the west, the tradewinds, pungent with island blooms, were building up momentum for another day of steady breezes.

Sticky-skinned and sleepy-eyed, Decker joined a handful of passengers already on deck. He was relieved not to find Leslie or Danielle or any of the raucous crowd of the night before, but an older group who apparently, like Decker, had had trouble sleeping. Decker had woken at five, his mind racing with all the logistical problems inherent in the Justin Grammer story, while

Rebo, oblivious in the bunk below, snored away. Decker needed to talk to Danielle, to Ellen, to the local police, and he would have to do it without blowing his cover—or what was left of it now that someone had ransacked their cabin. Worse still, with his laptop gone, he would have to dictate his story over the phone, with Farlidge sniping at every word.

*Que será, será,* he told himself as he watched the morning mist rise in tendrils from the hills. Whatever will be, will be. Right. Well, too bad he wasn't Doris Day: he'd simply tell Farlidge he wasn't that kind of girl, dump the assignment, and go home. But here he was, caught up in the chase for celebrity dirt like one of those cocky reporters for the TV tabloids with the phony British accents, pretending that a Pulitzer hung in the balance. But, dammit, Rebo was right: It beat going back to Cincinnati and writing stories about the August heat.

He scouted the harbor. There were far more boats there than he had realized the night before. Dozens of white yachts and sailboats, a sprinkling of windjammers—although none as trim and fine as the *Southern Cross*—and sidled along the easternmost pier, a big cruise liner, vapor rising from its winged smokestack like an offering to the island gods.

He looked back across the deck toward the heart of Road Town, Tortola—the most populous city in the British Virgin Islands—and yet there were no high rises or gambling casinos or slick condos marring the view. Somehow Tortola had escaped the developers' greed that had blighted so many other Caribbean islands, and Road Town lay nestled like a pearl between the cleavage of its bright green hills.

A kitchen hand came up with a plastic tray full of mugs, coffee thermoses, sticky buns, and—for the diehard drinkers on board—pitchers of Bloody Marys. He set the tray on the bench across from the bar. On his heels was Leslie Stanton, looking quite different from last night, almost tomboyish, in a loose white T-shirt and khaki shorts. In daylight, Decker could see how deeply tanned she was—polished to a smooth bronze gloss—and how the sunlight had bleached her hair and eyebrows almost white. Her whole body seemed somehow to have fused with the sun and survived.

The early risers converged at once on the breakfast tray, including Decker. Leslie was there first. She filled one of the plastic cups with coffee and handed it to Decker.

"Here," she said. "You look like you could use this."

"That bad, huh?"

She smiled and he saw now what gave her eyes such intensity: They were a deep, deep blue, with threads of gold all raveling inward toward the blackness of her pupils, creating a kind of kaleidoscopic pull. He couldn't look at them for long without feeling a touch of vertigo.

"First night on a ship is always bad," she said. "You'll get used to it. Would you like creamer?"

"Yes."

She poured him some from a tin dispenser, then got some coffee for herself.

"Why don't we sit?"

They settled on one of the built-in railing benches, not far from the breakfast tray. Decker took a sip of his coffee and nearly spat it out.

Leslie chuckled. "A little briny, hmmmm?"

"Somebody must have added salt by mistake."

"It's the filters on the desalinator. I understand one of them is broken."

"They make their own water?"

"Such as it is. You'll get used to that, too."

"I take it this is your second week."

"Yes, but I've been on these cruises before. What about yourself?"

"First-timer."

"Hmmm, a virgin. Did you sign up for one week or two?"

"Just one."

"You'll regret it. Put another on your credit card."

"If I could get the time away from work," he said, and instantly wished he hadn't.

"Communications must be a very *demanding* line of work," she said. "What is it you do exactly?" She was all ears now, mug by her side, hands around her polished knees.

"Corporate communications."

He told himself it wasn't far from the truth, many newspapers being what they were these days. Still, he felt a bit like Peter as the cock crowed for the third time.

"Where?" she asked.

"Cincinnati."

"I've never visited there. I've been to Cleveland, though. I have an aunt there."

"There's a big difference."

She smiled. "Why? They're both in Ohio."

Decker let it pass. "Where do you live?"

"Washington."

"You teach phys ed there?"

"In Alexandria, actually. There's a *big* difference."

She got him to laugh, then he said, "Of course, you've wanted to be a phys ed teacher all your life."

"No, I always wanted to be an astrophysicist, but I failed calculus in college. I've learned to adjust." The blue eyes sparked with mischief.

He tried to get things back on track. "So how was your first week on board?"

She sighed. "Relaxing. The weather was perfect. A dearth of single men, however." She smiled again; Decker let that slip by, too.

"I heard one of the men disappeared. Is that true?"

"If you're talking about Justin, I don't think 'disappeared' is the right word."

"What do you mean?"

"Personally, I think he committed suicide."

"Really? How?"

"I think he jumped overboard in the night. That's been known to happen on cruises."

"Does anybody know why?"

She gave him a quizzical look. "Are you a policeman by any chance?"

"No, just curious."

"You sound an awful lot like one. You know, I used to date a cop until he had the audacity to inform me that my breasts were too small." She put her chin against her chest, tugged at her T-shirt, and inspected herself.

"What do *you* think?" she asked.

"I think you have a very bizarre sense of humor." He meant it as a compliment.

"Really?"

"Yes. And it's the cop's loss, not yours."

"How sweet of you to say." She fluttered her eyelids in mock embarrassment.

Decker tried to regain control of the conversation. "This Justin person who disappeared—what makes you think it was suicide?"

"Broken heart," she said, serious again.

"By whom, Danielle?"

"Whom? I like that. You have a real respect for the language."

"I'll take that as a compliment."

"You know what," Leslie said. "I think what you really are is a reporter."

"You think so?" He didn't know what else to say without lying.

"I know so. Because you always answer questions with a question."

He laughed, despite being angry with himself. "I'm that obvious?"

"Of course. But not everyone is as astute as I am."

He struck a confidential tone. "Can we keep it that way?"

She appraised him for a moment with the icy blue eyes. "I think so."

"All right, then, let me ask you something else. If Justin committed suicide, why isn't Danielle grieving?"

"Danielle isn't the grieving type."

"Really?"

"You'll learn that soon enough. What else would you like to know?"

"Could Justin have been hiding something somebody wanted? Drugs? Money?" Decker was thinking about the ransacking of their cabin—previously Justin's. It made no sense, unless the intruder had been looking for something and only by accident had discovered their electronic equipment. But then why steal and destroy it? If somebody wanted them off the ship, all they had to do was tell the captain.

"I doubt Justin had anything to do with drugs," Leslie said. "In fact, I never saw him take a drink. He was too much of a health nut. What makes you ask?"

"No reason, really. Just covering the bases."

"Oooh, nice metaphor. Is that reporter talk?"

Kevin suddenly shouted across the deck, "We need volunteers!" He was standing at the foresail, holding a halyard line that snaked a good twenty feet behind him along the deck.

"This is it." Leslie set her coffee down. "Come on now. You can play reporter any time."

Leslie went over and picked up the line behind Kevin. Decker decided what the hell and fell in behind Leslie. Half a dozen other men and women did the same.

Without warning, the voice of Judy Collins, as sweet and pure as the morning air, poured from the bar speakers, singing the first few notes of "Amazing Grace," and that's precisely when Kevin began heaving the line. Leslie picked up the slack right on cue, getting her weight into it, but Decker missed by half a beat and nearly lost his balance as the line went limp in his hands.

"Look lively, mates!" Kevin shouted. He was pulling line like a madman.

Decker at last caught the rhythm, putting his legs and back into it, so that the tension on the rope and the work of raising the sail was transmitted evenly down the line. The scenario was more than a bit hokey: a bunch of hungover cruise passengers playing at sailor while Judy Collins sang the movie score. Still, Decker broke out in goosebumps as he watched the foresail climb toward the brightening clouds, flapping and luffing, a wild bird eager to fly, while Sweet Judy Blue Eyes belted out that haunting melody, the notes rising and falling as irresistibly as the ocean waves:

A-a-A-A-A-zi-i-ING gra-A-Ace, how SWEET the sound, that sa-A-A-AVED a-a-a WRETCH li-iKE ME-E-E. I-I once wa-as LOST, but NOW I'm found. BLIND, but NOW I s-e-e-e-e . . .

The moment all three sails were in place, Captain Pearce brought the bow around to catch the wind. As if by magic, the sails filled and quieted and the deck creaked and keeled ever so slightly to starboard. Within seconds, the *Southern Cross* was headed east-southeast out of Road Town harbor on a close reach, chopping through the slate gray waters of early morning toward Virgin Gorda.

Leslie and Decker made their way across the slowly rolling deck and rewarded themselves with a second cup of saltwater coffee and some cake donuts. Leslie poured while Decker inspected his hands: He'd opened raw blisters across the tops of both palms.

Leslie caught him inspecting the damage. "Those look pretty nasty. I have some iodine down in the cabin."

"I'm all right."

"You should wear gloves when you're a novice. Sorry I didn't warn you."

"Tell me more about Justin Grammer."

"Like what?"

"Like what kind of person he was. Who did he hang out with? What was he doing on the night he disappeared?"

"I'm not the best one to ask."

"Just give me something to start with."

"All right." They sat and she tucked one of her tanned, muscled legs underneath her on the bench. She took a moment to collect her thoughts, staring off across the water, mesmerized, it seemed, by the passing waves while the wind rushed through her hair.

"He was rather eccentric, actually. He had this thing about wearing blue—blue shirts, blue pants, blue shoes."

"A New Age type?"

"I suppose. He believed the color blue was deeply relaxing, even curative. Something to do with light amplitude and brain waves, all that sort of thing."

"I understand he also carried an old Bible around with him."

"Yes, he would go off sometimes and read it by himself. He never proselytized, thank goodness."

"When was the last time anyone saw him?"

"I saw him on the ship around two A.M. Just before I went to bed. He was standing at the bow, looking at the stars."

"Was he acting strangely?"

"No, not really. Unless you think it's strange to look at the stars." She smiled impishly.

"No." He wondered if Justin had noticed the Southern Cross, just as he had the night before.

"Where was Danielle?" he asked.

"I have no idea. She could have been in Spanish Town. We were anchored there."

"We're headed there again tonight."

"Yes, I think so."

"What kind of place is it?"

"A little beach resort on Virgin Gorda. Pretty seedy, actually. One open-air bar after another, all the way down the beach. It's more popular with the locals than the tourists, but some people like that. I call it slumming."

"Did Justin go in?"

"I don't know. I stayed on board that night."

"Who did he hang with—I mean besides Danielle?"

"No one, really. Well, except Ryan."

"Who's Ryan?"

"A boy—about thirteen, I think. He's here with his mother and sister. He doesn't have anyone his own age on board, so Justin kind of took him under his wing."

"That was nice."

"Yes, Justin was nice. Very sensitive, I think."

Leslie was distracted by the approach of a tall, middle-aged man, who managed to look distinguished even in a pair of swim trunks and a Hilton Head T-shirt. He had the requisite touch of gray at the temples and the sharp features and piercing eyes of, say, Gregory Peck. He was lean and muscled and confident.

Decker was surprised to feel a pang of jealousy as Leslie watched the man stop at the serving tray and pour himself some coffee.

"Who's that?" Decker asked.

"I don't know. He's new." She was still staring.

"I could ask him to join us."

Leslie stared a moment longer, then turned to Decker and said, "What? Oh sure. The more the merrier."

Decker caught the man as he turned from the tray, coffee in hand, and introduced himself. "Would you care to join Leslie and me?" He pointed over to where Leslie was sitting, bronze legs tightly crossed. She grinned and hoisted her coffee cup in greeting.

"No problem," the man said, as if Decker had somehow imposed upon him.

His name was Tony Henderson, a former navy officer now working as a geological engineer for some offshore drilling concern in Houston. He spoke as though reading from the company's annual report—meticulous and self-important—but Leslie seemed to hang on every word. Decker decided she was a shameless flirt, albeit in the self-parodying manner that certain spirited Southern women seem to have. He doubted Tony would know that.

Decker was relieved when a deckhand breezed by ringing a handbell, alerting passengers to the first breakfast sitting. It was almost seven-thirty.

He promptly excused himself and found Mary Beth in the saloon, where he got a quick rundown on the day's itinerary, then returned to his cabin. He found Rebo still in bed, snoring noisily on his back, his size-twelve feet overshooting the bunk.

He poked Rebo's arm and the snoring went out of kilter. A few more pokes and the head rolled over.

"What?"

"You're missing some great sunrise shots."

Rebo stretched, yawned, grunted hugely, and ended the performance by smacking his lips. "We're not doing a travel piece, dammit. Let me sleep."

"Come on. Get your butt out of bed. We've got a big day to plan."

He ran down the day's itinerary. At noon, the ship was due to anchor at the Baths of Virgin Gorda—a pile of volcanic rocks at the southern tip of the island, reputed to offer some of the best snorkeling in the Caribbean. Launches would leave the ship every half hour between noon and two, then start bringing passengers back at four. At five, the ship would set sail for Spanish Town, a few miles north along the island, and anchor there for the night. Launches would leave every hour on the hour until one in the morning.

Decker ticked off their "To Do" list. Decker would have to talk to the Spanish Town police before filing his story that night, while Rebo got shots of the police and maybe the local bar scene. And while Decker wrote his story, Rebo would have to find his way by ferry to the AP office in St. Thomas, where he could develop his film and transmit his photos back to the *Eagle*—all before their 9:00 P.M. deadline.

"Is there any room in this tight-ass itinerary of yours for a little fun?" Rebo asked.

"We could do some snorkeling this afternoon."

"Breathe through a tube? No, thank you. I'll wait until I'm brain dead."

"Mary Beth also mentioned a place in Spanish Town called Rudy's. Eighteen dollars for all the lobster you can eat. I signed us up for tonight."

"Now you're cookin'."

* * *

They went up to the saloon together where they were greeted with the strong, appetizing aromas of bacon and coffee. Decker spotted Leslie in the middle of a crowded table, sitting next to Tony the Bore. Her eyes caught Decker's for a second, just long enough to let him know she was looking. He liked that, even if she was a shameless flirt.

Decker and Rebo found a table with some empty place settings and scooted into the wraparound bench. There were quick introductions all around. At the table was a pair of college-age twins from Virginia, Melanie and Winston, male-female variations on the same fresh-scrubbed beauty and soft brown eyes. Next to Winston was an attractive fortyish woman with auburn hair named Maureen Daugherty, with her two children, Connie, the Madonna wannabe who'd been gyrating with Kevin the night before, and her son, Ryan, whose face was buried in a Nintendo Game Boy. Decker remembered Leslie's mention of the boy as Justin's adopted orphan child.

When it was Ryan's turn to be introduced, his mother reached over and grabbed the Nintendo. "It's not polite at the table, dearie."

Ryan looked up, annoyed but compliant, and Decker saw in one heart-piercing glance the red hair, the blue eyes, and the singular flaw in the boy's All-American face—a harelip. The defect had been repaired, certainly, but the scar still tugged at the bottom of his nose, flattening it a little and skewing it toward the right side of his mouth.

While the adults conversed, Connie looked cramped and bored sitting between her mother and younger brother. She quietly scolded Ryan for leaving toast crumbs in the butter. Sulking, he started scraping them away. The boy was getting it from every direction. Decker decided to even the sides.

"Ryan, you plan on snorkeling at the Baths today?"

The boy looked up for a second, then down at his plate again. "I don't know. I guess—"

"Why not?" Decker said. "They say it's the best snorkeling in the Virgin Islands."

When Ryan didn't answer, his mother said straight out, "He's looking for a partner." Ryan blushed, heightening the paleness of the scar below his nose.

"You got one now," Decker said.

After breakfast—a Heart Association nightmare of sausage links, bacon, eggs, grits, toast, and pancakes—Decker and Rebo returned to their cabin. While Rebo fiddled with his stash of film, Decker grabbed his book and his sun block and went on up to the main deck. There he found the Caribbean morning in all its glory: deep turquoise sea, sky of silver blue, and along the horizon, mountains of sun-burnished clouds, billowing and growing like masses of living matter. In every direction, the view seemed to shimmer and pulse, a mirage concocted of sun and wind and sea. He could blink and it would all disappear.

The ship was several miles now into the open waters of Sir Francis Drake Channel and picking up speed. You could hear the muffled swoosh of the bow plowing through the waves, the ancient sound of creaking wood, and, every now and then, the wind humming eerily through the lines. They were leaving behind the moss green mountains of Tortola and tacking due east toward the outer, less-settled islands—Dead Chest, Salt, Cooper, Ginger—a string of emeralds leading north to the crowning jewel, Virgin Gorda. Scattered among even these smaller islands were tiny deserted islets, their rocky slopes covered in bougainvillea, mango, cactus, and banana, all tumbling down to the sea in a strange arid and tropical mix.

By 9:00 A.M., the sun was glinting off the waves in dazzling points of light and the ship's varnished deck was beginning to sizzle. The intensity of the sunlight was like none Decker had ever experienced: Individual photons, like tiny phosphorescent pearls, seemed to ricochet in the backs of his eyes. Even so, the heat was made bearable at that hour, or any hour, by the ever-constant trade winds.

Soon after breakfast, the passengers began their day of sun worship, stripping down to bathing suits, slathering on oils and lotions. Some popped pills or wore medicated patches to ward off the inevitable seasickness. Those who felt like chatting gathered in small groups around the bar, while the loners curled up with a book on one of the soft foam mattresses scattered about the deck. The more adventurous crawled out to the widow's nest—a loose netting of thick rope strung along either side of the bowsprit. There they could sun themselves a few feet above the ship's plunging bow, every now and then catching the spray.

It took Decker a while to find his sea legs as he made his way unsteadily around the ship. He refused to medicate himself against seasickness, believing it was simply a matter of asserting mind over stomach. Dizzy at times, he closed his eyes to block out the chaotic data beyond the ship—the wavering horizon, the swirl of sea and sunlight and screaming gulls. Like everything else in life, you concentrated on what was secure and tried to ignore the rest.

He walked loose-legged to the bar, ordered a Bloody Mary, and squinted around the deck looking for Danielle, his next and perhaps most important interviewee. He spotted the captain astern, head just above the pilot's wheel, his eyes fixed on some point along the horizon. Behind him, lounging at the railing, Rebo was pretending to be a camera-happy tourist. Every so often, he'd lift his Nikon to his eye and snap off a shot. Rebo was a genius at capturing people at precisely those moments when they forgot themselves and showed something that came from the core—silly or mean or childish or contemplative.

For now, he was operating like a Russian general: Shoot everybody, sort out the guilty later.

Decker finished his drink and headed for the bowsprit, thinking he could relax there and still keep an eye on the deck. He squeezed through the small opening in the foredeck rail just as the ship plunged into a nasty trough. His stomach dropped to his feet. He waited, gathering his nerve again, then squatted down to the bowsprit, gripped the thick timber between his knees, and scooted out until he was only a foot or so from its tip. Holding for dear life to the gib line, he turned and looked back across the length of the ship—a flea poised on the beak of an enormous white-winged bird.

He noticed something right away: First Mate Kevin was sitting at the stern with Teen Queen Connie. They looked very cozy together. Connie placed her hand on Kevin's cheek and kissed him. Kevin wrapped his arm around her waist. Connie's mother was nowhere in sight.

When Decker turned and looked straight ahead, the wind gusted in his face. He felt a sudden exhilaration. It was as though he were flying now, with nothing below him but bright blue water, his body rising and plunging with the endless swelling contours of the sea. He felt brave and free and strong, stronger than at any time since the canoe trip. He braced himself against the wind and declared himself captain of his soul—at least for now.

To his surprise, Danielle and Ellen came out to join him. Danielle led the way, shimmying up the bowsprit the same way Decker had. She was wearing her orange string bikini, sans sarong, and her long bare legs, wrapped around the timber, were sleek and firm and glistening with oil. Lyle would have fainted dead away.

Ellen moved cautiously behind her, dressed in a powder blue one-piece suit. There was a slightly veiny, translucent pallor to her skin, the badge of a true New Yorker, accentuated, perhaps, by a touch of seasickness. She was cute in a small, frail way (quite the opposite of Danielle), with big green eyes, a button nose, and a kind of soft, rabbity mouth that showed a little of her front teeth even when she wasn't smiling.

Danielle moved in close to Decker, a new kid wanting to join the treehouse club. He could smell the perfumed heat of her—coconut oil baking on young, suntanned flesh.

"How's the view?" she said.

"Nothing like it. Wanna trade?"

She nodded and slipped down into the widow's nest, bow spray beading on her thighs, and let Decker shimmy down next to Ellen before she climbed back onto the bowsprit. Holding to the gib line like the reins on a horse, she dropped her head back, swung an arm in the air and yelled, *Yeeeehaaaaaa!*

Ellen leaned toward Decker. "Such a child."

"But the packaging is all adult."

Ellen bristled at first, but her face softened into an ironic smile. "So you think it's just packaging?"

"Not at all. She's a true wonder of nature."

"She's the best I've ever photographed." Ellen's eyes were uniformly green and bright, a trait Decker attributed to a tint in her contact lenses.

"So you're a fashion photographer?"

She nodded into the wind. "And you?"

"Communications." He almost chuckled at himself when he said it this time. "You two traveling together?"

"Not exactly. We're on assignment. We're shooting a new line of swimwear on the islands."

"Of course, you needed a windjammer to get you there."

She smiled. "You take your tax write-offs where you can get them."

The bow began to drop deeper as the ship encountered

some rougher seas. Ellen steadied herself and Danielle let loose another rebel yell.

Decker unloaded his first real question. "Were you two here last week when that guy—what's-his-name—disappeared?"

What little color remained in Ellen's face seemed to vanish. "Yes," she said, pausing. "Why?"

"I don't know. I just heard people talking about it."

"What do people say?" Her rabbity mouth was set hard now.

"That he may have jumped overboard."

Ellen snorted.

"Did you know the guy?" He tried to sound casual.

"He was sharing a cabin with Danielle."

Decker said, "Oh," as if that were a sudden revelation.

Danielle swiveled her head and snapped, "Justin was a damned good swimmer."

Decker wondered why that was relevant, but said, "I see."

"I wish everybody would just shut up and quit talking about it," Danielle said. She turned away again.

Decker apologized, for the time being anyway.

"It's not your fault," Ellen whispered. "The gossip has been endless. The fact is, no one knows what happened to Justin. Especially Danielle."

"But I thought they were sharing a cabin?" He had gone one question too far. Ellen was glaring now.

"Are you a cop or something?" she said.

Danielle turned around and he was caught in a cross fire of accusing stares. He took a silent Fifth.

"He's too nerdy to be a cop," Danielle said.

"Thank you," Decker said.

"What are you, a journalist?" Ellen asked.

He nodded. Strike two for the day.

"You realize the captain has banned reporters from the ship," Ellen said.

"Feel free to turn me in." In a way, he liked that idea. End of assignment. Honorable discharge.

Ellen didn't answer. "What paper are you with—the *Post*?" She said the name contemptuously. Decker assumed she meant New York, not Washington.

"No, a paper in Cincinnati."

Danielle hooted. "Why does a paper in Cincinnati give a damn what happened to Justin?"

"Because that's where his family lives."

The two women were silent.

Finally, Danielle said defensively, "He never talked about his family."

Decker was surprised, but kept it to himself. Maybe Justin and Danielle had been too busy doing other things in their cabin to discuss their personal lives.

"Do his parents know?" Danielle asked. She was beginning to soften.

"They know he's been reported missing. They won't talk about it."

"You won't learn much from us, either," Ellen said. "Danielle wasn't even with him that night."

"She didn't go into Spanish Town?"

Danielle spoke up for herself, irritated again. "He went over on the first launch. I never saw him after that."

"Why not? Were you fighting?"

Danielle's mouth dropped—she was either appalled or startled—but she recovered enough of her venom to blurt out, "Why don't you just leave us the hell alone?"

# 3

When asked if he could locate the British Virgin Islands among the Empire's dwindling treasures, Winston Churchill replied that he hadn't the foggiest idea. Decker could have said the same prior to a stop at the downtown library on his way to the Cincinnati airport. There he found a couple of glossy travel books on the Caribbean and a short item in the Britannica's micropedia, most of it statistics. He learned that there are more than fifty islands in the chain, located about sixty miles east of Cuba, and that they possessed a total population of fewer than 12,000 people—barely enough to fill the blue seats at Riverfront Stadium. The islands were a British dependent territory but, like most of the Caribbean states, relied on the Yankee dollar for their currency. Tortola was by far the most populous of the islands, with 9,200 people, followed by Virgin Gorda, with a couple thousand souls at most.

Unlike the U.S. Virgin Islands, the BVI prided itself on its quiet, unhurried way of life and lack of development. Virgin Gorda hadn't a single telephone or paved road until the 1970s, and scores of smaller islands in the chain still had no electricity or plumbing. Nor any high rises, gambling casinos, or traffic jams, either, thank you.

At 11:30 A.M., the *Southern Cross* dropped anchor in Spring Bay about two hundred yards west of the so-called Baths of Virgin Gorda—a jumbled pile of truck-sized boulders at the south end of the island, formed eons ago when molten rock met ocean. Viewed from the ship, the boulders resembled a herd of fat sea turtles sunning themselves at the far end of the beach.

The launch dropped the passengers just north of the Baths, and Decker and Ryan scouted quickly for a shady, private place to dump their gear. It wasn't easy. The passengers had fanned out several hundred yards along the beach, some sunning themselves in the hot white sand, but most clustering in small bits of shade wherever they could find it.

Decker and Ryan settled on a spot under the loose branches of a sea-grape bush, just a few yards in front of the beach's only bar. It was a nameless, open-air establishment—hardly promising as a communications center, but Decker decided to try it anyway. He told Ryan he'd be right back and then approached the bartender, a young black man with a neatly trimmed goatee. He was lining up Heinekens for a trio of overgrown frat boys Decker recognized by paunch, if not by name, from the *Southern Cross*. Decker asked about a pay phone and the bartender nodded toward a narrow hallway to the right.

The closed-in space reeked of stale urine and cheap cherry deodorant. The tip-off was a poem taped to a restroom door: "If it's yellow, let it mellow; if it's brown, flush it down." Miraculously, at the end of the hallway, hanging crookedly on a plywood wall, was a nearly new touch-tone pay phone, courtesy of the Cable and Wireless Company, Birmingham, England. Dangling on a cord below it was a grimy phone book about the size of a paperback novel.

Decker was tickled to find it cost only a dime, tickled even more that it worked—until he pressed the number for the police and got no answer.

He waited ten rings, then hung up, redeposited his dime, and tried the number again, this time stretching his patience to the twelfth ring. He called the operator. She confirmed that he had a working number. He retrieved his dime, tried again. On the fifteenth ring, he slammed down the receiver and walked back to the bar.

The bartender was perched on a wood stool by the cash register. He seemed almost in a trance, gazing at the pulsing blue of the ocean over the heads of his customers.

"Excuse me," Decker said. "Can you tell me why the police don't answer their phone?"

The bartender glanced over his shoulder at an ancient electric clock. "Lunch," he said. It was 12:05 P.M.

"Lunch?" Decker repeated.

"Give dem a ring mebbe in an hour."

"Tell me, do the crooks around here take lunch hour, too?"

"No," the bartender smiled. His gold incisor flashed. "De crooks, dey in bed."

It was a little after one-thirty when Decker and Ryan left the water and, with raging appetites, raced each other across the stinging sand to the buffet table the crew had set up for lunch. Decker could hardly keep up. He was always a step or two behind the youth, even in the water, as Ryan chased fish after fish. At one point, he had to grab Ryan by the leg to keep him from pursuing a nasty-looking stingray.

They loaded their paper plates with the ship's high-caloric fare—beans, burgers, potato salad, a bit of sliced fruit—then grabbed some sodas from the cooler and settled into their patch of shade among the sea grapes. Ryan was strangely quiet as he ate.

"Are you going to tell your mother?" Decker asked.

"Tell her what?"

"Don't play games. About Connie, of course."

During a break in their snorkeling, they had gone off exploring the Baths, where they soon stumbled into a cave where Connie, Kevin, and several deckhands were sitting lotus-style in a circle and passing around a joint the size of a Cuban cigar. When Connie spotted Ryan, she tried to stand but her legs tangled up and she fell to her behind. She seemed dangerously stoned.

"Why should I?"

"Because she's your sister."

"She can take care of herself."

"Maybe. But don't you think your mother should know?"

Ryan shrugged and gobbled a big forkful of potato salad.

Decker imagined there was worse than pot on board the ship, and Connie seemed poised to try anything. He would tell Maureen himself if Ryan didn't.

"Mom's been real strange since the divorce."

"How do you mean?"

"Well, she doesn't like Connie seeing different guys."

"With Kevin, I can understand."

"Yeah, but Mom's been that way at home, too. Connie says she wants to go live with Dad."

"What about you?"

Ryan grabbed a handful of sand and tossed it. "I don't know. Dad and I never did much anyway. He was always doing stuff at work. And then he got this girlfriend, some lawyer who talks all the time and never shuts up—"

"I see."

Every once in a while a breeze kicked up and sent sand crackling like dry snow against the sea-grape leaves.

"Do you miss Justin?" Decker asked. He felt slimy, playing the reporter con game with a lonely kid, but he had to start somewhere.

"Sure. He was neat."

"Do you know why he might have disappeared?"

Ryan shrugged, stared at his plate. He looked hurt about something. "I don't know. We never talked much about anything. We just had fun. He showed me how to go troll fishing, and we went snorkeling a couple of times."

"Did he seem sad?"

"No. Why?"

"Did he ever mention anything unusual about the ship?"

Ryan took a huge bite from his burger, licked the ketchup from his fingers. "He said he was pretty sure the captain was boffing Mary Beth."

Decker hooted. The affair must have been common knowledge to every man, woman, and child on board.

"Did he ever say he was afraid?"

"Afraid of what?"

"I don't know. Certain people. Like maybe he was being chased."

"Nah. He told me once I should live every moment like it was the last, though. You know, carpe diem and all that. I figured he'd just seen *The Dead Poets' Society* or something. Mom rented it for me one night. It was pretty cool."

"Did he say why he believed that?"

"No, he just mostly wanted to have fun."

Decker could see he wasn't getting anywhere and pulled out his final question. "Do you think Justin might have committed suicide?"

Ryan ruminated on this a moment while finishing up his baked beans. He shook his head. "Nah."

"Why 'nah'?"

"Because he was just too cool for that. He was a funny guy—humorous, I mean. Always jokin' around. He did this great imitation of the captain, you know the funny way he talks and stuff. He was even better at imitating Stu."

"Stu?"

"Stuart Parnell. He was this stuffy old guy who was here last week. You missed him."

"Stuart Parnell—why does that sound familiar?"

"He's a big-shot politician, I guess. Mom was real impressed to see him on board."

Decker remembered now—Congressman Stuart Parnell, Southern conservative, big on defense spending. What the hell was he doing on a tub like the *Southern Cross?*

"Was Parnell here alone?"

"No, he had his wife. She was seasick most of the time. They were in the big cabin at the back of the boat. Mom says it's called the honeymoon suite. It has a kitchen and windows and everything."

"You mean portholes."

"Yeah, portholes."

A teenage girl with long dark hair came swaying down the beach in their direction. Decker recognized her from the ship: She had arrived earlier that morning with her mother. Both were variants on the same long-haired, high-hipped chic, with dark brown eyes, only the daughter, who was all of fourteen, still had some baby fat on her frame. She held her face and hair to the breeze like someone in an inspirational poster. As she walked by, she smiled and waved at Ryan. He barely nodded back.

"Come on," Decker said, jabbing the boy on the shoulder. "You can be friendlier than that. She's cute!"

"She's not so hot." He licked the uneven spot along his upper lip.

"You jerk, she was trying to be friendly. What grade are you in?"

"I start ninth next year."

"Well, then it's about time you had a summer fling."

"A summer what?"

"You know, a fling. Holding hands on the beach. Long talks under the stars. Kissing—" He thought of Janet for a panicked moment, felt himself drowning again. He took a deep breath and waited for it to lift.

Ryan was staring into the sand. "How do you know she'd be interested?"

"What does she have to do, jump your bones? Just be friendly and see what happens. Women are funny."

"What do you mean, funny?"

"They get their mind set on some guy for some damned reason, then watch out. They won't take no for an answer."

"You mean like my sister and Kevin."

"Yeah, except I think your sister is looking for trouble."

"My dad says all women are looking for trouble."

Decker ruffled the boy's hair. "Quit talking like a damned grown-up, okay?"

They had almost finished eating when Leslie came toward them down the beach, striding confidently in a white one-piece suit cut well above her hipbones. Decker marveled at the volute strength there, the leverage between the small waist and the strong, smooth continuous flow of her legs.

She stopped about ten yards up the beach and spread out her towel in the hard glare of white sand: no hiding from the sun for her. She had just settled on her stomach with a book when she turned and flashed Decker a big smile—certain he'd be watching—then settled down to her reading. Clearly, she wanted attention and Decker, feeling like a silly teenager, his stomach full of butterflies, obliged.

"Excuse me a second," he said to Ryan. "I just need to say something to Leslie."

"Uh huh," Ryan said.

"Shut up, you."

He crouched in the sand just beside her book and said, "Mind if I join you?"

She smiled again. "Of course not."

He sat down, leaned back slowly on his hands, the hot sand stinging his palms, warming his behind. He looked out to the sea

and sky and discovered anew the unrealness of their reality—
the endless shimmering mirage of blue that now formed the
background of their lives, that pulsed there even when they
closed their eyes. He looked down. Leslie had her eyes in her
book, her ankles crossed above a broad but very shapely behind,
the white suit barely concealing the cleft there. His heart tumbled into those rounded contours; he tried not to stare. She was
finishing up a page in an old library copy of *Anna Karenina.*

"Some pretty heavy reading you've got there," he said,
sounding stupid, but feeling the need to say something.

She looked up, sunglasses on. "I can't resist stories about
fated women," she said. "Besides, I needed something rather
lengthy for a two-week vacation."

"Very sensible," Decker said. "I always wait until I get to
the airport, then buy the trashiest thing I can find. That way I
have an excuse."

"You should read what interests you," she said with final-
ity, and smiled.

"I thought you might be interested in what Ryan and I just
saw back in the Baths. Kevin and some of the boys from the ship
were consorting with ganja. Connie Daugherty happened to be
there, too."

"Oooh. Do you plan to write an exposé?"

He was surprised by the sarcasm. "No, but I think it's
interesting that our crew uses drugs to seduce minors, don't
you?"

"I doubt if you'd find anyone on these islands who doesn't
toke occasionally."

"True, but I suspect there's more than just marijuana on
our ship."

"I see. And you're convinced that drugs had something to
do with Justin's disappearance."

"Not convinced. It's just a theory."

"Tell the police."

"I would, if I could reach them." He told her about his experience on the phone. She laughed and lifted the sunglasses. The icy blue eyes were still there.

"Tell me, have you noticed how the islanders never smile?" Decker said.

She patted his knee. "You shouldn't take it so personally. It's a difference in custom. West Indians reserve their smiles for something funny, or people they know and like."

Decker's eye caught something surprising at the southern end of the beach near the Baths: Ellen and Danielle were sharing a spot with Lyle Hughes in the shade of an enormous boulder. All three were yukking it up as though they liked each other.

"Would you look at that?" Decker said.

Leslie turned and glanced. "How sweet. Danielle must be starving for attention."

"You don't like her much, do you?"

"She's a master manipulator."

"And you're a shrinking violet."

She smiled. "Touché. Why don't you just relax and enjoy yourself? You can't work every minute of the day."

"I'm afraid I haven't had much practice at relaxing."

"Try."

"All right," he said. He closed his eyes and let his head drop back, the sun burning red holes through his eyelids. He listened to the endless roll and hiss of the surf, the circling cry of the gulls. Yes, he was almost there—a definite state of semirelaxation.

He opened his eyes when he felt something brush softly against his thigh. Leslie was lying on her side, her hand moving just above his legs, sifting tiny streams of sand through her fingers. It was a mindless, almost childish gesture that touched him deeply in an odd way. He closed his eyes again. Soon, as though time and motion had come to a standstill, he could feel every grain of sand that fell against his sun-warmed skin, one and another and another, tingling like crystallized bits of sunshine fallen from Leslie's hands.

The *Southern Cross* set sail again promptly at 5:00 P.M., heading north along the western coast of Virgin Gorda to Ft. Thomas Bay and the small harbor at Spanish Town, where the ship was to anchor for the night.

At five forty-five, Decker and Rebo boarded the launch to Spanish Town, hoping to make a 6:00 P.M. appointment Decker had managed to schedule by phone earlier that afternoon with the chief duty officer there, a Sergeant Oliver Kitchens. Kitchens told Decker he had not personally investigated the Grammer case, but that he would pull the files and help in any way he could. He sounded polite on the phone and, anyway, given the time constraints, it was the best Decker could do.

Decker had showered and put on long pants and a button-down shirt for the interview, trying to regain a semblance of professionalism, but Rebo had refused to change from his Hawaiian shirt and lime green trunks with the blue whale print. "I'm not burnin' up in this heat just to impress some backwater cop," he said.

The beach at Spanish Town was lined with open-air bars, a few with thatched roofs but most featuring the corrugated tin that, along with cinder block, seemed to be the only building materials on the islands. Beyond the beach was the Promenade, the town's lone paved street, crammed with narrow hole-in-the-wall shops and crumbling stucco motels. The police station was the one freshly painted building on the strip, spanking white with black shutters, two doors from the southern end of the Promenade, where the pavement just simply stopped and vanished into sand.

They found the station's double doors wide open. An old stand-up fan the size of a B-29 propeller was chasing warm air around. The room was gloomy and sparse: a couple of metal desks, some filing cabinets, and an empty holding cell in the rear. Kitchens was alone, standing by an open filing cabinet to their left as they walked in.

"Please have a seat," he said, and pointed to some straight-back chairs in front of his desk. "I was just preparing for our meeting." He spoke with the gentle precision of an educated islander.

After the introductions, Rebo asked if he could take some shots of the station. Kitchens broke into a thin, amused smile and said, "It's not Hollywood, but please be my guest."

Kitchens looked young, no more than a teenager, really, although he must have been older. His face was flat and broad and his eyelashes curly. He was dressed in the sun-blind uniform of the Royal Virgin Islands Police Force—navy pants with black side stripes and a dark gray shirt—a heritage no doubt inflicted upon them by the British.

"I'm afraid our files contain very little on this case," he said. He opened a folder on his desk and began sorting through the paperwork. The loose sheets riffled in the breeze from the fan. "A missing-persons report has been filed, of course."

"By whom?" Decker asked. Rebo was floating around the room somewhere behind him, his speed shutter clicking away.

"By a Thomas A. Pearce, captain of the *Southern Cross.*" Kitchens cited the date and time it was filed—a day after the disappearance, close to eight in the evening.

"Can I see?" Decker asked.

"Yes, you may." Kitchens handed over the yellow sheet.

There wasn't much. Justin's name and nationality. A physical description, which included the words "thin" and "pale

Caucasian." When and where he was last seen by the crew—"disembarking from a launch, near the northern end of Spanish Town beach, at approximately 8:15 P.M."

"So he didn't return to the ship?" Decker said.

Kitchens broke into his thin smile again. "There are several additional affidavits. Very interesting, you'll see."

Kitchens handed him four plain white typewritten sheets. The writing was single-spaced and riddled with typos, typical of cop reports everywhere. Decker started reading and jotting down notes.

The first statement was from Danielle Evans, attesting to Justin's sound state of mind prior to his disappearance. She testified she had not seen Justin after 8:00 P.M., when he boarded the launch to Spanish Town.

The next was from a Rasiq Khan, apparently the pilot of the ship's launch, who stated when and where he had dropped Justin off that night. He went on to testify that he had not seen Justin on any of the returning launches that night, which he promptly reported to the captain.

"But why did the captain wait twenty-four hours to notify the police?"

Rebo was in both their faces now, snapping close-ups from every angle.

Kitchens smiled again. The behavior of Yankee tourists was an endless source of amusement. "Perhaps some of the ship's guests find more interesting accommodations on shore."

The third affidavit surprised him—it was from Leslie Stanton—stating, as she had told him earlier, that she had seen Justin standing at the bow of the ship around 2:00 A.M.

"This is crazy," Decker said. "Weren't there any other witnesses?"

"None that would sign affidavits, I am told."

"So it's Leslie Stanton's word against the crew's."

"I am afraid so, Mr. Decker. There is, however, one more statement in your hand."

It was from a Franklin Dirk, a bartender at a Spanish Town establishment called the La Ti Da. Dirk stated that Justin had arrived at the bar about 11:00 P.M., had talked to several men there, then left alone just before one. The bartender noted that Justin had ordered two rum-punch specials.

"The bartender says Justin was drinking," Decker said. "I thought he never touched the stuff." He remembered it was Leslie who had told him that.

"Perhaps he was under unusual stress."

"Maybe," Decker said, and let it drop. "Have you tried dragging?"

"If you look closely at the missing-persons report, Mr. Decker, you find that the ship set sail for Long Bay at two thirty-five A.M. That would necessitate dredging an eight-mile stretch of coastline, from here to the northern tip of the island. And, I might add, based on the testimony of one witness."

"Eight miles doesn't seem like all that much to me."

"Obviously, you have never done any coastal dragging, Mr. Decker. Done properly, it is a slow and tedious process."

"So you doubt Leslie Stanton's testimony?"

"It was late, Mr. Decker. Two o'clock in the morning is very late, even for a cruise ship. Perhaps she only thought she saw Mr. Grammer."

"And you don't think the crew is hiding something? Maybe an accident."

"The case is not closed, Mr. Decker. We can always hope others will come forward with additional information."

Decker scribbled down the official quote and moved on to the next obvious question.

"What kind of place is the La Ti Da?"

Kitchens's thin little smile grew big this time, creasing the flat cheeks. "It is popular with certain tourists from the Continent. 'Poofs,' shall we say?"

"Poofs?"

"As you would say in your country—gays."

"Where can I find the La Ti Da?"

"Three streets behind our building, turn right at DeSoto Street. Look for a pink structure to your left."

The back streets of Spanish Town were dusty and empty, save for a friendly mutt or a greasy-looking hen pecking here and there in the grit. Half the houses along the street were unfinished and overgrown with weeds—missing windows or doors or roofs or, in some cases, everything above the cinder-block foundation. Decker wondered how they could start so many buildings and never finish them. Did they run out of money and materials, or simply lose interest? Perhaps Leslie would know.

The scene was livelier as Decker and Rebo turned the corner onto DeSoto Street. The islanders were gathered on street corners and hanging out of unshuttered windows. A woman sang out, "Goooooooood afternoon, geeeen-til-men," as the two walked by, but Decker couldn't tell if she was being friendly or sarcastic. The others paid them no attention. Down the street they came across a group of little girls in clean white dresses and bare feet taking turns twisting inside a red hula hoop. Rebo stopped and snapped some shots; the girls giggled and covered their teeth.

They passed an abandoned house occupied, it seemed, by a family of goats, their yellow eyes staring out from the empty window casements and doorways like the possessed children in that campy horror flick, *Village of the Damned*. Several buildings beyond that, on the same side of the street, stood a gaudy pink, three-story motel, with black security grates over the first-floor windows. Stenciled in flowery script above the vaulted entrance were the words La Tierra de la Mar.

The lobby was a sanctuary from the dusty streets—dark and cool and inviting, with a jungle of tall potted plants and wicker furniture spread over a terra cotta floor. But it was hardly your typical resort hotel: men paraded about clad only in white towels—materializing from hallways and elevators and disappearing into the sun-dazzled courtyard at the back of the lobby. The reception desk was empty, although keeping watch from its flanks were cement reproductions of *Venus de Milo* and Michaelangelo's *David.*

"All the art treasures of Europe," Rebo said, "right here in the Caribbean."

"Let's find the bar," Decker said.

"It's at the opposite end of the courtyard," said a smiling old gent in a wicker chair. His gray-fuzzed chest sagged above an open newspaper spread strategically over his lap.

"Thank you," Decker said.

"You're welcome," the gent said. Decker turned before the old man could lift his paper.

The courtyard was another discovery. In its center was a large blue swimming pool, maybe half Olympic size, and at each corner a tiered fountain topped by a statue of a little boy. The boys were holding themselves in the exaggerated way little boys do, peeing long arcs of water into the pool.

"I've got to get this," Rebo said, lifting his camera.

"They'll never print it."

"I don't care."

They stopped near two younger men standing naked in waist-deep water, their arms draped languidly along the marble ledge.

Rebo was clicking away when one of the men smiled up at Decker. "The water's lovely today. Care to join us?"

"No, thanks," he said, and pointing to Rebo, quickly added, "I'm with him."

Decker felt the same way about gays as he did about religious fundamentalists: Whatever they did among themselves was fine, so long as they didn't insist on a conversion.

Rebo continued to roam and photograph as Decker headed around the pool to the bar. It was built into the far end of the courtyard, sheltered by a dark blue canopy. The remainder of the courtyard was lined with numbered black doors, like any motel, with a curlicue railing on the second and third floors.

The bartender was behind the empty counter stocking shelves. He was a chunky, middle-aged Anglo—all chest and stomach propped on stick-thin legs—dressed in white bikini trunks that could have doubled as a satin jock strap. His hair was black and curly but his chest was mostly gray. He had a big crooked nose, smiling blue eyes, a chipped tooth. He sounded very British.

"Sorry, gentlemen, but we don't open until seven."

"That's okay," Decker said. "I'd just like to ask a few questions." He pulled his notebook from a back pocket. The yearbook photo of Justin was tucked just inside the cover. Decker showed it to the man.

"Look familiar?"

The bartender barely glanced at it. "Might I inquire as to who is asking?"

Decker laid the photo on the bar. "I'm a reporter for a newspaper in Ohio."

Decker offered his hand, but the bartender only grinned and broke into a tune. "Oh why oh why oh why-oh, why did I ever leave O-hi-o?"

"You should be on Broadway, you know that." Decker was only half-teasing; the bartender had a rich baritone voice.

"Many people have told me that—especially when they're looking for favors."

Decker edged the photo toward him. "Has he been here?"

"Why should I care about some muckraking journalistic enterprise in Ohio?"

"I'm from the kid's hometown. His parents are mighty upset."

The bartender turned his attention to Rebo. "Please inform your friend there that if he doesn't stop taking pictures, I'll call the constable." Rebo was sitting in a wicker chair by the pool. He had his long lens out, aimed dead on at the bartender's crooked nose.

"You tell him," Decker said. "He doesn't like to be told what to do."

"Say, you there! Stop that! This is private property, I'll have you know."

Rebo squeezed off about three more shots and put the camera down.

"You're avoiding the issue," Decker said. He tapped the photo with a fingertip.

"I don't need to look. I've said everything I'm going to say to the police. Why don't you go bugger them?"

"Then you must be Franklin Dirk."

"I have nothing more to say."

Decker checked his notes from the police station. "According to your statement, Justin Grammer left here Wednesday morning, alone, at one A.M. You served him two drinks, both rum-punch specials. Is that true?"

"That's what I told the police, isn't it?"

He'd snapped at the bait; Decker tried to reel him in. "Where did he go from here?"

"How would I know? I don't follow customers once they leave."

"Did he stay the night at the hotel?"

"Check with the clerk."

"I will."

Just then one of the wicker-backed bar stools made a crunching groan for mercy as Rebo settled his weight on it. He grinned and set his camera on the bar. He was still sweating from the walk through town.

"A Diet Coke, please."

Dirk glared down his crooked nose.

"The establishment is closed," Decker said.

"Listen, boys," the bartender said, "I'd really love to cooperate with you in your little investigation, but you already know as much as I do. Now run along, please."

"You're a bathhouse, aren't you?" Rebo said. He leaned his elbows on the bar, squared his big shoulders. It was good-guy, bad-guy time.

"You say bathhouse as if it were some kind of orgiastic temple. We run a safe, clean place here."

"Sunday afternoon tea dances, right?" Rebo said.

"We have rules. No more than two people to a room. No bringing in little black boys from the village. We're not promoting indiscriminate sex."

"Sounds downright puritanical," Rebo said.

"We've got nothing to hide here."

"Then just tell us what happened to the college boy."

Dirk grabbed the bar phone. "Must I call the police?"

"Forget it," Decker said, and snatched up the photo from the bar. He tried some last-minute guilt. "Too bad the family will never know what happened to their boy."

Dirk put down the phone and sighed out his crooked nose. "I'm afraid I can't help with that. We're in a bad spot with the police here. We're not their favorite people, you know."

"Just tell us where we can look for answers. Your name will be left out."

"I don't know where you would look, but I know what you might ask."

"What?"

"Find out who your young friend was supposed to meet here that night."

"You can't tell us?"

"I haven't a clue."

"How do you know he was meeting someone?"

"When you've been tending bar as long as I have, you know."

"A man or a woman?"

Dirk grinned. "He could have his pick, I'm sure."

"And you're certain he didn't leave here with anyone?"

"I'm not certain of anything."

# 4

Decker picked up the gold and ivory handset from the little wicker nightstand and punched the numbers for the *Eagle*. As the phone played out a fugue of coded sounds bridging land and sea, he lay back on the big bed and enjoyed all the kinky comforts of his room. He stared at himself in the ceiling mirror, a tired-looking man who had fallen to earth and somehow landed safely on a king-size bed with lavender sheets. The La Ti Da wasn't Decker's style, but it was the only motel in Spanish Town with private phones.

He rolled over and picked up his photo of Justin Grammer, next to his notebook, just as Farlidge came on the line.

"So what have you got?"

Decker ran down the little he'd learned so far, hearsay, contradictions, and all. When he finished, Farlidge said, "Go with the heartbreak angle. Lots of human interest. Can you file it tonight?" It was almost seven.

"You're not listening, Ron. I'm getting conflicting information. If Justin was gay, why would he care enough about Danielle to commit suicide?"

"Maybe he was bisexual."

Decker considered quitting. He could reimburse the *Eagle*, have a real Caribbean vacation. But then he saw Justin staring at him from the photo again, haunted, persecuted. *Have you seen this child?*

"I can't confirm that, Ron. At this point, I don't know much of anything. What I do know is we're invading this kid's privacy, and possibly libeling him, based on a lot of hearsay and gossip."

"He's dead. You can't libel a dead man."

"Dammit, Ron, I don't know if he's dead."

"All right, all right. Settle down. Give me a story based on the police report. When was he last seen and all that. We're always safe with public record; they can't sue us on that. Then give me lots of color on the islands and the cruise. We'll leave the rest until we have something more solid. When can I have it?"

"A couple of hours. I'll have to write out it in longhand."

"Longhand?"

Decker would have to break the bad news sooner or later. "Somebody ripped off our equipment, Ron. Rebo's sending all his stuff from AP."

"Decker, how in God's name did—"

He held the receiver away, then put his ear back in time to hear Farlidge say, "I want that story by eight-thirty. We're backed up as it is."

"You'll have it."

"Where can I reach you for questions?"

Decker gave him the number of the La Ti Da and the room extension. "Call back before nine, Ron. I'm paying by the hour."

"You're *what?*"

Decker set his legal pad on the wicker writing desk, moved the basket of potpourri off to a corner, and pulled up a wicker chair. He scribbled out the piece in an hour, motivated in part by the strain on his back from the flimsy chair and, less consciously, by a desire to see Leslie again.

Nothing had really come of their encounter on the beach, not after Leslie had broken the enchantment of her sand-sifting by saying, "You're afraid of me, aren't you?"

His feeble answer had been, "I don't like to be rushed." It

had sounded oddly feminine and brittle, and it seemed to smash into fragments all that had been fused between them just moments before. Maybe he was afraid.

He leafed through his notes for any important details he might have missed, then gave the completed story a quick once-over. By eight-fifteen, he was ready to call the metro desk, although his lead wasn't exactly a sizzler:

VIRGIN GORDA, BVI—A police investigation here into the disappearance of Justin Grammer is riddled with inconsistencies and unanswered questions.

Statements given to the Royal Virgin Islands Police Force conflict as to whether Grammer, 22, scion of one of Cincinnati's oldest and wealthiest families, was on board the ship the night he vanished . . .

The story went on to say that at least one passenger feared that Justin may have jumped or fallen from the *Southern Cross* while it was under sail that night, and that he was last seen, according to one eyewitness, standing near the bow around 2:00 A.M.

Decker added that no one on the crew had reported seeing Justin return to the ship that night.

He avoided any speculation about Justin's relationship with Danielle Evans, saying only that he had booked passage in the same cabin with the New York fashion model. He stuck to the facts again when he wrote that Justin had last been spotted on the island drinking at a poolside bar at the La Tierra de la Mar (the full name sounded far less flamboyant) and that records showed he did not check into the motel. Decker agonized over whether to mention the La Ti Da's reputation as a watering hole for gays.

"Why not?" Rebo said, back from his mad dash to St. Thomas. "It's relevant, isn't it?"

"How do we know?"

"How do we *not* know?"

"But is it fair to Justin? What if he isn't gay?"

"Hey, he chose to go there."

"All right, all right. I'll put it in. You should have been a philosopher, you know that?"

"I *am* a philosopher."

The story wasn't one Decker was proud of, although he knew it would be well read. It was mostly grist for the local gossip mill, but for now at least it would keep Farlidge off his case until he could sort out some answers. He was eager to get at the truth of the matter, for he found himself as intrigued now as any tabloid fan by the mysterious disappearance of Justin Grammer.

Rudy's bar and restaurant was at the southern end of the beach in Spanish Town, tucked in a coconut grove, a safe distance from the other bars serving a more local clientele. It was an open-air establishment, very rustic, with a big thatched roof spread over a dozen picnic tables in the sand. There was a pineboard bar in the very back, and behind that, a kitchen shanty made of the island's ubiquitous corrugated tin. The roof beams were festooned with nautical flags from nearly every country in the world and stapled with business cards and old Polaroids left by tourists who wanted always to be remembered there.

Decker and Rebo arrived at Rudy's in time for the $18 lobster feast. The service was excellent—island girls with smooth black shoulders and bright red lipstick, trained to smile in the mindless American way. The food was as good, and plentiful, as Mary Beth had promised. The lobsters were cut in half and drenched in melted butter, so big their tails and claws hung over the edges of the plate. There were avocado halves filled with sweetened lime juice for appetizers, homemade passion fruit dressing for the mixed salad, and a side dish of rice seasoned with saffron and bits of green olive and pimiento. In short, everything was fresh, clean, and tasting of the islands, including the rum-punch specials, which Rebo ordered for both of them, claiming it was necessary to their ongoing research into the drink's celebrated potency.

Decker had wanted to sit with either Leslie or Danielle, hoping to learn more about Justin's whereabouts on the night of his disappearance, but as it turned out, both were sitting at tables crowded with other passengers.

Decker and Rebo were joined by Art and Gretchen Kapinski, a retired couple from Long Beach, California, who were chatty and pleasant enough. Decker turned the subject around to Justin Grammer, but neither had known him, although, as Gretchen said, they remembered seeing "a nice young man devoted to his Bible study."

"Were you a friend of his?" Art asked Decker. He was a tall, lanky older man with a sharp nose and hawklike appearance, although his brown eyes were gentle. His wife was a contented butterball with a cap of dyed blonde hair.

"I'm just curious," Decker said. "Some people think he might have jumped overboard in the night."

Art stuck out his lower lip under the hawkish nose. "I don't know. It can happen, especially under sail at night. During the war, we had a young ensign jump during watch duty; no one suspected a thing until it was time for his relief."

"Did they know why?"

Art shrugged. "Mighta been trouble over some girl. He didn't leave a note. But I'll tell you this, there's something awful chilling about the sea at night, like there's no end to the blackness. If you've got a problem, it seems all the worse. I've seen it get to lots of men."

Decker's thoughts were drifting somewhere on a black

endless sea when Tony Henderson showed up at their table scouting for an empty spot. He had given his Gregory Peck looks a quick Don Johnson makeover, slicking back his graying hair and throwing a white linen jacket over a dark blue T-shirt. He was slim and handsome enough, though to carry off the look. He said a soft hello to Gretchen and sat down next to her. She lit up like a Christmas ornament.

Tony got the attention of the waitress and ordered the lobster feast without butter.

"Without butter," she repeated. She looked at Tony for just a second to see if he was serious, then scampered off to the kitchen.

Art Kapinski filled up the silences at the table with his gentle observations about the islands. He pointed out the steady peep, peep, peep of the tree frogs in the background. "They sound like baby chicks, don't they?"

"They're probably bats," Rebo said.

Gretchen smiled at everything and chewed slowly, methodically, taking small, careful bites. Every once in a while, she turned and said something to Tony, who answered politely enough but seemed distracted. His cool gray eyes wandered around the restaurant. At first, Decker thought it was random, but the glances kept coming back to Leslie and, beyond her table, to Danielle.

Later, Mary Beth stopped by their table, trusty clipboard in her arms, company smile on her face. "Is anyone here interested in the dive on Wednesday? They're doing the wreck of the *Rhone*."

"Oh, yes, the *Rhone*," Tony said, trying to impress. "Went down in a hurricane, I believe, about a hundred years ago."

He'd probably read it in a brochure, Decker thought.

Nonetheless, Mary Beth chirped, "Very good! It's one of

the best diving spots in the islands. The charge is eighty dollars for the day. We have a boat that picks you up and takes you out to the site, with all the equipment you'll need."

"Who else signed up?" Tony asked.

"Danielle, of course—she's been down several times already . . ."

Decker interrupted, "Several times?"

"Oh yes. The diving boat comes every Monday, Wednesday, and Friday. You can choose any day you like."

"Who else?" Tony asked.

"Let's see. We have Chris Watt . . ." She mentioned several other names Decker didn't recognize, although he knew that Watt was Lyle's roommate—a pompous-looking law student with a walrus mustache and little wire-rimmed glasses. Decker didn't know much about him except that he seemed to avoid all association with Lyle, which meant he couldn't be all bad.

She turned to Decker. "Rick?"

"Sorry, not this time," he said. He hadn't dived in years, not since he and Janet had gone to the Keys one summer, where they both earned quickie certificates.

Rebo said, "Don't believe I will. Can't stand things covering my nose."

Only Decker laughed. Rebo's humor was an acquired taste.

"Is there a senior citizen discount?" Art teased.

Mary Beth laughed. "I'm afraid not."

"Then count me out."

"I'll do it," Tony said evenly, as though doing Mary Beth and everyone else a favor.

"Well, I guess I made one sale," she said, and handed him the clipboard.

Toward the end of dinner, Rudy himself stepped out of the kitchen and into the center of the restaurant. He was as pleasant and substantial as the food he served: a stocky islander with a graying beard and sparkling, intelligent eyes. "Is everybody enjoying their meal?" he asked ceremoniously. He was answered with wild applause. He wiped his hands on his apron, bowed, and backed away to his kitchen.

Before Art could start in again, Tony leaned over the table toward Decker and Rebo. His steel gray eyes considered one, then the other, and found them both wanting.

"You two gentlemen always travel together?" he said.

"Yeah, we're real funny that way," Rebo answered.

Tony missed the sarcasm, or chose to ignore it. "I couldn't help noticing your wedding band," he said to Rebo. "Did your wife decide to stay at home?"

"That's right. She doesn't like the nosy folks you meet on cruises."

Tony smiled, softened the stare. It was possible he'd gotten the message this time. "You know, we had several black males in my Navy SEALs unit. They were fine sailors."

"Well, I'm glad to hear the brothers didn't do us no shame."

"No, they did not," Tony said, not a trace of irony in his voice. "They served their country well."

Decked decided the man was genuine but painfully devoid of social radar. It would seem to fit the SEALs gung ho profile.

Gretchen was crestfallen when Tony excused himself a few moments later and wandered over to an opening at Leslie's table. Decker winced to see her eyes lock on to Tony as he sat down. (It's up to her now, he thought, and tried to put it out of his mind.)

The Kapinskis excused themselves shortly thereafter.

Rebo rubbed the back of his neck. "Tell me, is there some kind of stupidity test for this cruise?"

"Stupidity, or insensitivity?"

"In the case of Mr. Kiss-My-Ass-I'm-a-Navy-SEAL, I'd say both."

"You have to admit, our being together is a bit strange."

"Strange because I'm black and you're white? Or because people think we're a couple of pixies?"

"Probably both, which makes it even more confusing."

"No more confusing than a lot of people on this cruise."

"I'll agree with you there."

Decker looked around the open restaurant again. Leslie's table had mostly cleared, including Tony, but she was still there talking to Lyle's roommate, Chris Watt. She was leaning in close, laying it on thick with the blue eyes. Watt was eating it up, crossing his arms in a sleeveless shirt to show off those great biceps and pecs. He resembled a young, blonde Teddy Roosevelt—muscled shoulders, a walrus mustache, little wireframe glasses that barely covered his eyes. Muscle Beach with Brains. Maybe Leslie was into that.

Decker turned away and finished off his rum special.

"You've got the hots for her, don't you?" Rebo said.

"Hots for whom?"

"Come on, you know 'whom.' Miss Southern Belle over there with them big blue eyes."

"Not at all."

"Oh man, listen to you. It's about time you started looking around again."

"I'm doing my job, okay?"

"Yeah, the job. That's the main thing. When's the last time you had any contact with the female gender?"

"None of your business."

"Yeah, none of my business. Meaning you haven't had a date since you broke off with Janet, and now you've got that hungry look that's sure to drive off any self-respecting woman who happens to come your way."

"What do you know, you're married."

"You should try marriage sometime. Would save you a lot of this moanin' and pissin' around."

"Give it a rest."

"You're the one who needs to give it a rest. Blues don't become you, boy. You're the wrong color."

"All right." Decker broke into an exaggerated grin.

"That's more like it. Now go over and make a run at Miss Daisy Duke there."

But just then they both noticed Lyle, Ellen, and Danielle vacate their table and, drinks in hand, amble off toward the beach.

"Ménage à trois?" Rebo said.

"Only in Lyle's wettest dreams. But I'll check it out. You hold down the fort."

"I'll need reinforcements." He pushed his empty glass toward Decker.

"How many have you had?" Decker asked.

"Three, and I'll need a fourth if I have to talk to one more yahoo on this cruise."

Decker went to the bar, ordered a rum special for Rebo and a tonic water for himself, then dropped off the rum and started through the palm grove toward the beach. He crunched over fallen fronds in the darkness, certain he had given away his lurking presence. Through a break in the trees, he spotted the threesome on the beach, ghostly forms sitting one, two, three on a giant log. They were talking and laughing softly.

He decided against barging in, instead circling back through the grove and emerging farther north along the beach. He strolled south to make it look like a casual encounter. As he had hoped, Lyle and Danielle insisted he join their little group.

Danielle had transformed herself into an island nymph for the evening, hips sleekly wrapped in a white minisarong and hair accented by a giant gardenia. Lyle was dressed in shorts and his best Hawaiian shirt. He was sitting between Ellen and Danielle, drunk but on his best behavior, and laughing good-naturedly as Danielle hit him with one verbal jab after another—about his clothes, his perfect tan, his insurance job. He had no choice but to take it. He was lovesick and eager for anything Danielle was handing out.

Ellen mostly sat there and smoldered, but she talked a little to Decker about the fashion shoot that day during the moments when Danielle and Lyle were absorbed in each other. Ellen was concerned that the Virgin Gorda backdrop had too much the look of an island paradise when what she had wanted to capture, she said, was the island's "volcanic texture—the roughness of rock and sand. You know, something almost primeval. But I'm afraid it's going to look like one more rip-off of the *Sports Illustrated* swimsuit issue."

"Nothing wrong with that," Decker said.

"Not from a male point of view. But I would like women to think they're buying a suit designed for a real human being. Not some ethereal ideal."

"You mean, not for the Danielles of the world."

Ellen smiled at him, lips shadowy in the dark, and for a moment, Decker thought she might be interested. "You're a perfect smartass, you know that?"

He glanced up at the sky and the stars seemed like thousands of tiny watchful eyes. He remembered what Art had said about the sea at night, the never-ending blackness that drowns all hope. He wondered when, and if, he would ever come out of the blackness left by Janet.

Rudy had hired a band for the night—a reggae trio of keyboard, drums, and rhythm guitar—and the instant they began to play, Danielle was on her feet and bouncing back to the restaurant. Lyle scurried after her, drink in hand. Decker and Ellen stayed behind.

"They certainly make an interesting couple," Decker said.

"Couple? You mean someone to keep Danielle from being bored. Anyone with a prick would do."

"Did that include Justin?"

Ellen seemed to jump at the mention of the name, but she sounded calm and a bit sad when she said, "They were friends."

"Yes, but how close?"

"Is that all you care about? Getting dirt?"

"As long as it's true dirt."

"At the expense of everyone's privacy."

"It stopped being private when the police stepped in."

"Can't you just leave it alone for one night?"

"Not until you answer one thing for me. If Justin and Danielle were such good friends, why doesn't she show it? Where's the pain and worry over a missing friend?"

Ellen bit her lip. "Because she knows something she's not telling—not even me."

"About what?"

"Why don't you ask her?"

"Maybe I'm trying to respect her privacy."

She jabbed his arm playfully, his kid sister again, then suddenly jumped from the log and took his hand. "Come on, let's dance. You can ask smartass questions later."

Inside Rudy's, the picnic tables had been cleared away and a tight cluster of passengers—Danielle at center—was dancing in the sand. Decker was surprised to find Rebo among the five or six men pressing around as Danielle held an impromptu clinic in lambada.

Grabbing one man from the circle at a time, she would swirl around his body in a series of quick brushing and clinging maneuvers—arms around his neck, thighs around his leg, ass against his crotch—while her dazed partner could only grin and try to retain his balance. Lyle and Rebo were her principal victims, but so were Chris and Tony and any other males who wanted their moment with the Maybelline Girl.

Ellen tried to smile as she danced with Decker, but he could see her heart wasn't in it. She stole glances every now and then in the direction of Danielle.

A group of island children soon materialized on the fringes of the restaurant, dancing in the shadows just behind the band. They had holes in their T-shirts, bare feet, smiles that never stopped. Danielle went out and drew them inside like a flock of small pets, and after a moment of self-conscious giggles, the children began to dance among themselves again. Their small bouncing bodies added a festive note of innocence to the gathering.

The officers of the *Southern Cross* arrived a few minutes later dressed in outrageous garb—well-rehearsed antics for the amusement of the passengers. The captain sported wild-colored shorts and a T-shirt that read SHOW US YOUR TITS. Kevin was a pirate and Mary Beth, who must have changed in the restroom, a comely harem slave.

Danielle drew them instantly into her magic circle—everyone, it seemed, except Ellen, who kept up the brave show a while longer before thanking Decker and excusing herself.

"Is there anything I can do?"

"Yes." She smiled. "You can stay here and enjoy yourself."

After Ellen had drifted outside and into the dark, Leslie tapped him on the shoulder. He felt a kind of redemption when he saw her smile. She was packaged in a white terrycloth romper with a zipper down the front. There was a big metal ring attached to the zipper, asking to be pulled.

"Why aren't you dancing with Danielle?" she said. "All the *real* men are."

"Maybe I don't like competition."

"Yes you do. You're a reporter."

She smiled and took his hands and, before she could take the lead, he swept her away in a quick two-step. She retaliated by pressing against him, thigh to thigh, heat to heat. They were taking their cue from Danielle.

"Tell me," Leslie said, setting her glossy cheek next to his, "what *do* reporters like in their women?"

"Answers." He hoped she wouldn't pull away. "Like who Justin Grammer was supposed to meet the night he disappeared."

She separated, but just enough to look him in the eye. "Maybe you *should* be dancing with Danielle."

"What if I told you Justin Grammer was gay," Decker said.

Leslie smiled, unimpressed. "Try bisexual, dear. It seems to be an epidemic on this cruise."

"Does it take one to know one?"

Leslie lost a beat on her step. "Does it matter?" she said coyly.

"In terms of what?"

She pulled away completely now, the heat of her gone. "You really enjoy playing the innocent, don't you?"

"I'm not the one playing."

"Of course you are. You're a reporter. That's all you do is play."

"For a phys ed teacher, you know an awful lot about reporters."

"I know a lot about people."

"So *are* you?"

"Am I what?"

"Bisexual."

She slipped into her best Southern drawl. "Darlin', a woman has to keep a few secrets to herself, or she may just lose her feminine a-llure."

"You're something else, you know that?"

She pressed against him again, but now it was different. He wasn't sure how he felt about Leslie's latest revelation, or even if it was a revelation. Perhaps it was just one more sly come-on. He'd known only one openly bisexual woman in his life, and there had been something so hard and predatory about her that Decker hadn't been interested. But he was, in fact, interested in Leslie, which made the possibility of her bisexuality both exotic and, at the same time, intimidating. He doubted he was secure enough to compete against other men, much less women, for Leslie's affections.

But perhaps Leslie was right. Maybe it didn't matter, not here in the sea and sun and perfumed sweat of the Caribbean. He thought: Where everything was strange, nothing was strange.

They were quiet for a while as they danced, trading turns watching Danielle and her circle of worshipers. Decker had one more question to get off his chest.

"Tell me," he said, "why are you the only one who saw Justin return to the ship?"

She stiffened. "Who says I'm the only one?"

"The captain and the launch pilot both testified he never returned from Spanish Town."

"And you believe that?"

"I don't know whom to believe."

"There you go with your 'whoms' again. It's so endearing."

"Who else saw Justin back on the ship?"

"Why don't you ask around? That's your job, dear."

"Fair enough."

Leslie was watching Danielle's performance again. "You

know, I think your friend Rebo is the only one who can really handle her."

Decker swung Leslie around and looked. It was true. With Rebo in charge, the lambada became a dance instead of a one-person assault. Limbs entwined, the two went twirling and dipping like a couple of mating pumas, one black, one white, tumbling in counterpoint through the jungle.

Decker was pulling Leslie closer when she suddenly lifted her head and said, "Uh oh. Déjà vu."

She swung Decker around in time to see Lyle cutting in on Rebo, only Danielle wasn't having it.

She dispensed with Lyle in a couple of quick dance moves and went back to Rebo and that was that. Lyle was left standing there, rejected and empty-handed, a repeat of last night's mini-drama.

Decker seemed to witness twice the rush of events that followed: once in anticipation, a second (and in a strange way, less vividly so) as it happened. Lyle grabbed Danielle by the waist and pulled her away from Rebo. She wheeled around and slapped him hard. The music died, eyes turned. Lyle took a second to compose himself, arms loose at his side, before trying to retaliate. But an instant before his backhand could reach Danielle's face, there was a soft squishy thud, a sudden implosion of flesh. Rebo's fist had rocketed over Danielle's right shoulder—a short, quick jab, that's all—but enough to send Lyle reeling backward into the sand, right at the feet of a waitress, who shrieked as though his body had fallen from the roof.

Lyle was still flat on his back when the captain and Mary Beth ran over and began checking vital signs. The island children gathered round, their eyes wide with excitement and curiosity.

"Is he dead?" the waitress wailed.

"No," Mary Beth said, "but he may wish he was when he comes to."

The captain, proving very British despite his outlandish garb, calmly asked Rudy, who was standing behind the bar, to bring a glass of ice water. With a splash in the face, Lyle snapped to, blinking and shaking his head. His return to consciousness was greeted by an almost audible sigh of relief around the restaurant, perhaps more for Rebo's sake than Lyle's. Lyle appeared none the worse, save for a reddish crescent above his left cheekbone that was rapidly changing to purple.

As Kevin and the captain got Lyle to his feet, the band started up again, but there were few takers. It seemed that the party would break up early until Rudy stepped into the crowd and announced drinks on the house.

Decker took his leave from Leslie, who was still smirking like a know-it-all. He found Rebo sitting down at one of the picnic tables. Someone had brought him a glass of ice water and he was soaking in it the three fingers he could fit.

"You didn't tell me you were a Golden Glover."

Rebo examined his swelling knuckles. "I feel like a bone-head. I haven't lost control like that in years."

"You had pretty good reason."

"There's never a good reason to hit a drunk. It's not worth the energy. Listen, pal, I've had enough fun for one night. Are you heading back?"

"I'm still trying to corner Danielle."

"You and about a half dozen other men. I'll catch you back on the ship." Rebo got up and walked away, leaving the ice water on the table. The island children, giggling from the shadows, followed after him at a worshipful distance.

Decker looked around for Danielle. She was gone. So was Leslie. He waited several minutes, thinking they might have gone on group safari to the women's room, but neither showed up again.

Decker headed off through the coconut grove, hoping to catch Rebo and the next launch, but when he got to the beach, he saw the boat already chuffing back to the ship. He was stranded now for at least another half hour.

He thought about taking a walk along the beach, but decided against it: He was suddenly bone-tired and thick in the tongue from two rum specials. Instead, he found an empty hammock strung near the beach and curled up in it. There he could see the entire reach of the bay, black and shining now in the cold moonlight, the froth of its crashing waves a ghostly white. A breeze played through his hair the way Janet's fingers had sometimes done, distractedly, as they lay side by side. It seemed cruel that she wasn't there with him now.

He was on the edge of sleep when he heard footsteps approaching through the grove, crunching over the carpet of desiccated fronds. The sound stopped just a few yards behind him. He was too settled to lift his head and see.

Someone was sniffling and a soft feminine voice began to soothe, "There, there, baby. It wasn't your fault."

"But it *was*. It's *always* my fault. When they're like that, I can't help myself."

"Hush, baby. Hush now. Let's just be together now. Just you and me."

There was the creak of weight settling slowly into a nearby hammock, then a low moan and the moist sounds of unhurried kissing. Fully alert now, Decker felt like the worst kind of voyeur, yet he was too embarrassed to do anything but lie there. He lay curled and alone in his hammock, a tingle of jealousy running through him like a current as he listened to the soft give and take of women's voices sighing in the dark.

# 5

When the bell rang for the first breakfast sitting, Decker grunted and buried his face deeper into his pillow. It felt like he'd crawled into bed just minutes before. With the ship's air-conditioning busted, he had slept in the widow's nest until the rain started pouring down sometime in the wee morning hours. He'd scuttled off to his cabin and had slept fitfully since then in the stuffy room, amazed that Rebo could snore so strenuously and not wake himself.

Soon breakfast aromas came seeping into the room from the saloon upstairs, and he dreamed in snatches that he was drinking a perfect cup of coffee in a greasy spoon on Amsterdam Avenue, the one he had haunted during his Columbia University days. He was still sipping when he woke in earnest a minute later. There was an urgent knocking at the door.

Rebo interrupted his snoring long enough to emit a pained, semiconscious groan; Decker slipped from his bunk, down the ladder, and groped his way through the dark. Without a porthole, it was impossible to guess the time. Decker thought it might be Ryan at the door, wanting an early start on the day's snorkeling.

He stuck his head out the door, blinked a few times, and there was Ellen. Her hair had been hastily brushed back from her face and the dark circles under her eyes were deeper and darker than ever. There was panic and defiance in her hard glare.

"Is she in there?" It was an accusation, not a question.

Decker was in his underwear, but hardly conscious of it.

He blinked some more and licked his lips, trying to loosen his dried-out mouth.

"Uh, who in here?"

*"Danielle.* Is she?"

Decker was only a few heartbeats from being fully awake. "I don't think so," he said. He turned and was about to look for his shorts when Ellen burst through the door and snapped on the light.

Rebo groaned again, angrily this time, like an animal pursued to its lair. There was no Danielle.

Ellen sobbed and quickly left the room. Decker found his shorts on the floor and went out to investigate. Ellen was just a few feet down the hallway, her face buried in her hands.

He placed a hand on her shoulder and felt her whole body tremble.

"What's wrong?"

"I don't know what to *do.* She's just not here. She's not anywhere on this whole damned ship."

"Did you ask the crew?"

"I've asked every person I've run into this morning. No one has seen her since last night. *No one.* I just don't know what to do." She shook her head, raked her fingers down her cheeks.

"I'm sure she's somewhere on board. Did you check the widow's nest?"

"Yes," she said, her voice breaking. "Everywhere. Even the launch."

"When was the last time you saw her?"

She took a deep breath and reflected; it seemed to calm her a little. "We were both sleeping on deck. Way at the back of the ship—the stern, I mean. Anyway, when it started raining—I don't know, it was around two or three in the morning—I got up but I couldn't get Danielle to budge. She said to leave her alone, so I went down to the cabin by myself. When I went back again this morning, she was gone. Vanished. No sign of her at all, not even her blanket. Like I'd just imagined her there."

She looked up at Decker with red-rimmed eyes and smiled miserably. "If she's playing a prank, I'll kill her, I really will."

"Have you told the captain?"

"Told him what?"

"That Danielle is missing."

Ellen looked at Decker now with the eyes of a frightened child. He'd said the dreaded word.

Apparently, it had been a long night for the captain, too. They found him in the saloon—cheeks stubbled, eyes glassy, red nose several shades redder. He was having a cup of coffee with Mary Beth, all cozy in their nook. Decker told him they had something urgent to discuss—in private.

"May I ask what this concerns?"

Ellen blurted it out. "Danielle's missing."

The captain blanched and glanced around the saloon to see if any passenger had heard. "I'll meet you in the deckhouse in five minutes."

The deckhouse of the *Southern Cross* was the glory of the refurbished ship, a gleaming cubicle of varnished wood and brass-lined portholes located on the aft deck between the jacuzzi and the raised door leading down to the honeymoon suite. The inside, however, was strictly business. Plywood benches had been slapped together on either side of a Formica tabletop, and the table and built-in shelves were crammed with electronic gear: several radio sets, a mobile telephone, a radar screen and, like any commercial operation, a desk-top copier and a FAX machine.

When Ellen and Decker arrived, the captain, shaven now and dressed in his formal whites, was already seated on the far side of the table, Kevin beside him. The two parties sat facing each other and the encounter quickly took on the feeling of an official inquiry. More at ease playing the ship's fool than its chief guardian, the captain strained to look concerned and in charge. His hands were folded on the table, his posture properly British. Kevin sat poised to take notes on a legal pad. The first mate looked comically serious and a little nervous, no doubt remembering that Decker had seen him toking with a minor.

"Now, to the best of your recollection, Miss Freedman," the captain asked, "what was Miss Evans's state of mind when you last saw her?"

Ellen threw up her hands and looked at Decker, then back at her inquisitor. "State of mind? You mean, was she thinking of suicide?"

"Let me ask it this way: Was she depressed? Angry? Frightened? Was there anything troubling her?"

"No. Certainly nothing that would have driven her to suicide. There was that thing at Rudy's, of course, with Rebo and Lyle—but you saw that. Besides, Danielle had forgotten about it by the time we got back to the ship. She was amused by the whole thing. A silly boys' game."

"Was she intoxicated?"

"She'd had a few drinks, yes—but no more than the night before."

"About how many drinks?"

"I don't know. Maybe three or four; and that was during the entire time we were at Rudy's. But what does that have to do with anything? She disappeared hours after we got back."

"All right then. When, exactly, was the last time you saw her?"

Ellen turned to Decker. "When do you think the rain started last night?"

Decker shook his head. "I didn't look at my watch."

"I believe it was around three-fifteen," Kevin volunteered. "I know, because I left my porthole open and had the devil to pay in wet sheets."

"You and who else?" Decker said, grinning. Kevin laughed nervously.

"Fine," the captain said, "we've established the time of rainfall. Now, when was the last time you saw Miss Evans?"

"Both of us were sleeping on deck last night, and when it began raining so hard, I got up to go downstairs."

"To your cabin," the captain added.

"Yes, but Danielle refused to get up."

"Refused?"

"She was either too tired or too hung over. I don't know. I couldn't just drag her off."

"And you didn't see her again?"

Ellen repeated what she had told Decker earlier. She had gotten up around seven, gone upstairs to wake Danielle, and found no sign of her.

The captain cleared his throat for the next question. "And you're, uh, certain she didn't spend the night in someone else's cabin?"

"I've asked everyone who even remotely knows her," Ellen answered directly.

"Did she have any further 'contact,' shall we say, with Mr. Hughes last night?"

"Lyle? No, not after what happened on the dance floor. She wanted nothing to do with him."

"Did they exchange words?"

"Exchange words?"

"Did they argue, Miss Freedman?"

Ellen reflected on this. "No, not really. Lyle tried to apologize—it was while we were on the beach waiting for the launch—and she told him to leave her alone. Actually, to use her exact words, she said to leave her 'the fuck alone.' And he did, as far as I know."

"You didn't see him on deck later that night?"

"No, but I was sleeping. Until the rain came and then—" Ellen sniffled and rubbed her nose. The tears were coming again. "This is just so awful," she sobbed.

Decker put his arm around her shoulders.

"Miss Freedman," the captain said, his voice softening. "I assure you I'll do everything within my power. The crew will conduct a complete search of the ship. It's possible Miss Evans may have holed up in some corner of the vessel and is sleeping there now."

"And if you don't find her?" Ellen sniffled.

The captain took a deep breath. "We'll have to contact the police, I'm afraid."

Suddenly, he turned his attention to Decker. "May I ask, sir, what your interest in this matter is?"

"To help in any way I can," Decker said.

"Are you a lawyer by any chance?" There was a skeptical look on the captain's face. Meanwhile, Kevin was staring down at the table.

"No, I'm not a lawyer."

"He's someone I can trust," Ellen said flatly.

Decker knew she was exaggerating for effect. Theirs was an uneasy alliance: journalist and source against a mutual foe. It was the closest thing to trust any reporter knew.

The captain turned again to Decker. "My crew informs me that you've been asking a good many questions among the passengers, Mr. Decker. Mostly about Justin Grammer."

"Your crew informs you correctly."

"Then I take it you're either a journalist or a private investigator, and I won't tolerate either aboard my ship."

"I'm a journalist," Decker said, and caught Kevin's eye.

"I've been fascinated by how your crew takes a very personal interest in entertaining certain under-age passengers. It might make a good travel piece."

"What's all this about, Anderson?" the captain said. Kevin would have looked pale if it hadn't been for his deep tan.

"Nothing, sir. I'll discuss it with you later."

The captain turned to Ellen. "I'm sorry to have strayed so far from the purpose of our meeting. I'll have the crew begin the search immediately."

And then to Decker: "I'll settle affairs with you at a later time."

When Decker returned to the cabin, Rebo was sitting on the edge of the bunk in his underwear, head cupped in his hands as if it were about to fall off his neck.

"You feel as bad as you look?" Decker asked.

"I couldn't look that bad."

"Brace yourself for some startling news. No one can find Danielle."

That got him to release his head. "Since when?"

"Since this morning. Ellen said she was sleeping on deck last night. There's not a trace of her."

Rebo shook his head, carefully. "This is some crazy shit goin' down here."

"I'd get a move on. We've got a busy day."

The search of the ship was conducted quietly by Kevin and a single steward, so that nothing should seem out of the ordinary. That one passenger had disappeared, especially someone as eccentric as Justin, was merely troublesome, but once word got out that Danielle had vanished—the femme fatale of the *Southern Cross*—there might surely be a panic. Hence, no announcement from the captain.

For nearly everyone else but Ellen and Decker and Rebo, morning on the main deck progressed as usual, with passengers coming up from a hearty breakfast and devoting themselves to their books, their drinks, and their tans while admiring the new sights.

Around one-thirty the night before, the *Southern Cross* had set sail from Spanish Town and dropped anchor a half hour later at Long Bay, ten miles north along the western coast of Virgin Gorda. It was a cove more than a bay, really, a tiny recess nestled at the foot of Gorda Peak and rimmed by a crescent of deserted white beach. The island at that location was lush and green, more tropical than arid, with thick groves of mango and banana along its shores.

The Caribbean sun performed right on schedule, burning off the island mist and spilling over the calm waters of the bay like liquid gold. By nine, all traces of last night's rain had disappeared, and the water in the cove was a bright translucent blue, unreal, like mouthwash.

While Ellen cleaned up, Decker kept watch from a bench at mid-deck, waiting for Leslie to appear, anxious to get her private reaction to the latest developments. When she still hadn't appeared at nine-thirty, he considered rousting her from her cabin, but then Rebo came slapping from the stern in his mammoth flipflops. The back lid of his camera was dangling wide open.

"I've just been censored," he said, sitting down heavily on the bench.

"The captain?"

"Him and cabin boy Kevin. No more picture-taking on the good ship Lollipop."

"Damn. Farlidge is going to have a fit. Did you lose any good shots?"

He shook his head. "Just the spot where Danielle allegedly

slept last night. Nothing that shows anything. At least I've still got the film I shot at Rudy's."

"Good—in a safe place?"

Rebo patted the pocket on his whale trunks. "I don't leave nothin' in that cabin."

From the top of the companionway, Ellen spotted Decker and started their way. Her dark hair was wet and gleaming from the shower.

Rebo stood up. "I'll leave you to your investigative duties, pal. Catch you at noon."

For privacy, Decker and Ellen moved nearer the stern, not far from where Danielle had slept the night before. Decker let Ellen talk things out, hoping she might inadvertently shed light where his questioning had failed. Mostly she talked about Danielle, about how impulsive and unpredictable and stubborn she could be. Decker lent a sympathetic ear, waiting for the right moment to pop his next question. Timing was everything; any reporter, or con artist, could tell you that.

"Were you lovers?" he asked, wanting to confirm last night's tryst in the grove.

He blew it. Ellen turned away. "It's just a story to you, isn't it?"

"Yes," he said, and fell back again on his only defense, "but I also want the truth. You won't find many others interested in that." Part of that, too, was selfish. The best stories, the most satisfying ones, radiated truth like unflawed gems.

She stared him hard in the eye, skeptical but also contemptuously proud. "Yes," she said, as though announcing it to the world. "And why should it matter?"

"Why shouldn't it?" he said evenly.

She blinked and considered a moment, then gave him the hard, proud stare again. "All right, then, it does matter."

"How long?"

"For two years—until Danielle broke things off."

"And now?"

She lowered her head. "We started again last week."

"Leaving Justin out in the cold."

"It's not that simple."

"What do you mean?"

"I don't know. I'm not sure Justin and Danielle even slept together."

"Not sure?"

"Danielle refused to talk about it—until last night. He was just someone she'd met in New York, and they decided to make the trip together."

"And you tagged along?"

"Danielle asked me. She said it would make a great tax write-off if we took some pictures."

"Were either of them into drugs?"

"What makes you think that?"

"Nothing, except they might have been keeping the wrong company. Danielle never touched drugs?"

"No, absolutely not. Although a lot of models do. They do coke instead of food. Danielle despises them. She calls them 'nose eaters.' "

"What about Justin?"

"Justin, I don't know. I guess there were times when I thought he might be stoned. But I don't know if it was booze or drugs or his own internal bliss. He was kind of spacey."

"What about the night he disappeared?"

Ellen shrugged. "I didn't see him at all that night. Danielle was trying to avoid him."

"Why?"

"She said she was tired of him. You have to know Danielle. She tires easily of anyone who adores her."

"So you think Justin adored her?"

"In a way. She seemed to be his feminine ideal, someone who could use men instead of being used."

"Can I take a look at Danielle's things?"

"Why?" She eyed him suspiciously.

"It might give us some clues."

"She wouldn't like it."

"She doesn't have to know. And, besides, she might have left us a trail."

Decker felt a twinge of guilt to see how quickly Ellen brightened. Even the most dubious hope was better than none.

"Let's go," she said.

Decker pulled a black leather shoulder bag from under the bunk—a Gucci with just enough wear to give it that soft, almost fleshy feel—set it on the mattress, and started unzipping compartments. There were surprisingly few clothes, most of them flimsy bathing suits and lingerie, all of it, Ellen assured him, quite expensive. Decker felt like a voyeur just touching them.

Her makeup case was another surprise. Just a bottle of aloe vera, a tube of lip balm, some eyeliner. None of it Maybelline. And a jar of bee pollen, which Ellen said Danielle applied religiously to her face at night. "Every model I know has some sort of superstitious routine," Ellen said. "Otherwise they go crazy thinking about how they're getting older everyday."

In one of the side zipper pockets, he found a paperback copy of *A Year in Provence*—new and never cracked—and a small brown address book. Decker riffled through the latter and jotted down the name and phone number of every listing in the book. It might come in handy later.

He dumped the contents of the other pocket onto the bunk and found maps, a couple of guidebooks, a pack of Kleenex and, dangling from a silver chain, a St. Christopher medal. Ellen held it a moment in her palm.

"I remember when her mother sent this," she said, starting to sniffle now. "It was supposed to protect her in godless New York."

"Let's hope it worked here, too."

He checked under the bunk again and pulled out a large blue athletic bag. Inside was a hot pink diving mask, hot pink fins, and a lavender snorkel tube: Barbie goes to the beach. Underneath these items, however, he found a diving journal, bound in gray and sheathed in a clear plastic case. He slipped it out and flipped to the last written page, about a quarter of the way through. There were three recent entries there—two from the previous week, a third the day before she disappeared.

"A serious diver, I take it."

"Very much," Ellen said. "It's one reason she booked the cruise."

"And you?"

"I took some lessons years ago in the Caymans, but I haven't done it since. It hurts my ears."

"You're supposed to swallow a lot."

"I did—only my mouth was always dry."

Decker started repacking the bag, but Ellen took over, careful to make sure everything was put back just where Danielle had left them. She was collecting the maps and guidebooks when Decker noticed something—a small box for a videocassette tape, the 8-millimeter kind. It was about the size of a cigarette case.

"Did Danielle bring a camcorder?"

"Not that I know of."

"Then why would she have a tape?"

"I don't know."

He looked inside. "It's empty."

Ellen shrugged. "Does it mean something?"

"It could mean a lot."

\* \* \*

When Decker and Ellen left the cabin, Leslie was just leaving hers, three doors down the hall. She shot them a suspicious look, blurted, "Good morning," and started up the spiral staircase ahead of them.

"She gives me the creeps," Ellen whispered.

"Why?"

"She's always staring at Danielle and me. I think she's a homophobe."

"You think she knows?"

"Some people can tell. Not everyone is as dense as you are."

By eleven that morning, Ellen and Decker were talked out and lying side by side in the widow's nest, drenched in the heat of the sun, cooled by the moist caresses of the trade winds. There were two ways, Decker found, of dealing with the Caribbean climate: You could fight it by running to the shower three or four times a day, or you could give in to it, the way the crew did, letting the sun and sea salt mingle with your sweat and coalesce into a kind of coppery-smelling glaze, not unpleasant at all. Decker had gotten comfortable with this new skin while Ellen hadn't. She was about to go back to her cabin and shower before lunch when Mary Beth stopped by the widow's nest and said quietly that the captain would like a word with both of them in the deckhouse. They went quickly.

Kevin and the captain again were seated on one side of the makeshift Formica table; Ellen and Decker sat down to face them.

"Well?" Ellen's voice was small and helpless.

"I'm afraid we haven't found her," the captain said. "What I would suggest now, Miss Freedman, is that we go to the BVI police."

"The police," Ellen sneered. "They can't find Justin, now you want them to find Danielle?"

"We have little choice," the captain said. "We happen to be anchored in their territorial waters."

Kevin spoke up. "Sir, if you don't mind, I might suggest that this time we contact the detective division in Road Town. They appear to be a much more professional lot."

"Yes, that's true," the captain said. "They train at Scotland Yard."

"What about the American embassy?" Decker said. "Can't they be brought in?"

"I wouldn't think that's necessary at this time."

"But the embassy could call in the FBI," Decker said.

The captain sighed impatiently. "Yes, that's true, Mr. Decker. And I would think we should try that—but only as a last resort. It might take the embassy several days to arrange such an investigation. And they may insist that we sail to St. Thomas and anchor there for the duration. That could mean days, perhaps weeks, of delay. I rather doubt anyone on board would want that—not even you, Miss Freedman."

"I don't care about delays!" Ellen burst out. "I just want to find Danielle!"

"Believe me," the captain said, "nothing would please me more. But there are fifty other passengers aboard this vessel whose comfort and convenience must be considered as well. I beg you to at least give the Road Town police a proper go. If their work is unsatisfactory, we'll go straight to the embassy."

Ellen turned to Decker, looking for advice. Her eyes and nose were as red and raw as if she'd taken a beating.

Decker faced the captain, saw the tense expectancy in the troll-like face. It was true: The feds were notoriously slow and not always better than the locals. It might mean weeks of being tied up on shore.

"It's worth a try," he said.

"Okay." Ellen sniffled.

"One more thing," the captain said, turning aggressively toward Decker. "I've decided that you and your colleague may stay aboard this ship, but on two conditions."

"No pictures is one of them, I assume."

"Absolutely. You have no right to violate the privacy of my passengers, not so long as they remain on this ship, which I remind you is private property. Secondly, if I hear from any passenger that you have been intrusive, badgering, or otherwise a pest, I will personally deliver you to the nearest island. Now is that clear?"

"Perfectly," Decker said.

Kevin was staring at the table.

Sgt. Lansforth Baines and Inspector Malcolm Givins were on board within the hour. They were a professional-looking duo in dark suits and white shirts, their black skin gleaming against starched collars. In the British tradition of law enforcement, they carried no firearms, just a look of unassailable dignity.

At noon, the captain assembled the passengers on deck. He introduced the two investigators, explained what they had come to do, and asked everyone's full cooperation.

"Now let me tell you briefly how this will work. Each of you will be interviewed in your cabin, starting with the lowest number and working on up to the highest. Mary Beth will come to fetch you as you are needed. Once you are dismissed, you may go about your normal business. The more smoothly this goes, the sooner we can all return to making this a holiday you won't forget." A few passengers chuckled at the ambiguous choice of words.

That said, the captain switched back to his role as the ship's MC and stand-up comedian. "We will be serving lunch in the saloon shortly, and afterward, those of you who are finished 'being grilled,' so to speak, may board launches to the beach. Then, later tonight, at twenty-one hundred hours—nine o'clock for you landlubbers—we will start a little bonfire on the beach here. We'll have toasted marshmallows, of course, and singing, as well as a joke-telling contest. Now, how does that sound?"

The passengers applauded, but the gossip and buzzing began almost immediately as the captain led the two investigators below.

Art Kapinski was standing close to Decker: "Makes a damn beach party seem kind of dull, don't it?"

While Rebo went off to the loading deck to sneak pictures of the cove, Decker decided to grab some lunch. He wanted to sit with Leslie, but found her already preoccupied with Tony and Chris, who seemed to be squaring off now for her affections. Gregory Peck versus the Muscle Boy. Decker wasn't about to enter that race.

Instead, he sat down with Ryan and his mother Maureen and his very subdued-looking sister Connie, who sighed every now and then and pushed her food around her plate. Clearly, it was the end for her and Kevin, who had no doubt been given a hands-off order from the captain.

Like many passengers, Maureen was wondering aloud if she should cut the family vacation short.

"Aw, Mom, we can't go now," Ryan whined. "It's just getting fun. Jenny and I want to go scuba diving tomorrow. I'll miss the wreck of the *Rhone.*"

"The wreck of the what?" his mother said.

"It's a British mail steamer that sank about a hundred years ago," Decker said, remembering something Mary Beth had said.

Connie spoke up. "As far as I'm concerned, we can leave this very second. The whole vacation's been a drag."

"Mom, don't listen to her."

Maureen clapped her hands to her ears and shook her head. She turned to Decker. "What do you think? Is the ship safe?"

"It's hard to say. Certainly, Justin and Danielle were known to each other. I suspect their disappearances are linked. They might have even taken off together, for whatever reason. Who knows? At least now there are police on board."

Mary Beth called out Decker's cabin number. It was just past one. Decker excused himself from the table. "Maybe after my little interview I'll know more."

Decker was first to reach the cabin, where he found the investigation had already begun. Rebo's few remaining pieces of photo equipment—mostly lenses and film—were spread out on the floor. Givins, the graying senior of the two investigators, was sitting on the bottom bunk with Decker's duffel bag open on his lap, poking a hand around the insides. Meanwhile, Baines was in the bathroom checking out items in the medicine cabinet.

Givins rezipped Decker's bag and tossed it lightly on the bed, then stood and shook hands.

"Inspector Givins, BVI homicide. Most pleased to meet you." His eyes were slightly bulging and jaundiced in the puffy face. The lids drooped a little, imparting a look of arrogance, perhaps undeserved.

Decker glanced around the room. "I thought you needed a search warrant for this sort of thing."

Givins smiled patiently, suffering one more Yankee tourist. He spoke with a precise, uninflected British accent. "We have the permission of the captain, Mr. Decker. Under international maritime law, a captain's authorization is the same as a bench warrant. So, would you care to have a seat, please?"

Givins continued standing while Decker sat.

"Sgt. Baines, I'd like you to meet Mr. Decker." Baines came

out of the bathroom, a clipboard in his hand. He was younger and taller than Givins, and quietly handsome. He could have given Sidney Poitier, in his prime, a run for his money.

Baines asked Decker for his passport. Decker dug through his duffel bag and handed it over.

"I see you are a resident of Cincinnati, Mr. Decker." Baines pronounced the name of the city with a stress on every syllable. It sounded almost exotic.

"Correct."

Baines checked off something on his clipboard, then smiled. "I know the baseball team. The Reds. They are very good, yes?" Baines had more of the island patois in his voice, a kind of choppy Cajun accent.

"They *were* very good," Decker said. "Now they're a bunch of crybabies."

"I remember. They used to call them Redlegs, yes?" Baines grinned as though this were a private joke.

"During the Cold War," Decker said. "Only Commies were Reds back then."

"I see," Baines said, still grinning.

Givins spoke up. "Redleg means something quite different to us here, Mr. Decker. It refers to the first white slaves on these islands—Welshmen, I believe. Their skin, of course, turned bright red as they worked in the fields under the hot sun. Today it has become a slang term for, shall we say, 'less civilized' white people. I'm afraid that many American tourists are called red-legs."

"Thanks for the language lesson."

"You are most welcome."

When Rebo came to the door, Baines asked politely if he would wait on the main deck. "One interview at a time, please," he said, and then lapsed into dialect. "We fetch you coming, Mr. Johnson."

Rebo glanced anxiously at his precious equipment spread in disarray across the floor, but kept quiet for a change. He backed out of the doorway and closed the door.

Givins turned to Decker. "You and Mr. Johnson work for an enterprise known as the Cincinnati *Eagle*, am I correct?"

"Yes." There was no use lying even if Decker had felt inclined. Their gear was plastered with ID stickers.

"And you are on assignment?"

"Yes."

"Perhaps you are writing a travel piece?" Givins asked all the questions while Baines scribbled on his clipboard.

Decker toyed with answering yes—loosely defined, Justin's story *was* a travel piece—but he feared that stretching the truth now would come back to haunt him later.

"We were sent to do a story on the disappearance of Justin Grammer."

Givins and Baines exchanged even glances, then Givins turned back to Decker. "And I take it you're doing this story with the full cooperation of Captain Pearce?"

"I wouldn't say full cooperation—but, yes, he knows."

Givins got down to business. "You and Mr. Johnson, I understand, were both at Rudy's restaurant last night."

"Yes."

"Until what hour?"

"We came back separately. Rebo about a half hour before me, around eleven-thirty, I think. I returned at midnight."

"Tell me what transpired between Mr. Johnson and another passenger at the restaurant that night, a Mr. Lyle Hughes."

Decker gave them a quick rundown leading up to the one-punch knockout.

"Would you say Mr. Johnson is prone to violence?"

"Not at all. I've never seen him throw a punch until last night. Under the circumstances, I'd say it was justified."

Givins smiled a little. "Perhaps." He moved on. "When did you last see Miss Evans, Mr. Decker?"

He wondered for a moment whether he should tell them what he had heard while lying in the coconut grove. He decided against it. After all, he hadn't "seen" anything.

"It was at Rudy's. Around eleven."

"And what was her state of mind then?"

"She was angry," Decker said.

"At whom?"

"With Lyle, of course."

Givins began asking Decker in detail where and when he had slept on deck that night, and at what time he had returned to his cabin.

"And when you returned to your cabin, Mr. Johnson was already in bed?"

"Yes, and snoring like a monster."

"Would you describe yourself as a light or heavy sleeper, Mr. Decker?"

"Sometimes light, sometimes heavy. It depends on how wound up I am."

"What about last night?"

"I didn't sleep very well. The AC was out."

"Did you notice Mr. Johnson leave the cabin at any time after your return last night?"

Decker was surprised by the question. "No, of course not."

"But he may have."

"What do you mean?"

"If you were sleeping at any point—"

"Yes, but what's that got to do with Rebo?"

Givins buried his chin into his tie. His neck ballooned like a frog's bellows. "We have a witness who says Mr. Johnson was seen on deck at about three-thirty A.M. this morning."

"What witness?"

"That's not your concern, Mr. Decker."

"Are you implying that Rebo had anything to do with Danielle disappearing?"

"We are not implying anything, Mr. Decker. We are simply trying to ascertain the facts. You did not see Mr. Johnson leave your cabin at any time during the night?"

"No, I did not."

Givins turned to Baines to see if he had any questions. He shook his head and deferred to Givins.

"We thank you for your time. Now if you would please notify Mr. Johnson that we are ready."

Decker scrambled up to the main deck and found Rebo sitting on a bench near the bar. Next to him was Leslie Stanton, her slim brown legs crossed and turned toward Rebo like weapons.

She smiled and rocked her foot a little as Decker approached. "I was just getting to know your colleague here," she said, her voice teasing. "You didn't tell me how fascinating he was."

"I'm sure he filled you in." Then to Rebo: "I need to talk with you—alone."

"Ooh," Leslie mocked. "Official newspaper business?"

"You might say that."

"Well, I won't stand in the way of working journalists. I'll catch you two later."

Decker watched as Leslie strutted off. She had a way of leading with her hips, a straight-on, athletic walk, unconsciously sexy.

"Thank God you showed up," Rebo said. "That woman was about to eat me alive. She asked everything except my penis size. I swear—"

"Listen, were you up on deck around three this morning?"

"Yeah, for a while. Why?"

"What the hell were you doing?"

"I couldn't sleep, so I did some laundry. What's the big deal?"

"Laundry?"

"I washed out some things and hung 'em out to dry. Ain't nothin' goin' to dry down in those cabins."

"Why in the middle of the night?"

"I told you, I couldn't sleep. I was sicker 'an a dog from those damned rum specials."

"Someone told the police they saw you."

"So what?"

"It places you on deck around the time Danielle disappeared."

"So, there were a lot of people on deck. What are you so worried about?"

"I don't know," Decker said, shaking his head. "I have a bad feeling about this whole thing."

"You have a bad feeling about everything. The sun shines, Decker has a bad feeling. A woman makes eyes at him, Decker has a bad feeling. Why don't you go with the flow a little."

"Because the flow is always downhill."

"That's deep, Rick. Really goddamn deep. Sign me up for your course in the power of negative thinking."

# 6

At 9:30 P.M., Decker and Ellen boarded the last launch to the beach, where the bonfire for the late-night beach party was already blazing—a neon dome of orange pressing upward against the blackness. Decker had persuaded Ellen to leave the ship to get her mind off the investigation. He also hoped to get her talking more openly about Justin and Danielle. He was all sympathy and, at the same time, shamelessly manipulative, a duality Decker had long ago come to terms with as a reporter, and was no longer even conscious of it.

Rebo had left in the early afternoon for yet another trip to St. Thomas, both to send off his film and to dictate Decker's handwritten story over the phone. (Using the ship's cellular phone, while convenient, would have meant waving a red flag in front of the captain's nose.) Decker expected Rebo back by ten, assuming he could find someone in Spanish Town harbor willing to ferry him the ten miles up the coast to Long Bay.

Meanwhile, life on the *Southern Cross* had changed in subtle ways since the police interrogation began: A touch of paranoia was in the air, as well as a kind of collective denial. Mary Beth moved about the passengers most of the day, assuring them of their safety and offering a full refund to anyone upset enough to cut their vacation short. There were few takers, Decker learned. Most of the passengers seemed determined to have a good time. In fact, some refused to believe that foul play was involved in either disappearance. The gossip, or perhaps wishful thinking, was that Justin and Danielle had run off together to live somewhere on the islands.

Decker had heard that from someone as sensible as Art Kapinski, although Art couldn't support it with a motive. "Who knows with these young ones today?" he said. "They all seem to be running from something. Drugs. Marriages. Their awful childhoods. Of course, they blame every damn thing on their parents, as if we didn't have plenty of problems of our own."

Ellen and Decker walked north along the beach, away from the bonfire and the marshmallow toasting and the camp songs, and found an overturned skiff where they could sit together with their toes in the fine white sand. The bay that night was a velvet painting: glassy waves of white on black, a silver dollar for a moon. Most of the stars were hidden behind the sky's cold lunar brilliance, all but the brightest planets and the four dazzling points of the Southern Cross, plunging, as always, toward the sea.

Decker was surprised at how comfortable he was just being with Ellen, despite their obvious differences in background and sexual bent. Decker had never befriended a lesbian before, and although he was savvy enough to know they weren't all fat, androgynous types with glandular problems, he was pleasantly surprised by Ellen's softness and vulnerability and her willingness to accept him, a man, on his own terms.

Ellen did most of the talking, and the subject somehow turned to families. She told Decker about her father, a Wall Street banker, and her mother, a social worker who at one time had been a card-carrying member of the American Communist Party.

"Quite the odd couple," Decker said.

"Not if you know the whole story. My mother's mother came from Russia and worked in the sweatshops in the garment district. I think my mother hated the system that had oppressed my grandmother, but she also wanted the security of a rich husband."

"And what about your father?"

"Daddy was head over heels because Mom was gorgeous. Really, you wouldn't know from me—she looked a lot like Lauren Bacall when she was young. He couldn't believe that anybody so gorgeous would have wanted him, too—even with all his money."

"That's a pretty cynical analysis."

Ellen shrugged. "Relationships *are* cynical. It's all about power, isn't it? There's always one person in control. There has to be or it falls apart. In my parents' case, it was my mother."

Decker tested the theory against himself and Janet, whether she had been the controller, he the controllee. In the end, she had been the one with the power to walk away and take up with someone new. Then again, hadn't his cowardice forced her to? That he had put his own life ahead of hers proved he didn't really love her. Forget the extenuating circumstances; pure love was a matter of absolutes, of finalities and eternities. Was it not?

Ellen took Decker's hand, squeezed it. "I didn't mean to depress you," she said. Her touch brought a sudden flush of shame. She was trying to ease his pain even as he was trying to exploit hers.

"Tell me," he said, "are your parents happy?"

"As happy as any married couple their age, I suppose. Mom's still the boss, she always has been. They sleep in separate bedrooms now."

"Have you told them about yourself?"

"About myself? Oh, I get it. You're afraid to say the 'L' word." Ellen smiled and touched his arm. "No, but I think Mom suspects. I dated a lot of guys when I was younger, but they never did much for me. There was an older man, a widower with a couple of sweet kids, that I almost married. I don't think I really knew until I met Danielle."

"I take it Danielle always knew."

"Danielle is in love with Danielle. She's attracted to anyone who comes worshiping at her altar."

"Seems to me that would be a lot of people."

"She told me once—I think just to hurt me—that she was never happier than when a man was inside her, but what she couldn't stand was when they started moving. She didn't like the feeling of not being in control."

Decker had never thought of it that way: Seeing things from a woman's point of view was always a little unsettling, especially in matters of sex. Most men, of course, would rather not know.

"It's hard to believe, isn't it?" Ellen said, staring across the moonlit bay. "Here we are in the middle of paradise, at a time when we shouldn't have a care in the world, and we're both on pins and needles. If Danielle suddenly turns up again, I don't know what I'll do. Maybe kill her."

They both laughed, but Decker knew that with the passing of every hour the chances grew slimmer that Danielle was alive. He'd seen it too often as a reporter—families frantic for hours, then days, over a missing child, a loved one, and then . . .

As if reading his thoughts, Ellen asked, "There's still hope, don't you think? I mean there's *always* hope. She could have asked a deckhand or somebody to take her back to Spanish Town. She could be in a hotel room somewhere now, taking a *real* bath instead of those awful lukewarm showers."

"Anything's possible," Decker said. He told Ellen what Art had suggested. Ellen found no comfort in it.

"Why would they engineer anything so fantastic?"

"To escape the past, perhaps."

"What past?"

"I don't know. Maybe a crime. Or a jealous lover."

"Danielle wouldn't run from an ex-lover. She'd laugh in his face."

"Or her face."

"True, but if Danielle is running from anybody, it's debt collectors."

"Seriously? I would think Maybelline pays her a nice chunk of change."

"Danielle spends it faster than she can make it. When she first moved to New York, she was like a kid at FAO Schwarz. In a couple of months, she was in debt up to her eyeballs and it only got worse. I had to find her one of those bankruptcy consultants to straighten things out."

"Then how did she pay for the trip?"

"She didn't. She promised to reimburse me from the money we'd earn from the swim photos."

Decker's mind stirred with new possibilities. It made the blackmail angle that much more plausible.

"But what about Justin? Couldn't she have borrowed the money from him?"

"She said he was borrowing the money, too. He was your typical shoe-leather actor—always broke, always looking for work."

"But his father is worth millions."

"If it's true, Danielle never mentioned it."

Decker's thoughts returned to the empty cassette box. "But you still don't think Danielle could have been blackmailing someone?"

"I can't imagine that. Danielle would more likely be the person blackmailed."

"Justin could have put her up to it." Especially if Daddy had cut him off, Decker thought. He'd have to check into it.

"I doubt it," Ellen said. "Justin was as helpless as she was.

Danielle told me he didn't even have his own apartment; he moved around and lived with friends."

They cut the conversation short when they saw Maureen, Ryan, and his new girlfriend Jenny walking toward them up the beach. The two young teenagers were practically skipping through the sand.

"I'm sorry to butt in like this," Maureen said, "but these two nuts insist on going night snorkeling. I told them they could go, but only if a responsible adult went along."

"Aw, Mom, you've seen *Jaws* too many times," Ryan said. "There're no sharks out there."

"Yes, but there are plenty of other things. And besides, it's dark, young man."

"That's the whole idea, Mom."

"I'd be glad to," Decker said, thinking he had an airtight excuse, "only I didn't bring my gear."

"Jenny has an extra mask," Ryan said excitedly.

Decker looked at the two young eager faces, then turned to Ellen. She hugged herself and said, "I'll be all right. Go ahead. It sounds like fun."

"All right," Decker said to Ryan, "but no chasing after fish. You got that?"

Decker felt his whole body loosen the instant he plunged into the bay. It was a baptism of sorts, the water warm, silky, infinitely calm—only the lip-tingle of salt as a reminder of the sea.

He could see the moonlight rippling in waves across the sandy bottom. The visibility was astounding—fifteen, maybe twenty feet in any direction—and there, at the outer reaches of sight, the darkness gathered until it became a black wall, holding behind it all the mystery and terror of the sea.

They had swum out from the beach, but not so far that

they couldn't touch bottom, when they noticed tiny sparks of light, like fairy dust, swirling from their fingertips.

Ryan signaled the group to surface. "Wow! What is this stuff?"

"It's a kind of algae," Jenny answered brightly. "It lights up whenever something touches it."

"It's beautiful," Decker said. "I've never seen anything like it."

They plunged in again and swam round and round until the whole bay seemed to glitter with the phosphorescent creatures. Decker felt like one of the kids in *Peter Pan*, chasing Tinkerbell around the bedroom.

They didn't see a single fish until they came across a school of baby tarpon, their sleek bodies shimmering like knife blades in the moonlight. Decker wondered where the other fish were, if they slept in caves at night, or if they were all hiding beyond that wall of darkness farther out to sea.

Ryan signaled and they surfaced again, heads chilled in the night air, bodies warmed by the sea.

"Hey, why don't we swim out to the ship?" Ryan said. "There's always lots of fish hanging out there."

"Why don't we?" Jenny piped in. "It's not that far."

Ryan swallowed his mouthpiece and was about to dive back in when Decker shouted, "Whoa! Wait a minute! If we do this, we do it as a team."

Decker scanned the distance across the bay. The *Southern Cross* was anchored about 150 yards out, a couple of degrees or so off to their left, its brightly lit hull casting an inverted, ghostly image on the smooth black water. They were already about a third of the way there, with the bonfire and the beach some 70 yards behind them.

"It's not that far," Decker said, "but I'm not sure about the currents."

"Aw, come on," Ryan pleaded. "We'll stay real close together. Won't we, Jenny?"

She nodded and pulled her mask down as though the matter had been settled. Decker was outnumbered.

"Okay, but if we don't stick together, I'm taking both of you back to shore. Hear me?" His answer was a couple of splashes as the two dropped below the water.

Decker was the only one without flippers, and he had a hard time keeping up with his younger charges. Several times, he had to grab Ryan by the ankle to slow him down. The currents proved not to be a problem, however, and they closed the distance to the ship with ease.

It was eerie when they reached the deeper water and couldn't see bottom, as though they were flying over an abyss of uncharted depth. Decker shivered and tried not to imagine what lurked down there.

Within fifty yards of the ship, they could see the penumbra of soft yellow-green light below the waterline. As they swam closer still, the submerged hull came into view, dark and massive, its long floating bulk defying gravity and all common sense.

The two teenagers picked up speed; Decker kicked faster to keep pace. Within ten yards, they could see fish—all kinds of fish—gleaming like Christmas ornaments in the ship's fringe of light. Grumpy-looking snapper with downturned mouths. Slinky, pipe-shaped gars. Rows of iridescent squid. And a battalion of pink jellyfish, like paratroopers dropping from the sky, dotting the water at every level.

Ryan grabbed Decker's shoulder and pointed. Just below the layer of fish was a granddaddy of a barracuda, maybe five feet long, with a nasty overbite of sharp, snaggled teeth. It hung there motionless, sleek and shiny as a sword, biding time until its next meal.

Ryan could hardly contain his excitement. He swam back

and forth several times between Jenny and Decker, making certain they had spotted the barracuda as well.

Decker led them in a wide berth around the old codger as they swam away toward the bow. They stopped to inspect the anchor chain. Decker took hold of it and climbed downward a few feet along its long curving length, watching it slope away in the direction of the beach and disappear into the abyss.

They rounded the bow to port side, where Decker discovered a troop of small black sea horses bobbing just below the waterline. He signaled for the others and Jenny came quickly to his side. Ryan, however, was nowhere in sight. Decker signaled Jenny to the surface.

"Where the hell did he go?"

"He was just here. I was—"

"Shhhhh! I hear splashing. Over there!"

They swam straight out from the bow and were soon met by Ryan, who surfaced instantly.

"Hey, you guys, I spotted a whale!" He was breathless and pointing. "Right out there. It's huge!"

"You sure it's not a sea turtle?" Decker said.

"It's way too big. Come on, follow me!"

"Hold on, Ryan. Could it be a shark?"

"No, it's too slow for that. It's *huge.* Come on! We'll miss it!"

"All right. But let's stick together this time."

Decker guessed it was a log or maybe a big manta ray feeding on the surface. As far as Decker knew, whales didn't migrate to the Caribbean until winter, and even then a sighting was extremely rare.

Ryan and Jenny stayed back with Decker for a short while, then raced ahead, leaving him in the wake from their flippers. They swam straight out for twenty or thirty yards, veered left as Ryan corrected his course, then suddenly veered right as he corrected again. Decker was ready to call it off. Every yard they ventured beyond the ship, the water seemed to grow deeper and colder, the darkness more forbidding.

Decker caught up and signaled them to the surface.

"I can't believe it!" Ryan said between gasps for air. "It was just here!"

"Let's forget it," Decker said. He was breathless himself now with trying to keep up.

"But it was just here!"

"It probably swam away," Jenny said.

"I swear I saw it, I swear!"

"We've seen plenty for one night," Decker said. "Let's head back."

Ryan slapped the water. "Aw, come on, Rick. We're having a great time."

"Just a few more minutes?" Jenny pleaded.

"I'm pooped. Now let's go."

"Aw, ma-a-a-n," Ryan said. "Just when it was getting fun."

Decker took a fix on the bonfire and plunged ahead; Jenny and Ryan fell in behind. They had gone maybe twenty yards toward shore when Decker felt a sharp tug on his left foot. He whirled around, ready to face an angry shark, a barracuda, but it was Ryan, pointing frantically to his left.

Decker dived in front of Ryan, blocking the boy's way, then squinted in the direction he had indicated. Something was out there, all right. Something very difficult to explain.

It was drifting at a forty-five-degree angle, five or ten feet below the choppy surface, just inside the fringe of their visibility: a large gray object, cocoon-shaped, its loose edges flapping in the current. Possibly a sea turtle snagged in a fishing net, but Decker couldn't tell at that distance, even in the moon's cold, pure light.

He signaled the others to the surface. "I'm going out for a closer look. You two stay here."

Ryan protested. "But *I* found it."

"Stay here. I'll let you know if it's safe."

Closing within ten feet of the object, Decker dived again. The gray cylinder was now more defined: ragged patches of white at either end, thin spiraled stripes around a bulging middle. It was like no creature Decker had ever seen.

When Decker surfaced, Ryan and Jenny were right on top of him.

"Dammit, you two! Stay back!"

"What is it?" Jenny asked.

"It's not moving," Ryan said. "It can't hurt us."

"Just stay the hell back."

Decker swam ahead now with an icy dread in the hollow of his stomach, a heaviness in his thighs. His instincts told him what he would find, and diving again within two or three feet of the object, his worst fears were confirmed. He saw a rolled blanket, loose edges undulating in the current, and a white cord, looped tightly around the swollen torso. And then something that convulsed his stomach: human feet, poking from the higher end of the blanket, the flesh mangled, the bone gleaming in the moonlight.

Decker popped to the surface and there was Ryan, teeth chattering like a wind-up toy.

"It's D-d-d-d-d-anielle, is-is-isn't it?"

"Let's go. Both of you. Back to the beach."

"Is it?" Jennifer demanded. She was a few feet away, treading water.

"I don't know. It could be anyone. Now let's get back to the beach, do you hear me?"

Jennifer sobbed sharply, once, the sound echoing through the cove, again and again, never coming to a rest—a lost soul tossed on a black and endless sea.

# 7

Givins and Baines had no sooner returned to Road Town that night than they were called back to the *Southern Cross*. They arrived by police boat forty minutes later, close to eleven, and asked that Decker assist them during the dragging operation. They decided to use the ship's rickety launch for the job; it was slow but big enough, and besides, speed wasn't the important thing.

Baines boarded the launch with a black satchel, bulky and official-looking, and both he and Givins carried heavy-duty flashlights for the search. Three deckhands came along as well: one to steer, the other two to maneuver the fishing nets on either side of the boat. The two investigators sat in front while Decker was consigned to a spot behind the engine casing, surrounded by activity.

Givins asked Decker to direct them to where the body had last been seen. As far as Decker could remember, that was about fifty yards from the bow of the ship, in a north-northeasterly direction. The problem was, the wind had picked up, alternating from the west and southwest, and the position of the bow kept changing. Gone, too, was the moonlit calm; nothing seemed the same now in the bay's dark, choppy waters. Decker gave it his best guess, operating on instinct more than anything. The tiller-man changed course half a dozen times until Decker said, "This is the spot," although he wasn't at all certain.

The tillerman cut the engine, and the boat settled into the chop and drifted forward. They were about fifty yards from the ship, in a direct line between the bow and the northern outreach of the cove. The water looked cold and mean in its blackness; no more romantic notions about velvet paintings. Decker's thoughts went back to that old barracuda they'd seen waiting under the ship, bloodless, deadly, biding its time.

Givins turned to Baines. "What would the tide do at this hour?"

"Goin' to sea, I think, but—"

The tillerman interrupted in a fast patois. Decker couldn't decipher a word, but apparently Givins and Baines could.

"Then we should work our way back toward the beach," Givins said.

Baines passed the instructions with a nod back to the tillerman. The deckhands lowered their nets, Givins and Baines took their positions in the bow, and the dragging was on.

The launch zigzagged across the bay in slow, lazy S curves—a procedure as tedious as it was nerve-wracking. Decker grew increasingly nauseated from the engine's oily fumes, but couldn't move without getting in the way of either the net handlers or the tillerman. He kept his eyes fixed ahead on the sweeping movements of the flashlights, and whenever a bright circle lingered on some uncertain form, his heart began to pound. But after more than an hour of searching through endless chop, nothing had turned up except a couple of curious dolphins, whose playful shadowing of the boat seemed a mockery of its mission.

About forty yards short of the beach, the tillerman idled the engine while the deckhands emptied the debris from their nets. Decker was surprised to see how full they were, mostly with wriggling eels and garfish, although there were a few good-sized snappers. These were tossed at Decker's feet, where they thrashed and popped like spring-loaded toys before giving up their cold-blooded ghosts.

The dragging continued, and half an hour later Decker

began to wonder how much longer Givins would press the fruitless nighttime search.

"Look, mon! Off de starboard!"

The tillerman was on his feet and pointing north along the beach. About fifty yards up, near the very tip of the cove, a long, narrow object was rolling in the shallow surf. In a kind of perpetual tug-of-war, one wave would send the object spinning toward land, the next would pull it back to sea.

The tillerman opened throttle on the old diesel and the whole launch vibrated as it sped forward. He eased off an instant before they plowed into sand and scraped to a stop. The object was to their left, about ten yards away.

Givins and Baines pulled off their shoes and socks and rolled up their pants legs while the deckhands set up the ladder for a wet landing. The water there was knee-deep, but the waves were coming in about a foot higher. Baines went in first, holding the briefcase above his head, followed by Givins and then the net handlers, one of whom carried a long fish hook over his shoulder. Decker decided to stay put.

The landing party regrouped briefly on the beach, then Baines, the younger one, took the fish hook and waded out far enough to reach the rolled blanket and snag it by a loose cord. But when he tugged, the cord snapped and the body slipped back into the waves. Baines rejoined the group on the beach and there was a lot of loud talking back and forth in Pidgin English. Finally, the two deckhands waded into the surf and each grabbed a loose flap of the rolled blanket. They grunted under the strain as they dragged the body onto dry sand.

Baines performed the remainder of the dirty work. He produced a pocket knife from his briefcase and, covering his nose with a handkerchief, knelt by the blanket and cut the rope in several places. Standing again, he used the fish hook to unwrap the soggy blanket.

The men coughed as Givins swept a flashlight over the length of the body, quickly at first, then slowly, top to bottom. From where Decker sat, it was only a gray, glistening heap—some decaying thing disgorged by the sea.

Givins spoke to the deckhands and, without a word, all three started back to the launch. Then Baines went back to his briefcase and pulled out a two-way radio. He mumbled something in cop talk. Decker made out the words "Spanish Town" and "transport."

In a minute or two, Givins called out politely, "Mr. Decker. Would you come here, please?"

Decker took his time getting down the ladder and into the water. It was warmer than he expected. He walked up the beach and around the body, aware of its presence but not looking at it, and stood next to Givins, who offered him his handkerchief. Decker held it to his nose and looked down to where Givins was holding the light.

The face was bloated, gelatinous, mangled at the fringes; sea creatures had torn away bits of soft flesh from the nose and ears and cheeks. It could have been anyone, no one. Decker turned to Givins and shook his head.

"What about the hair?" Givins asked. He spotted the flashlight and Decker looked again. Blonde hair. Straight. About the right length.

"It could be her," he said.

"Was she wearing a gold necklace?"

"I don't remember."

He spotted the flashlight on her neck and Decker saw the unmistakable man-made brutality: a deep crescent gash across the lower neck from ear to ear, like a swollen, hideous smile. Decker took a deep breath and looked away.

"I told you I don't remember," he said.

"And the bathing suit?"

Givins moved the beam down to the chest. Decker remembered the suit from Rudy's: an orange bikini top. The triangular patches dug now into the soft, gaseous flesh. He could hardly believe this had once been Danielle's proud body, the altar at which so many had worshiped.

"She was wearing an orange suit that night."

"A two-piece?"

"Yes. With a wraparound skirt."

"This one?" The light moved to a flowered sarong spread out next to the body. The corners of the sarong had been knotted but were now untied, revealing a collection of work tools—wrench, hammer, power drill, more.

Decker nodded and said, "It's hers."

Givins turned off the flashlight and the body vanished again into darkness.

"The ballast was hardly sufficient," Givins said. "Our murderer was clever, but not clever enough to know that warm sea water greatly accelerates the decaying process, producing large amounts of gas."

"But why tools?"

"Convenience, Mr. Decker. One of the deckhands recognized them from the ship. They were left unattended last night, following the repair work on the air-conditioning."

"So you think the killing wasn't planned?"

"It is difficult to say. Perhaps the murderer didn't mind if the body were found. Certainly we won't find any fingerprints. The salt water will have taken care of that."

Givins turned on the flashlight again. "All right, Mr. Decker. You may return to the launch. Sgt. Baines and I have further business here."

The two cops kept the others waiting while they snapped photographs and collected bits and pieces of things in plastic bags, like cops anywhere. Twenty minutes later, Givins returned to the launch and left Baines behind to watch over the body. The boat chugged back to the silent mother ship. As the deckhands were tying up, Givins asked the search party not to speak about what they had seen. He then boarded the ship and disappeared up the aft gangway to the main deck.

Rebo and a handful of curious passengers were lined up quietly along the side deck. Ellen was there, too. Her sad, hollow stare told Decker she understood everything.

Rebo helped Decker out of the launch, but by then Ellen was gone. They retreated farther aft where they could talk alone.

"Him or her?" Rebo asked.

"Her. Or what was left."

"Murdered?"

"Throat slashed. Body rolled in a blanket. The killer used tools to weigh it down."

"Somebody in the crew then."

"Not necessarily. There were tools in the cabin hallway last night."

Decker felt suddenly exhausted, drained, his legs wobbly from the hours of swimming that day. He felt anger, too, a slow-burning rage like molten metal weighing down his limbs. He wanted to strike out at something, but he didn't know what. He told Rebo he'd like to sit. They moved to a bench behind them.

"You okay?" Rebo asked.

"Yeah, just tired, and a little rattled. I never thought things would get this twisted." He thought of poor Ellen, how much worse it would be for her.

"Now what?" Rebo said, although he knew the answer.

"We call Farlidge, give him the dirt."

"The nearest phone's in Spanish Town."

"Then we'll have to wait till morning. Did you have any trouble getting back?"

"Nah. I lifted a ride from some Aussies hanging out at Rudy's. They were headed back to Jost van Dyke anyway. Wouldn't even let me pay for drinks."

Decker rubbed the back of his neck and said, "Tell me, Rebo, is your heart still in this?"

"In the story? Sure, man. Like my daddy always said, somebody's got to follow the parade and shovel the shit."

"I guess that's what we do, isn't it?"

"It's a livin'." Rebo's voice brightened a little. "Did I tell you? I got my own studio now."

"No kidding. Where?"

"Downtown. An old walk-up off Sixth Street. Used to be a bail bondsman there."

Decker tried to think of downtown Cincinnati. Of tired pavement and wheezing buses and people stopped obediently at corners for traffic lights. It belonged to another world, another life.

"You know, I plan on quittin' in a couple years," Rebo said. "Takin' up portraits and fashion spreads and the like. Let the people come to me for a change."

"You'll get bored."

"I could use some boredom."

"Me, too—someday."

"Someday, huh?"

"Right now I want to find the bastard who'd slit a woman's throat and dump her body like so much garbage."

"Most likely a dangerous bastard, but I'm with you."

Decker elbowed his partner. "Portraits? Come on."

Rebo stood and stretched, the flat of his palms touching the overhanging deck. "Shut up and let's get a drink. Maurice is keeping the bar open late."

"As long as it's not a rum special."

"Don't even say the word."

It was almost two in the morning, but they found a handful of other passengers still at the bar. All ears seemed to prick up when Decker arrived, but no one was crass enough to ask about the dragging—no one except Leslie, that is, who was waiting in the shadows, ready to ambush. She brought her drink over and stood next to Decker, so close the heat of their arms touched.

"So, was it *her?*"

Decker nodded.

"Suicide or murder?"

"Which would you prefer?"

The comment startled her for a moment. "Contrary to what you might think, I never wished her dead."

"Too late to tell her now."

She glared for a long angry moment, the deep blue eyes pulsing, and he thought she might slap him. Instead, she smiled a little, as though she pitied him, and walked away.

Decker went down to Ellen's cabin and found her sitting on the lower bunk, elbows on her knees, face in her hands. She turned her palm to stop him as he walked in.

"Don't tell me—please," she said.

Decker stayed by the door. "Okay."

"I thought it would be better knowing."

"It is, and it isn't. At least now you can start putting it behind you."

She looked up at him. "You saw her, then?"

"Yes—"

"And you're certain it was Danielle?" Her voice clung to a final bit of hope.

He didn't know how to answer without crushing her. "You can never be certain."

"But how was she—? No, don't tell. I don't want to know. I just want this whole thing to be over with. I just want to go back to New York and live my normal crazy life again and pretend that none of this ever happened."

"You will," Decker said.

She threw her head back and sobbed. "Oh, God, what do I tell her parents?"

"The truth—eventually. It won't be easy."

"But you don't understand. They always said I took such good care of their baby girl." She rubbed her nose. "Her mother, Dorothy—you know what she calls me? 'Elle's guardian angel.' Honest to God. They never knew—about us, I mean. Danielle never told them. I don't think they could even conceive—"

"Danielle wasn't a baby," Decker said.

"She was," Ellen said, openly sobbing now. "She was always a baby."

She turned her head away, her hand motioning him to leave.

Decker returned to the main deck and found the bar closed, the lights out, the empty deck awash in moonlight. A dusting of pale sparkling white, like hoarfrost, seemed to cling to everything— railings, masts, benches, spars—a ghost ship under a cool pure sky.

"Rebo?"

"In the deckhouse," answered a soft voice in the dark.

"Who's that?"

"Me."

He squinted and Leslie's outline materialized on the other side of the bar. She was sitting on a bench, her arms stretched along the railing. He wondered why she was there alone, but he kept quiet.

"You'd better go check," she said. "The cops are grilling him."

"Yes, I'd better."

"Aren't you going to thank me?"

"Thanks."

"Any time, honey."

He thought he could see her Cheshire smile floating in the dark.

He walked across the empty moon-washed deck, past the humming jacuzzi. He felt a sudden chill at the back of his neck, turned and looked, but no one was there.

At the rear of the deckhouse, he found the door wide open, the insides burning with light. A bare bulb hung from the ceiling above the table, its harsh glare on the black, sweaty faces of Rebo, Givins, and Baines. All three closed their mouths when Decker appeared in the doorway.

He stepped inside. "What's up?"

"Ask these two gentlemen," Rebo said. His mandibular joint was twitching away, grinding up all that anger between his clenched teeth.

A pair of swim trunks had been spread on the table—Rebo's lime green trunks with the blue whale print. The pattern was blotched by what looked like large rust stains.

"Do you recognize these?" Givins asked Decker.

"Who wouldn't?" He was still standing near the door.

"We found them rolled and hidden inside one of the lifeboats."

Decker looked to Rebo.

"I told 'em," Rebo said. "I washed the trunks last night and hung 'em out to dry, and that's the last I've seen of the damn things until now."

"And you didn't report this theft to the captain?" Givins asked.

"Theft? Who cares about a pair of ugly-ass swim trunks? I thought maybe somebody hated 'em so much they threw 'em overboard."

Baines smiled, but only a little.

"Just the same, Mr. Johnson," Givins said, "I would like you to come with us for questioning."

"On what grounds?" Decker asked.

"No grounds," Givins said pleasantly. "I am not charging anyone. In fact, it would be for Mr. Johnson's sake that I would be detaining him. We would conduct tests that would prove his innocence."

"What if I refuse?" Rebo said.

"Under BVI law, I have the right to hold and question anyone suspected of a capital offense for up to forty-eight hours."

"So I'm a suspect."

"For the time being, yes."

Decker slammed the flat of his hand against the door. "I can't believe this! Anybody could have taken those trunks."

"In which case, Mr. Johnson has nothing to fear," Givins said.

"Are you jailing him?" Decker asked.

"We will pay the cost of his hotel. In the morning, when the tests are done, he is free to return to the ship."

Rebo strode across the deck far in front of the two escorting officers. Captain Pearce was waiting on the receiving deck when the trio arrived. Rebo refused his help down into the police launch. He settled into the backseat of the old Chris-Craft looking relaxed and bored, a teenager waiting for the start of an amusement ride.

"I'll see you in the morning," Decker called from the rail.

"Tell Farlidge I want a decent lawyer. Don't let the assholes cut corners."

"If you need a lawyer, we'll get the best. Don't worry about a thing."

The deckhands threw the lines and the police launch took off with a deep thrum, cutting the water into ribbons of white and black. Decker watched as it headed south across the channel, disappearing into the dark melancholy of the sea.

# 8

Ellen and the captain boarded a BVI police boat at six forty-five the next morning. Ellen was wearing a loose flowered skirt and white blouse and holding a small black purse on her lap. The captain was dressed in his formal whites. Like a retired couple on holiday, they sat squarely in the middle of the boat, side by side, no talking, no touching. Decker watched as the boat powered off and veered south toward Spanish Town, ripping apart the early morning calm.

He stood at the railing a moment longer, stalled by some last-second ethical considerations. Did he have the right to search Ellen's cabin? No, not legally. (And in the States, it would land him in jail.) Morally? Yes, if it meant gaining information that would clear Rebo, an innocent man. Still, he didn't feel any less squeamish about what he was about to do.

He decided to be done with it and went quickly, then, to Ellen's cabin. His hand was on the doorlatch when he stopped himself: Someone with even fewer qualms had beaten him to the punch. He could hear the sounds of a frantic search inside— drawers squeaking, thumping, objects going bump on the floor.

His heart jumped inside his chest: He'd found the killer.

His hand was still on the latch, immobilized by fear, by conflicting impulse. Should he hold off, get a good look as the killer left? Or should he count on the element of surprise?

In the end, his curiosity was the deciding impulse. He had to see.

He opened the door a crack, ready to retreat at the first sign of trouble, but then smiled: Leslie was tugging the mattress off the top bunk.

"Good morning," he said brightly, stepping inside.

Leslie jumped. The mattress in her hands slipped and thudded sideways to the floor.

"Close the door," she snapped.

There was a pile of clothing and personal items in the middle of the room. "Starting a bonfire?" he said.

"Why can't you mind your own business?" She picked up the mattress and jammed it back in place.

"I could ask you the same."

"Ask away, Reporter Man."

She sat down on the lower bunk in a kind of pout and crossed her legs. She was wearing red running shorts and a rumpled Opus T-shirt. Her hair had lost its thick luster and her eyes looked puffy: signs of a bad night and no stomach for the ship's lukewarm shower.

"All right then," Decker said, "what's your interest in all this? Professional or amateur?"

"Look who's talking? You've been like some kid walking across a minefield. You have no idea what a mess you've landed in."

"Are you a cop?"

Her eyes sparkled. "Sort of."

"A PI?"

"Maybe." He was hearing an echo of his own amateurish replies, he thought.

"You're working for the Grammers, is that it?"

"I never disclose my clients, darlin'. That wouldn't be discreet." He wasn't sure if she was being facetious.

"I guess you didn't find what you were looking for in my cabin, did you?"

"What do you mean?"

"Oh, come off it. You ransacked our cabin the first night Rebo and I came on board."

"Don't flatter yourself."

"Then who did?"

She shrugged.

"I suppose you've solved the whole matter of Justin and Danielle," he said.

"Not all of it, but I'm light years ahead of you, bub."

"I think I like bub better than darlin'. Can you stick with that?

"Anything you say, bub."

"So what happened to Justin?"

"What if I told you Justin was perfectly safe?"

"Where?"

"If you promise to leave this ship and get the hell out of Dodge, I'll land you an exclusive interview."

"I would," Decker said, "only my partner has been hauled in by the cops, and there are too damn many unanswered questions floating around. For one thing, if Justin is alive, why was Danielle killed? And more importantly," he said, bluffing his way now, "where's the videotape?"

Leslie was silent a moment. When she spoke again, her voice had lost its sarcastic edge. "How do you know about the tape?"

"Maybe I'm not such an amateur after all."

"Who told you? Ellen?"

"Ahn-ahn. I don't show my cards until you show yours." Which wasn't much. All he'd seen, really, was the empty video jacket among Danielle's things.

"Why should I trust a reporter?"

"All right, a truce then."

"On what terms?"

"We work together, share information. Two heads are better than one."

"That depends on how much you intend to print." She folded her arms. "My clients are concerned about their privacy."

"Murder is hardly a private matter."

"I can assure you, the Grammers had nothing to do with Danielle's murder."

"The same goes for Rebo."

Leslie shrugged. "I have no idea who killed Danielle, but I can guess who gave the order."

"Who?"

"Will you help me find the videotape?"

"Yes."

"A deal then." Like a couple of kids ending a playground dispute, she reached out and they shook hands. Her grip was small but firm.

"All right," Decker said. "First question: Where the hell's Justin?"

Leslie swung her legs up on the bunk and settled, catlike, on her side. "He's safe. He's hiding out in Spanish Town."

"He never returned to the ship that last night, did he? You lied to the police."

"I was only trying to protect Justin."

"Why?"

"Because his life's in danger, obviously."

"Don't get smart. It's because of the videotape, am I right?"

"How very perceptive of you, Rick. Let me ask *you* something. Have you ever heard of a congressman named L. Stuart Parnell."

"He was on the cruise last week, wasn't he?" Decker couldn't remember who had told him that.

"Yes, and he's a very powerful man. He heads several

important committees. One of them oversees the health insurance industry."

"I think I've heard that. Isn't he involved in some sort of AIDS legislation right now?"

"He sponsored a bill allowing insurance companies to screen and reject anyone at risk of AIDS."

"That's right. Gays are in an uproar. There've been protests."

"Not just protests. Justin had something more specific in mind."

"Blackmail," Decker said.

"Very good, Rick. You show promise."

"Tell me the particulars."

"Parnell came with his wife. She spent all her time in the cabin, green to the gills, while Stu came out to play."

"Why did he book this tub? He could have had his own yacht."

"And be stuck with his wife the entire time? You have to think like Stu."

"Let me fill in the rest. Justin and Danielle booked the cruise with the idea of Danielle getting it on with Parnell. They videotape the action, then tell the congressman he'd better change his mind about that little piece of AIDS legislation." He paused, then added, "But how did they know Parnell would be on the cruise?"

Leslie tucked her legs up, all cozy and sweet on the bottom bunk. "I'm impressed, Rick. You're really quite analytical. I'd like the answer to that myself."

"Tell me how you got involved."

"Somebody in New York, one of Justin's friends, tipped off his parents. They were afraid for Justin."

"So his parents hired you?"

"An attorney of theirs, actually."

"Why you?"

"Are you referring to my gender, perchance?" She batted her eyelids for effect.

"No, but I don't understand why the Grammers would hire a PI in Washington when Justin lived in New York."

"My reputation precedeth me, darlin'."

"All right, then, what about Danielle? What was in all this for her?"

"Money. The greedy bitch wanted tons of it."

"So what went wrong?"

Leslie sighed. "What didn't? Danielle and Justin started fighting the moment after they'd made the tape. Danielle wanted money, Justin wanted political leverage. Their original plan was to wait until they got back to New York, make copies of the tape, and then contact Parnell. Only Danielle couldn't wait. She didn't believe Justin would ask for the money, so she hid the tape, ran to Parnell, and threatened blackmail on her own. Only one problem: Parnell didn't cave in."

"He didn't?"

"He said he'd see them both in hell before he paid the first dime. Poor dumb Danielle didn't have sense enough to know you don't blackmail someone unless you have copies of your evidence—lots of copies."

"And Parnell's a tough cookie."

"Tougher than you can imagine. He went back to Washington and got the DEA and customs people involved. Justin and Danielle were targeted as international drug couriers. They'd be grilled at customs and arrested unless they turned over the tape."

"But then why didn't Danielle go into hiding?"

"Because Danielle doesn't scare easily, and because she knows where the tape is. Knew, I should say. I assume her plan was to have someone release the tape the moment she was threatened with arrest."

"That someone being Ellen."

"Now you know why I'm here."

"Then why risk killing Danielle?"

"You never told me how."

"Her throat was opened. Ear to ear."

Leslie untucked her long legs and sat on the edge of the bunk. Her eyes were blank, fearful, the sockets pale against her tan.

"Does that sound like Parnell?" he said.

She shook her head, staring at the floor. "He sent someone—I don't know, a professional killer—to board the cruise after he left. There were six new arrivals this week." She looked up at Decker. "One of them was you."

"I take it that explains your sudden attraction on the dance floor."

She smiled coyly. "Part of it, darlin'. The rest was your animal magnetism."

True or not, he liked hearing it. "Who are the others?" he asked.

"Tony Henderson. Chris Watt. Jennifer what's-her-name—Ryan's cutie—and her mother. And, of course, Rebo."

"Can we eliminate me?"

She smiled again. "Only if you cooperate."

"So, if Justin Grammer is to return to New York and continue his illustrious acting career, we have to find that tape."

"You got it, bub." She hopped off the mattress and stood by the pile on the floor. "Would you care to help?"

"As long as you search the undies drawer."

She touched his arm. "Such a prude."

\* \* \*

They systematically tore the room apart, Decker taking the bathroom and dresser and Leslie continuing her work with the suitcases and mattresses. Decker was down on the floor checking for loose boards when he heard Leslie gasp.

"What?"

"Somebody's at the door."

Decker shot outside, but the hallway was clear. He thought perhaps he'd heard a door close. He listened a moment to his own heavy breathing and returned to the room. Leslie was standing in the same place, looking unhinged.

"Did you get a look?" he said.

She shook her head. "I just noticed the door open, and I saw a hand."

"A man's hand?"

She nodded.

"A white man?"

"Yes."

"Well, that's a start," he said.

She shivered a little, very undetectivelike. "Let's finish this and leave."

Decker took a good look at Leslie as she put things back in Ellen's bag. She looked more like a lifeguard at the neighborhood pool than a detective.

"How does a sweet kid like you end up a PI?" The "sweet" was dripping with some of Leslie's own honeyed sarcasm.

She flashed him an exasperated look, as though she'd had to explain this many times before.

"I started out as a divorce lawyer, got bored and frustrated with it. Most of what I do is routine—credit checks, lie detector tests, undercover stings on dishonest employees. Forget all the glamorous stuff you read in books."

"Do you carry a gun?"

"I'm licensed, never use it."

He was almost persuaded, but he couldn't help thinking she had her own interest in the tape.

"Assuming Ellen has the tape, what would she do with it?" he asked.

"She could try to blackmail Parnell herself."

"Oh, come on. She'd just as likely destroy the tape to protect Danielle."

"Either way, my client is screwed. Besides, you're too trusting. There's power in that tape. And power corrupts."

"Thanks for the ninth-grade civics lesson. Now when do I get my interview with Justin?"

"Soon, if you'll get close to Ellen first."

"How close can a guy get to a lesbian?"

"Closer than I can. I think she hates me."

"All right, but I want my interview tonight."

"That's up to Justin."

"Persuade him."

"All right, all right. I'll reach him this afternoon. Let's start cleaning up this mess. I'm afraid a steward will pop in any second."

Decker was putting items back into the rusty medicine cabinet above the sink—shampoos, rinses, facial creams galore—when he picked up a large plastic squeeze bottle of contact lens solution. It seemed empty. He shook it. There was a dry rustle inside. He unscrewed the cap, turned the bottle upside down, put his eye to the opening.

"Ah, yes," he said.

He set the bottle down by the faucet and zipped open a small white makeup kit he'd left in the sink. He found what he needed—tweezers—and went to work.

With some gentle twisting and pulling, out came a small white envelope, only slightly damaged by the retrieval.

Someone had penciled a diagram on the outside. It looked

like an unsolved geometric proof: a skewed rectangle, leaning at a forty-five-degree angle, with a half moon shape inscribed in the top right-hand corner. More baffling still, a line had been drawn from the half moon to the opposite side of the rectangle. Where the two lines intersected was the number twelve.

The final bit of information was scribbled in the upper left-hand corner of the envelope, where a return address would normally appear. Four letters, all caps—RMSR.

"Leslie, come here."

She was at the bathroom door in a flash. "Did you find something?"

"Look."

Leslie snatched the envelope and pulled it taut between her thumbs. "It's some kind of map."

"A map of what? The Leaning Tower of Pisa?"

"Where did you find it?"

"In an empty bottle."

She moved the diagram back and forth, squinting at it. "It must mean something to someone."

"Yes, and she's dead."

She sounded out the letters slowly—"RMSR. Why does that sound so familiar?"

"Real Men Seek Riches?"

"Quiet, I'm trying to think. R-M-S-R—"

"Royal Majesty's Secret Railroad?"

"Royal Majesty's . . . Royal . . . Rick, that's it! The RMS *Rhone!* The wreck of the *Rhone!* That's where she hid the tape!"

She jumped once and clapped her hands, then leaped on Decker with a huge hug. He put his arms around her, feeling the solid warmth of her, dizzied by the smell of her hair. A second later, she broke free and he felt suddenly empty.

"I'd better sign up," she said, a worried look on her face. "I think the dive is sometime this afternoon."

She bolted for the door.

"Wait a minute. What about me?"

"Do you dive?"

"I can get by."

"There's no need for you to come, really. I can do perfectly well on my own."

"I'm sure you can."

They found Mary Beth on the main deck lying by the jacuzzi—working on her tan until her captain returned—and signed up for the 2:00 P.M. diving expedition. They celebrated with a cup of coffee in the saloon. At nine, the tables were mostly empty, just a few of the kitchen crew talking in a corner near the galley window. The room's *Treasure Island* motif, with its hurricane lamps and leather benches and faux stained-glass windows, seemed an appropriate setting as Leslie pulled out the envelope and spread it flat on the table between them. They were touching arms again, comrades in a game of treasure hunt.

"I'm almost positive I recognize that half-moon shape," Leslie said, tracing the outline with a well-manicured fingernail. "I was down there last week. There's this huge hole in the bow section of the hull."

"What about the intersecting line here?"

"My best guess is that it points to a beam. The number twelve probably means it's the twelfth from the end. But it's hard to say. We'll have to see once we're down there."

"How much time will we have?"

"The rental tanks last about forty-five minutes. That should give us plenty of time."

She held up the envelope, poised to rip it in two.

"Do we need this any more?"

He shook his head.

She ripped it once and then into smaller and smaller

pieces, sprinkling the confetti onto a paper napkin. For good measure, Decker crumpled the napkin into a ball and dropped it in his half-filled coffee cup, where it quickly soaked through. Leslie kissed him quickly on the cheek, smiled, and stood. "I'll meet you back here at one forty-five, okay? And then it's off to the *Rhone,* darlin'."

"Off to the *Rhone,*" he repeated. He watched her turn and walk away, a new buoyancy in the thrust of her hips. Leslie Stanton, girl adventurer. He succumbed for a moment to a triple sinking feeling—lust, despair, unworthiness—then got up and went looking for Mary Beth.

He found her in the deckhouse this time, filling out paperwork. She had slipped her white purser's blouse, front open, over her black bathing suit, reclaiming some semblance of rank.

He asked if he could use the ship's cellular phone. "It's an emergency," he said, only a half lie.

She looked concerned. "The captain usually gives the okay, but I can't see why not. We can charge it to your cabin."

She showed him the phone, wrote down the access code on a slip of paper, and politely disappeared. Decker punched in the long list of numbers and waited. The microwaves beamed, the fiber optics pulsed until, voilà, a phone rang—a phone Decker knew sat on a corner of Farlidge's big oak desk, next to the Glamour Shot of his plumpish wife in a black-lace bodice he'd probably gotten her out of a Victoria's Secret catalogue for their last anniversary.

Over the line came the smooth voice—"Metro Farlidge here"—no break between the words, as if to say Farlidge was his name, newspapering his game.

Decker felt a reassuring silliness in it all until Farlidge said, "Listen, I've got bad news. I just heard from Rebo—"

"Have they charged him?"

"No, that's the good news. The bad news is that Captain Pearce won't let him back on the ship."

"But we had an agreement!"

"He told Rebo it would cause a stir among the passengers. They met this morning in Road Town."

"Ron, he can't do that. Call our lawyers!"

"Just calm down. Listen, I'm flying Rebo back tonight. From what he tells me, the police don't have squat. They just want to make sure they have prints and samples for a match in case they do find anything."

"What about his trunks?"

"We had our lawyer talk to the cops. They admit the trunks had been used in a quick mop-up job. Anybody could have grabbed them."

"So now what do we do for pictures?"

"We don't. I'm bringing you home, too."

Home? The word seemed quaint. "Forget it, Ron. I'm staying."

"It's no good, Decker. The last thing the paper needs is one of you charged with murder, or killed."

"I'm staying, Ron. I've got a story coming that will knock your patterned socks off. Besides, I'm *this* close to landing an exclusive with Justin."

"You know for sure he's alive?"

"Yes, from what I think is a reliable source."

"You think?"

"Never mind. Just check on a couple of things for me, okay? Find out everything you can about Congressman L. Stuart Parnell. I think he's from one of the Carolinas. Committees he sits on. PAC donors. The names of all his aides. Can you do that?"

"I'll get Simmons in Washington on it."

"Have the wires picked up anything on Danielle's disappearance?"

"A short story went out on the AP this morning. Very sketchy. Evidently, they can't reach the ship and the police down there won't comment. Better brace yourself for a blitz when the TV tabloids latch on to this."

"I'm way ahead of 'em. One more thing, Ron. Find out if a Leslie Stanton is registered as a private detective in D.C. Check Maryland and Virginia, too. Got that?"

"Leslie with an 'ie'?"

"Yes. Stanton, S-T-A-N-T-O-N. A female."

"Simmons can handle that, too. If you're staying, Decker, I want a story filed by nine tonight—and a damned good one. You hear me?"

"All too clear."

"And stay out of trouble. Any more legal fees and we bust our budget."

Decker hung up and looked at his watch: It was only ten in the morning, but it seemed hours later. He felt tired and on edge. He decided to retire to the widow's nest, slather on the sunscreen, and catch up on some of the sleep he'd been missing. There wasn't much he could do anyway until the captain and Ellen returned.

He tried to read his book at first, a submarine thriller loaded with technical terms, but the letters drifted in and out of focus in the brilliant morning light. Already, the sun's intensity was tingling on his skin, ricocheting in the backs of his eyes.

His thoughts drifted toward Leslie, idly at first, but then he began to wonder what she would be like as a lover. Direct and uncomplicated, no doubt, the way Janet had been once. But you never knew that about a woman until it happened; nor, when it was best, did she. Soon, though, his speculation gave way to memories, not of scenes or words but of feelings, atmospheres long buried. And as he drowsed and drifted toward sleep, he felt himself enmeshed in Janet again, in her essential Janetness, that is. Lost in the orange-scented smell of her skin, the solid warmth of her body, burrowing deeper and deeper into the cocoon of his past.

Judy Collins's throaty tremolo vibrated through his skull: "I-I o-o-nce was lo-ost/ but now I'm found/ blind but now I se-e-e-e."

He blinked and looked up from the widow's nest and saw the stirring sight of white sails rising against a bright blue sky.

They were due that morning to sail north to one of the smaller outer islands, Jost van Dyke. But when the sails had filled, the ship listed heavily to port side and began to turn around sharply toward the west and south. The sails luffed and slapped like trapped birds and finally quieted as a spanking wind picked up from the west. Within minutes, the *Southern Cross* was plunging southwesterly on a close reach across Sir Francis Drake channel, the bow sending up a fine warm spray.

So much for Jost van Dyke. Decker wondered where they were headed now. He sat up, rubbed his sun-weary eyes. He would have to find the captain and Ellen.

He was sitting up, collecting his things when Ryan and his sister Connie appeared at the railing, just a few feet from the widow's nest. Connie looked bored, as usual, but Ryan was fidgeting. Decker could tell the boy wanted to talk about something.

"Where we headed, sailor?" Decker asked.

"Back to Spanish Town."

"Did the captain say why?"

"No."

Connie spoke up, sounding irritated. "He probably wants us closer to the police station."

"That I can understand."

"Are you diving the *Rhone* today?" Ryan said, a small note of pleading in his voice.

"I doubt it," Decker lied. "I lost my certification. I haven't been diving in years."

"That's okay," Ryan said, adding quickly, "there's a class you can take, and then the instructor goes down with you."

"What about Jenny?" Decker asked, wondering if their summer fling was already over.

"Her mom won't let her," he said.

"I'm sorry, Ryan. I can't. Maybe tomorrow, okay?"

"Sure." Ryan was silent a moment as Decker finished wrapping his things in his towel, then the boy turned to Connie and asked if she would like to go.

"Not with some lunatic who scares all the fish away."

The sharpness of Connie's answer was no surprise to Decker. Kevin had been carefully avoiding her.

Connie softened the blow by adding, "Why don't you play with your Game Boy or something?"

"It's broken."

"Way to go, Clyde. How much did mom pay for that thing?"

"I didn't break it."

"Then who did?"

He hesitated a moment. "Danielle," he said quietly.

"Oh, sure. Blame it on a dead person. Get real, Ryan."

Decker stepped carefully from the bowsprit back to the deck. "How did it happen, Ryan?"

The boy shrugged. "She asked if she could borrow it. She's a Super Mario fiend."

"And she returned it broken?"

"She said she knew some guy in New York who could fix it."

"She didn't promise to buy you a new one?"

"They're expensive, like ninety bucks."

Danielle really *had* fallen on hard times, Decker thought.

"I don't like playing with it anyway," Ryan announced. "It's kids stuff."

Decker smiled, amused and pleased. "Is that so?"

"I'm sorry, but the captain is unavailable at the moment," Kevin said. He was standing at the pilot's wheel, navigating the big ship across the channel—the only time he seemed truly like an adult.

"I assume that means he's with Mary Beth."

"You're very good at picking up on things, aren't you, old man?"

"I'll consider that a compliment—only because of your tender age."

Kevin clenched his jaw, kept his eye on the compass.

Decker went off to find Ellen. She was in her cabin, facedown on her bunk, clutching her pillow as if it were her only friend. She still had on the white blouse and flowered skirt.

Decker sat on the mattress by her knees. "Have you been back long?"

She shook her head. "Just before we sailed." She shivered a little and said, "My cabin was searched."

"Really?" He pretended shock, looked around. They had tried to put everything back in order, but there was only so much you could do. "Do you think it was the crew?"

"It doesn't matter." She was silent again.

"Do you want me to go?" he asked.

She lifted her head from the pillow. "No. Please stay."

"How did it go with the police?"

She smiled forlornly. "You know, it was funny," she said. "I'd thought I'd accepted that she was dead. I knew it the moment you men went out in the boat last night. But looking at that face in the morgue this morning, I just couldn't believe it was her. It was just some slimy *thing*—I don't know—not really a person at all."

"Did they show you the swim suit?"

"Yes, I recognized that. We bought it together at Bloomingdale's."

"But you're still not certain?"

"What does 'certain' mean, anyway? I know she's not here and then they show me something that used to be Danielle, with her throat cut like some piece of meat." She bit her lip to get control of herself again. "I guess that's about as sure as I'll get."

Decker thought back to the death of Turk Nystrom, his mentor and the best reporter he'd ever known, who had crashed and burned in a suspicious car accident. Decker was never asked to make an identification: There hadn't been enough left of Turk to fill the ashtray in his Honda.

Ellen took a deep breath. When she spoke, her voice was quavery but determined. "They're sending for her dental records. I called her parents and told them. Not everything. I couldn't. Not all at once. I told them she'd drowned."

Decker thought that a bad idea, but he didn't say so. Truth was like a junkyard dog: You only made it meaner by trying to hide from it.

"I was surprised," she said. "Her parents were almost stoic about it. I mean, after the initial shock and all. Her father wanted to come down from Boise on the next plane."

"What did you tell him?"

"I told him there was nothing he could do. There isn't, really. He has emphysema anyway. Smokes like a fiend. I told him I'd take care of everything."

Decker popped the question he'd been wanting to ask since their conversation began. "Did Danielle ever talk to you about Stuart Parnell?"

"You mean 'Stu'? Of course she did."

"Is that what she called him?"

"That's what everybody called him. Good ol' boy Stu—your friendly neighborhood congressman."

"Did she tell you she had sex with him?"

Ellen looked stunned, then shook her head, eyes shut tight for a second. "I made a point of never asking."

"Does it surprise you?"

"Nothing surprises me when it comes to Danielle."

"Did she mention a videotape of her and Parnell?"

She sat up now on the edge of the bunk. "What are you getting at, Rick?"

"I'm sorry to spring this on you, Ellen, but here are the facts: Danielle and Justin made a tape of Danielle having sex with Parnell. They tried to blackmail him with it and now, it seems, Parnell, or someone working for Parnell, is taking care of business."

Ellen glared at him. "Where do you come up with these things?"

"I have it from a good source."

"A source," she said, her voice pure scorn. "Danielle didn't even own a video camera."

"She could have borrowed one. Or maybe Justin had one."

"Are you saying Danielle deserved to be murdered?"

"Of course not. I'm saying there's a reason she was murdered, and what worries me now is that you might be in danger, too."

"But I don't know anything about a tape."

"What about a map?"

Ellen was silent.

Decker tried again. "Did Danielle say anything about a map?"

She closed her eyes and nodded. "A little."

"What's a little?"

"She told me where it was, but that was all. I was supposed to hand it over if anyone ever threatened us."

"You didn't ask her what it all meant?"

"No, because I didn't want to know." She sniffed. "We were back together. That's all I cared about."

"The killer may not realize that, which is why you need to get off this ship."

Ellen clutched her pillow again, closed her eyes. Then she said softly, "Would you do something for me?"

"What?"

"Would you just hold me for a while?"

In minutes she was asleep, clinging lightly to his neck, her mouth moist and warm against his shoulder. He didn't want to wake her, but he had to get on with his day. It was almost eleven.

He carefully removed her arm from around his neck, then sat up on the edge of the bunk and slid away. She was still sleeping when he closed the door to the room.

His grumbling stomach reminded him again that he'd missed breakfast, so he stopped in the saloon, picked up a roast beef sandwich from the galley window, and took it to one of the empty nooks. There was a sweaty pitcher of ice water and a stack of plastic cups still on the table from breakfast. He was two bites into his sandwich when Leslie strode in, cleaned up now, wearing a white one-piece suit and a big straw hat. She looked strong and confident and glowing, a textbook illustration of the Ideal Woman.

She sat next to him and grinned. "So, how is little Miss Innocence?"

"Asleep. She was exhausted."

"She knows nothing about the tape?"

"She knew about the map, that's it."

"That's it?"

"She said Danielle told her to hand over the map if she were ever threatened."

"Oh, come on. Do you believe that?"

"I don't know what to believe. It doesn't matter now, anyway. When do I talk to Justin?"

"You don't give up, do you?"

"It's the whole reason I'm still here."

She looked hurt. He liked that. "All right, I'll try to arrange it for later tonight."

"When?"

"That's up to Justin."

"How do you reach him?"

"That's my business. We'll talk about details later." She touched his shoulder and stood. "I'm making a quick trip into Spanish Town. I'll be back at one-thirty."

"You'd better. I might go treasure hunting without you."

"Watch it, bub."

This time when she turned and walked away, Decker didn't watch. He went back to eating his roast beef sandwich, the meat dry and papery thin. He was about to leave it when Art Kapinski stopped by on his way to his cabin. Decker liked the old man. He was the voice of sanity among a ship of fools.

"You hear the news?" Art said ominously.

"What now?"

"We're sailing back to Road Town tonight."

"Road Town? I thought we had two more days."

"The captain just announced it. They're cutting the trip short because of mechanical problems; it's the generator, I guess. We're all getting half our money back for the week. The ship's sailing tomorrow for Antigua, although I think they're crazy. They lose their generator, they lose everything—lights, communications, weather instruments."

Decker could guess the captain's strategy. Dump the passengers and do an end run around the legal mess with Danielle. He wondered how that would sit with Givins and Baines.

"Well, it was nice knowing ya," Decker said grimly.

Art walked over to the table and lowered his voice. "The wife and I thought we might spend a few extra days in the islands. We found a nice little resort on the other side of Virgin Gorda. You're welcome to be our guest—I mean, if you're in no hurry to get home."

"That's nice, Art. I may take you up on that."

"Feel free. We have a whole suite of rooms."

They both stiffened when they heard the scream come up from the cabin deck. Decker was the first to reach the spiral staircase. He spun down to the narrow hallway; Ellen's door was wide open. He found her huddled on the floor by the bunk, crying and shaking.

"He tried to kill me," she sobbed. She was clutching a pillow case in her hands. There were red marks on her neck.

"Who?"

She shook her head, speechless, and sobbed again.

"You didn't see?" Decker asked.

She threw the pillowcase to the floor. "He put this thing over my head. He tried to strangle me."

Art was at the door. "She all right?"

"Are you?" Decker asked.

"Yes." She sniffed. "He said he'd kill me if I didn't tell him where it was."

"Did you tell him about the map?"

"I told him I had a map, but someone took it. When he let go, I screamed."

She started to rise on wobbly legs. Art and Decker helped her sit on the edge of the bunk, where she buried her face in her hands.

"What about the voice?" Decker asked. "Did you recognize it?"

She raised her head, took a deep breath. "Not really. He was talking in this deep, deep voice." She laughed miserably. "I thought he was joking at first, then he started choking me. I rolled off my bunk and landed on the floor screaming my head off. That's when he ran."

"Which way?"

"I told you I didn't see."

Decker went outside and looked. The rear companionway was just two doors down from Ellen's cabin. He took the stairs two steps at a time and emerged just in front of the jacuzzi. The mid-deck was empty. On the port bench, however, Chris Watt was lying on his back, a thick law textbook propped against his raised knees. The muscles in his thighs were massive, clearly defined. A Braves baseball cap protected his eyes.

Decker stood next to him. "You see anybody come up the stairs just now?"

Chris was motionless, nose still in his book. Decker moved in closer, just above the bill of his Braves cap, and repeated the question.

"Huh?" Chris snapped to. The book landed with a thunk on the deck.

"Never mind." Decker walked away. If Watt hadn't been sleeping, he deserved a major acting award.

He looked around to see who else might have had a view of the companionway. He spotted Maureen among a lively group of passengers near the end of the bar.

"Come join our little farewell party," she said as Decker approached. She was standing next to Martha, a feisty retired schoolteacher with a cap of silver hair. They hoisted their freshly ordered rum specials and touched glasses.

"To our last day in paradise," Maureen said. They both

giggled. The alcohol had taken years off their ages, and their IQs.

"Did either of you see someone come up the companion-way a second ago?"

The two women looked at each other, shook their heads, giggled.

"No one here but us drunks," Maureen said. More giggles.

Decker went down the portside gangway to the loading deck and into the saloon. Just inside the open bulkhead was Tony Henderson, standing by the coffee urn, filling up his cup. He turned and gave Decker a single flash of the cool gray eyes—calm, disinterested. So what, they seemed to say.

Decker disappeared down the staircase and returned to Ellen's room.

Art and Ellen were sitting on the bunk together, Art's long arm around her shoulders.

"You find out anything?" Art asked.

"I saw Tony in the saloon."

Ellen sniffled. "You think it was him?"

"He could have ducked into somebody's room, stayed there until the coast was clear. It's like musical chairs around this place with no locks on the doors."

"What if he comes back?" Ellen said, clearly frightened.

"You're getting off the ship," Decker said.

"But my plane doesn't leave until late tomorrow."

"Find a hotel on Tortola, and lock your door."

"You're welcome to stay with the wife and me," Art said. "If you can stand the boredom, that is."

Ellen cheered up a little. "I would love some boredom."

Decker thought of Tony again, of the cool indifference behind those gray eyes. He wished he could reach Leslie.

# 9

At one fifty-five that afternoon, a sleek white catamaran roared into the overheated calm of Spanish Town harbor and sidled up to the ship's receiving deck. Leslie and Decker were the first to set foot on the boat, cleverly dubbed the *Cat Men Do*. The pilot, François, told them in a heavy French accent to stow their gear under one of the benches on either side of the tank racks. "Zat way, we heet bad water, no proh-blem, yes?"

They found some bench seats underneath the boat's blue canopy and out of the glare of the midday sun.

Beryl Thompson, one of the diving instructors, came by and introduced himself. He looked like Poseidon himself, a burly, midthirtyish man with a tangled beard and a sun-streaked mane. His body was tanned to a deep bronze and most of it, including his shoulders, was matted with sun-burnished hair. He was one more flirtation for Leslie.

"So, back for another plunge, ay?" He had the sledgehammer accent of an Australian.

"You know us Southern gals—always looking for adventure."

He turned to Decker on a more official note. "And your name, sir?" He checked the name against his list. "Are you properly certified?"

Decker nodded, softening the lie by adding, "I haven't been down in years, though."

"I'd urge you to join the resort class and stick close by."

"But what if I'm with Leslie here?"

"She's a fine diver, and a fine lady, I might add. Just the same, we're liable if anything was to happen."

"Can we both go with the resort class?" Leslie asked.

"That's fine by me." He smiled.

When Beryl had moved on, Decker turned to Leslie. "Are you crazy? Do you want an audience while we're down there?"

"Don't worry. We'll break away from the class."

"I just hope you know what you're doing, because I sure don't."

"Trust me, darlin'."

About ten other passengers had lined up on the loading deck and were being helped by deckhands down to the catamaran—Ryan not among them. Decker guessed he hadn't found a partner after all. He felt bad for a moment, but it dissolved into a new concern when he spotted Tony near the back of the crowd.

He nudged Leslie. "We've got company."

Tony was toting a diving bag made of a silvery synthetic material, shiny as an astronaut's suit. Kid's stuff, but not the diving knife strapped to his right calf. It was a big, gleaming knife, showy in a high-tech, gruesome way from its bright blue plastic grip to its mean-looking jagged edge. Chances were it could cut through bone.

Without glancing in their direction, Tony trailed off toward the back of the boat and sat on one of the benches there. He dropped his diving bag between his feet, zipped it open, and pulled out his wet suit. It was half Day-Glo blue, half Day-Glo lavender, split down the middle like a circus suit.

He made a show of pulling off his T-shirt. Tony's build lacked bulk, but there was menace in it despite his age: pecs and abdomen flat and hard as body armor, ropy arm muscles twitching just below the skin. If you struck him, by God, you'd hurt your hand. He looked that lean and mean at forty.

Leslie nudged Decker. "There's more," she whispered.

Chris Watt and Kevin were laughing hearty male laughs as they stepped onto the catamaran. Watt had a ton of gear—a heavy-duty diving bag slung over each shoulder, a long fishing spear in his right hand. He grinned at Leslie through his bushy mustache. Walrus lust. Kevin caught a glimpse of Decker and quit smiling altogether.

The pair went off together to the back of the boat and settled next to Tony.

Decker turned to Leslie. "What's the deal with Watt's spear? I didn't realize this was a fishing expedition."

Leslie placed her hand on his back. "You worry too much, Rick. Lots of divers carry spears. It's a phallic thing."

He smiled. "I see. Like a Neptune complex."

"That's it."

The diving site for the *Rhone* was a relatively calm spot midway in the Salt Island Passage. It was about a mile east of Dead Chest, the tiny deserted island where, more than three hundred years ago, Bluebeard set off fourteen mutinous mates with a phony treasure map and a bottle of rum, then sailed away and let the poor buggers starve to death. Folklore had transformed the incident into a grim ditty for kids: "Fourteen men on a dead men's chest. Ho, ho, ho and a bottle of rum . . . "

Ho, ho, ho, indeed.

The site was about the size of a football field, marked off by small red buoys and dotted by a small fleet of leased yachts. Stretched across gleaming white decks were expensive young women—"professional bimbos," Leslie called them—their gold, sleek bodies flashing like so many hard-won trophies in the sun. Here and there, one would deign to crane her neck, bored and slightly annoyed, to catch a look at the *Cat Men Do* as it idled into place.

While the other divers collected their gear, Decker caught a glimpse of Tony leaning forward from his seat. He held a whetsone in his left hand and was snapping his big knife across it with quick, fluid motions of his wrist. *Snick-snack, snick-snack, snick-snack.* . . . The sound made the little hairs at the back of Decker's neck stand on end.

Beryl whistled from the pilot's wheel. "All right, resort class. Everyone without a diving certificate, over here, please!"

Decker was still watching Tony's knife, its blade flashing like a signal light in the sun, when Leslie nudged him to go.

They joined the others gathered round Beryl—the North Carolina twins, Melanie and Winston, dressed in identical light-green suits, and Martha, the retired schoolteacher, and her equally game female friend.

Beryl laid out the day's expedition. The certified divers, all six of them, would descend first, followed by the resort class with Beryl in the lead. There was time to explore only the bow section of the *Rhone*, he said, explaining that the steamship had broken in half on the rocks at Salt Island before going to bottom.

Leslie leaned toward Decker. "That's the section we want."

Beryl talked on. "The bow is upside down on a sand reef, just off our starboard, in approximately eighty feet of water. We'll be entering the hull through a small tear in the ship's bow, then exiting at mid-deck. I warn you: When we first enter the hull, it will seem claustrophobic, but there's no need for anyone to panic. Once you're farther inside the ship, it's easy to see your way clear. Any questions?"

There were only blank stares among the class members, their thoughts scores of feet below water.

"All right, let's get moving."

Leslie handed Decker one of the boat's thick, standard-issue wet suits from a pile in the middle of the deck. He was surprised by its weight. The foam liner was sopping from the last dive. When he stepped into the suit, he had to tug, twist, cajole the thick rubber over his thighs and torso. He shivered. It was like squeezing into a cold, wet sponge.

"You have to learn not to fight things," Leslie said.

"That's easy to say if you don't have love handles."

She laughed a little as she slipped into her suit like a second skin. "Just stay close while we're down there, okay?"

Decker crouched unsteadily on the edge of the boat's diving platform, weighted down with fifty pounds of diving gear, a boulder with legs. His heart was pounding in his ears as he reminded himself of the two most important rules of diving—never hold your breath, and never rise too quickly. The first could burst your lungs, or worse, throw an air bubble to the brain; the second could fry your insides with compressed nitrogen, a condition known as the bends.

When Leslie's plume of bubbles disappeared, he had no choice. He took a giant step out from the platform and broke the surface: There was a loud smack, a frantic rush of bubbles around his ears. He popped to the surface again almost immediately, pressed the release valve on his buoyancy vest, and went under a second time for good.

The instant the water closed over him, Decker felt calmer, safer. He was weightless now, sheathed in another world, warm and benign. He stopped a second and stared: All around him was the clearest, brightest blue he'd ever seen—Justin's blue—pressing in and yet expanding away in every direction for hundreds and hundreds of feet until the blueness gathered, like dusk, into impenetrable twilight. It was that dark, almost violet blue of the distance—mysterious and slightly menacing—that reminded him of Leslie's eyes.

The other resort divers were already far below, spaced evenly along the diving line, their plumes of silver bubbles rising, spreading, conjoining into a single curtain. Decker traveled down the line slowly, hand over hand, pinching his nose every few feet and blowing to equalize the pressure in his ears. At times, he felt as though he were dreaming: a slow free-fall from the sky, thrilling and frightening. Each foot of depth compounded the pressure on his mask, his ears, his chest, the sensation that, at any moment, his body might implode. At bottom he saw Beryl, a tiny blue-gray smudge at the end of the diving line. And there behind him, an enormous beast, collapsed and quivering in the watery distance—the shifting gray outlines of the *Rhone*.

Decker took long, slow, deep breaths, calmed by the regulator's steady hiss as he sucked air in, again by its glottal closure as he forced air out. *Pffffffffff*-pop! *Pffffffffff*-pop! *Pffffffffff*-pop! His second heart.

When Decker reached bottom, Beryl formed the group in a circle in the shadow of the *Rhone*. Decker moved in next to Leslie, who flashed him the OK sign—thumb pinched to forefinger. He signaled back OK but she stared deep into his eyes for a moment, looking for signs of panic. The intensity of her concern made him feel childish, vulnerable.

The bow of the wreck loomed above them on the crest of a sandy ridge, upside down and listing heavily, a three-story building on the verge, it seemed, of collapse. The metal plating was thick with barnacles and sea vegetation, a patchwork hide of purples, greens, and browns. Tiny fish hid like parasites in all the crevices. At mid-deck, where the big boilers had blown, the exposed beams formed a series of metal arches, some collapsed, some still standing, like ribs on a rotting whale. Divers drifted in and out, scavengers among the metal bones, and there among them he spotted Tony—or at least someone in the same half-purple, half-blue clown suit. He touched Leslie's shoulder, pointed, but by then, the diver was gone, back into the belly of the beast. Leslie was confused. He flashed her the OK sign and they continued on.

In the meantime, friendly gangs of yellowtail and potato cod had converged around the class. Beryl reached into his diving pouch and brought out bits of shrimp to feed the beggars. The smaller yellowtail nuzzled all around his hands and face, but the potato cod—with dour faces and huge downturned mouths—waited as patiently as nuns, and having gotten their due, swam politely away.

Decker wondered when Leslie would break away—he was getting anxious about their time—as Beryl led the class along the bottom of the ridge below the wreck. Their weightless bellies skimmed above the veiny lobes of sea fans and the tentacles of soft coral swaying in the current. Blues and greens and purples were the only colors now, the harsher reds and oranges blocked out by the depths of the sea. Justin would have liked that.

They stopped in a small gully where part of the deck had settled, and found a huge, rusted wrench, as thick and long as a stevedore's arm, half-buried in the sand. Beryl had them take turns hefting it, curling it like a barbell, before leading them up the slowly cresting ridge to the wreck's starboard bow. They stopped and regrouped just below a ragged opening in the hull. The tear in the plating was five or six feet above the ridge, just wide enough for a single diver. The inside was black as night.

Decker looked at the hole and felt a tightness in his throat. The old fear. Water and blackness. The endless nothingness pulling him down, suffocating him. And only Janet to reach for.

He was startled by a touch on his shoulder. Leslie was behind him, signaling him to wait.

Beryl swam in first and was quickly devoured, followed by each of the twins and the diving schoolmarms. Leslie waited a beat or two, got the OK from Decker, and went in.

Decker held back, took one last look around: There was a lone diver at the bottom of the slope, moving fast above the coral, spear in hand. Was it Watt? He was perhaps fifty feet away—too far to identify.

Decker decided the time had come. He drew a deep, slow breath, narrowed his eyes, and plunged in. For a second or two, he saw only blackness, as though he'd stepped through the door of a spacecraft and fallen into the absolute emptiness of space. The current through the hole pushed against him, the ship's cold, exhaling breath. He kicked harder.

*Krrraaaaaang!* A sudden jolt set his scalp tingling. His tank had struck something, an overhanging beam perhaps. He fumbled for the release valve on his air vest, jabbed it until he dropped an inch or two. He continued on, conscious now of his breathing, fast and mechanical, the regulator hissing and popping like an overworked sump.

Where were Leslie and the others?

A heartbeat from total panic, he detected light again. It was a cold, gray light—soulless—but reassuring just the same. The source was far uphill: the tilted half-moon shape in Danielle's map where the vessel had ripped in two. He stopped and looked around. He could make out the cavernous insides of the hull now, an abandoned cathedral, all its corners lost in quiet gloom.

Leslie was just ahead, drifting slowly, reverently, it seemed, a safe distance behind the others. Beryl was far out front, outlined against the half moon.

Leslie signaled Decker before veering sharply to her right. He soon noticed what Leslie had already discovered—a single shaft of light, like an errant laser beam, striking one of the hull supports midway between deck and bottom. Clearly, it was the intersecting point on Danielle's map.

Leslie went to work. She started at the top of the support beam and worked down, carefully frisking both sides of the

encrusted metal with her bare hands. Decker held back and
drifted, alert to everything around him. He had an eerie sense
that they were being watched. He turned suddenly, but he could
see nothing but the huge void inside the hull.

He closed his eyes, concentrated. Something was playing
at the edge of his consciousness, a steady sound, barely percepti-
ble. It was a continuous screeching of sorts, a high-pitched
vibration through the hull's watery space. He hadn't a clue what
it could be, unless it were somehow the voices of those who had
drowned here a hundred years before. He shivered at the
thought: men, women, and children, terrified, sucked into this
watery grave by the murderous innocence of the sea.

In a kind of vision, he could see it: the sinking bow—
capsized, free of the ocean's thrashing surface—rotating in its
slow descent. It skims the crest of the sunken ridge and plows
down its lee side, scraping and thundering against rock and sand
before reaching this, its angle of repose.

Leslie wasn't having any luck. She had worked her way to
the bottom of the beam, barely visible in the gloom, where she
continued digging around in the ocean floor. They should have
brought a flashlight. Dumb. Very dumb. He considered whether
to give up his guard post and help, but he waited a moment
longer, hearing again the chorus of wailing voices inside the ship.
They seemed to be calling him now, pleading, louder and
louder, then dying again, rising and falling in waves of storm-
tossed emotion. He shook his head to block the sound, but it was
steady and unbroken, a siren song of peace, paralysis. He closed
his eyes.

The tug on his leg came with such sudden force he thought
he'd snagged his flipper on a loose beam—until the snag began
to pull him downward.

He screamed into his mouthpiece, a silent scream. Leslie
was oblivious to everything but her search.

He bent his body in two, saw the plume of another diver below him in the gloom. He kicked, twisted, kicked again, and broke free.

He dove toward Leslie, his breathing so frantic now that the regulator vibrated against his teeth. He was a foot or two away, his hand just above her floating hair, when his whole body jerked backward as though on a string.

Decker spun and kicked like mad, but the diver clung to his waistbelt. An arm coiled around his neck, a blade flashed above his head. Decker arched his back, braced himself for the hot plunge of steel, but it never came, only a quick tug on his regulator, then the fast boil of air all around his ears. His head was lost in a shroud of bubbles.

He resisted the reflex to breathe—the sea would come pouring in now. The severed hose was whipping above him like a snake. He grabbed the loose end, tried to stick it in his mouth, but the surge of air was too great, like sticking a garden hose full bore into your mouth.

The voices started again, wailing in desperation now. They were pulling him downward into the gloom, their watery chorus vibrating in his aching chest. He thought: Why not inhale now? Why not let the voices in?

But then he saw Tony start for Leslie.

He swam in a blind rage. No thought now for air or breath, only a single focus: reaching Tony, taking him down. He somehow snared Tony's flipper strap, slowed the leg action, then grabbed his ankle with both hands and held on, fingernails digging. Tony kicked, somersaulted, slashed with his knife, but Decker felt only the bluntness of the blows that fell across his hands. He clamped his jaws shut against the convulsing in his lungs. He was a machine now, a death machine for Tony, taking him down to where the voices wailed.

He was still holding on when he saw the half moon again

and Leslie silhouetted there, entering the safety of the light, vanishing into it. A moment later his arms and legs gave out, suddenly, completely, like someone flipping a switch. Tony disappeared into the gloom. Decker was a dead thing now, limp and immobile, adrift in liquid space, and yet not alone.

The sea began pressing in. It pried gently at his lips at first, poked its burning fingers inside his mouth, seeping like acid down his throat. He looked up at the half moon, cold and unfeeling, farther and farther beyond his reach. He gagged and choked, life's annoying reflex clinging to the last, as the half moon dimmed and disappeared.

Suddenly, a second sight flickered at the backs of his eyes—surprised him—as though the blood there were boiling. Liquid reds and yellows bubbled up from nowhere, hot and bright as lava. He seemed to be peering inward now, deep into the molten core of his brain.

He wasn't afraid: The hot glow there was peaceful, inviting. He thought, So this is death, and wasn't scared or discouraged but only surprised that he had come to this other place and that it seemed so strange and confining, not what he had expected at all. The wailing voices grew louder as his mind's sight plunged ever deeper into the hot orange glow. In a moment, or perhaps an infinity, he would be safe, at peace, the long journey ended.

The shock to his face seemed a violent intrusion. Someone was clawing at his lips, banging against his teeth. He shook his head, trying to tunnel deeper, wanting refuge in that blood-warm sanctum, but all that was not him came pouring in—bitter, angry, choking—spilling into his throat and lungs. He vomited. The acid burned up through his nose, behind his eyes, into his skull.

Big hands worked both sides of his face now, squeezing, jamming the thing between his teeth. He took a burning breath.

Then a second, a third—each one cooler, more soothing. On the seventh, something clicked inside his brain, like flipping on a video camera, the world in instant focus.

He saw Beryl's gentle eyes staring deep into his own.

He lay a long while facedown on the diving platform, coughing until his throat was raw. His lungs and sinuses felt as if they'd been seared with a blowtorch. His hands were on fire, too. Why, he didn't know.

Beryl yelled to François. "Bring the first aid kit!"

Beryl reached down and examined what was left of Decker's regulator hose. "What the bloody hell?" he said. "It's sliced clean through."

Beryl and Leslie helped Decker to his knees, then Beryl unbuckled his vest and removed his tanks. Instantly, he felt lighter, but also light-headed, as though the weight on his back had helped anchor his straying consciousness. They moved him to a bench where he sat and caught his breath, resting his burning hands on his knees.

An audience of divers gathered around. Leslie glared and they scattered.

She sat down and hugged him carefully around the shoulders.

"I can't believe you're alive," she said. Her voice was near to breaking. It brought a smile to his bruised lips.

"You were *amazing* down there," she said. He liked that even more.

"You think so?"

"Oh, shut up." She hugged him again, rocking a little.

He felt more than pride in how he'd handled his encounter with Tony. He felt a kind of redemption, as though he had recovered a part of himself that had been lost since that moment in the river when he saw the scratches on Janet's face and realized they were his. He was no longer frightened of who he was.

François came with the medical kit and gingerly took one of Decker's hands. For the first time Decker noticed the bloody gashes across his knuckles and the tops of his hands, and nearly blacked out.

"Merde," François said, inspecting the damage. "You need a doctor for dees, yes?"

He had Decker hold out his hands, and while Leslie looked away dribbled the contents of an iodine bottle over the cuts. The initial sting was an icy shock, followed by a long, slow burn. Decker's mouth formed an *O*, his breath whistling. Quickly, François wrapped one hand in gauze, then another, and taped them.

"Zat ees all I can do. We take you to a clin-eek, okay?"

"Where's Tony?" Decker asked.

Beryl was standing near. "We were asking the same. He hasn't returned yet."

"He won't," Decker said. "He tried to kill me."

"Are you sure?" Beryl said.

"I saw him, too," Leslie said. "Just before you came back to find us."

"Well, he can't get far," Beryl said. "He's very nearly out of air."

Decker looked out to the diving site and the dozen or so yachts anchored there, all of them with motorized dinghies in tow. Tony could easily cut the line to one and be on his way.

"Under normal circumstances, we'd send out a search team," Beryl said. "But in this case, I think we'll make an exception."

François took Decker's wrists and held his hands vertically in the air. The bandages were beginning to seep.

"We must go," he said to Beryl. "He ees losing much blood."

The two men headed to the pilot's wheel, and a few seconds later, the catamaran shot off like a rocket.

Decker and Leslie were alone.

"Did you find it?" Decker asked.

*"Yes,"* she whispered.

She unzipped her wet suit, reached just under her left breast and pulled out a small sealed plastic bag. It was filled with wet pebbles. Like a Babushka toy, there was another plastic bag inside and, inside that, a cartridge box. Her fingers plucked out the box, then slowly opened it on her lifted palm like a tiny treasure chest.

Inside was dry, white sand.

# 10

It was almost four when the diving boat reached the ship at Spanish Town harbor. After boarding, Leslie led Decker straight to her cabin.

"Sleep," she said, pulling back the sheet on her bunk. "You can always worry later."

He lay down, feeling better than he would have expected, perhaps because of the medication, perhaps because he was still floating on the calm of his self-discovery, almost oblivious to the pain in his hands.

They had found a doctor at the Peter Island Resort, a luxury hotel half a mile southwest of Dead Chest, only ten minutes from the diving site. His name was Larry Silbermann, a vacationing plastic surgeon from Glen Cove, and he was tanned and good-looking and very adept with sutures and needle. He was finished in several minutes—twelve stitches to the right hand, eight to the left—then wrapped Decker's hands and knuckles in pressure bandages, leaving only the thumbs and tips of his fingers exposed. He told Decker to keep the bandages on for a week and handed him enough pain pills to get him through the night.

Decker offered to mail him a check, but he refused. "This one's on Hillary," he said.

Decker's throat was still raw. When he spoke later in Leslie's cabin, his voice rasped. "I can't believe Danielle was that clever. A decoy map—and *we* fell for it."

"It was desperation," Leslie said, going to her dresser at the foot of the bunk. "She knew Tony was closing in. She must have planned to disappear, just the way Justin had. The map was meant to throw Tony off for a day or two."

"But how?"

"She knew Tony would go straight to Ellen the moment she was gone. *He* was supposed to find the map—not us."

"So now what? Danielle's dead and the tape could be anywhere."

"We'll find that tape, believe me."

With equal determination, she pulled down the straps on her bathing suit and, without losing a beat on the conversation, stepped out of it and deposited the tiny scrap on her dresser. "I'll find it even if I have to string up Ellen by the thumbs."

She stood there proud and naked, hands on her hips, showing off her nut brown body as though it were the most perfectly natural situation in the world. She was as sleek and contoured as a statue, even her small tuft of blonde hair, triangulating to a fine, soft point.

Decker could hardly speak. No one since Janet had been that open, that intimate. Finally, he managed to croak, "Why won't you give Ellen a break?"

"Don't be a fool. Ellen told Tony we had the map."

She continued to pose, naked and unashamed. Decker swallowed and said, "You mean he forced her to."

"Allegedly, darlin'. I wasn't there to see it, nor were you."

His heart pounded, thinking she might come toward the bed now, but she stepped into bathroom instead and reappeared a moment later, cinching an apricot bathrobe around her waist.

He felt relieved, but also disappointed—both the pressure and the excitement were gone.

"So how did Ellen know we had the map?"

"She knew her cabin had been searched. She could figure out the rest."

"That's where I disagree. Tony knew something was up when we both signed up for the dive."

She sat down on the mattress next to his thigh. It seemed he could feel the soft weight of her body perched there.

She smiled and said, "Except Tony didn't count on getting such a fight." She leaned down and kissed him lightly on the forehead.

He took her face in his hands, bandages and all, and kissed her on the lips. She opened up for him like a tropical flower, tasting of the warmth of the sun, the saltiness of the sea.

She stood suddenly and slipped out of the bathrobe, and then lay down beside him, cool and sleek and polished, not at all like Janet's ample warmth. He put his arm around her, awkward, a bit unsure, his hands in those damned bandages like a pair of ragged claws. His fingertips traced her hip, her rib cage. A wind-tunnel contour. She tugged at his trunks.

"Isn't this a little fast?" he said.

"Is there a reason to go slow?"

"Maybe."

They kissed again and then she left his mouth and started planting soft kisses on his neck and down his chest, his heart racing as her destination became abundantly clear. She fingered the waistband of his trunks.

"Leslie, are you sure—"

"Just be quiet," she said softly, "and let it happen."

When she took hold of him, he gripped the headboard and steadied himself against the slow rocking of the ship as he seemed to fall deeper and deeper into the enveloping warmth and sway of the sea.

When he woke, she was gone, but the perfumed smell of her was still with him in the bunk. She had left the bathroom light on and a small, battery-operated alarm clock on the floor by her bunk. It was six thirty-five. His hands were throbbing under the bandages. That's what woke him.

He sat groggily on the edge of the bunk and the memory of an hour or two ago came back to him in flashes of sensation and emotion, like a dream half-remembered upon waking.

Leslie had performed as anticipated—the straightforwardness of her sexual maneuvers, the greediness of her need—but what surprised him was that she had been tender enough, artful enough, that he'd had no trouble responding in kind. She'd taken definite precautions, too, about AIDS, a sensible girl, although it bothered him a little that she didn't trust him, not completely, although what did he expect in this day and age. Afterward, as they lay tangled and exhausted in the bunk, she began to cry, silently. He could feel the tears run warm on his chest. She wouldn't tell him why, and when he insisted, she told him they should hold each other and sleep.

In a while, she seemed to stop crying and her breathing became as slow and deep as the tides. He held her, thinking, I could hold her like this forever. He took her with him then as he fell toward sleep, back to the molten spring inside where everything was warm and safe and glowing, and that was the last he remembered.

He got up slowly and found his pain pills and his trunks set out neatly on the dresser. There was a handwritten note beside them: "I promise you Justin tonight. Meet me at 10—courtyard of the La Ti Da. Love, Leslie. P.S. Our friend Ellen has scrammed. Mary Beth said she left for the airport at 3."

He took a quick lukewarm shower and forced himself to gulp down a full glass of the ship's briny water. He decided against another pain pill, wanting to be sharp for his interview with Justin. Then he left Leslie's cabin and went up to the main deck and back to the deckhouse. It was only seven, but it felt and looked much later as the sun began to set behind a bank of thick clouds, marbled gray and pink, mounting on the horizon. The wind had picked up from the north and west, carrying with it the smell of rain. He filled his lungs and felt his head begin to clear.

He peeped through a deckhouse porthole to make sure it was empty, then went inside and shut the door behind him. He used his right thumb to press the numbers for the Road Town police. When the call went through, he asked for either Givins or Baines but was told they were not at their desks. With a bit of bravado, he left a message for them that he had broken the Danielle Evans murder case "wide open" and that if they wanted the details they should meet him at 8:00 P.M. in Rudy's restaurant. The male clerk who took the message had no reaction to the message at all, except to ask, "Would you spell your title, sir?"

"Reporter. R-e-p-o—"

"No, mon. Your title, please."

"I don't understand. I have no title."

"Then you are plain Rick, no title?"

"Yes, Rick Decker."

"Okay, Decker is your title. Spell it, please."

"D-e-c-k-e-r."

"Okay, mon. Ah leave dis message."

Decker wondered if Berlitz offered a cram course in West Indian. He hung up and dialed Farlidge's number on the metro desk. A clerk answered: Farlidge was still tied up in the six o'clock news meeting.

"Get him out," Decker said.

The clerk put him on hold, and that's when Mary Beth stepped in.

"I'm sorry," she said, doe eyes blinking. "Were you making a private call?"

"Just finished, thank you." He hung up. A bad connection. Farlidge would understand.

"I'll come back later," she said, heading for the door.

"Really, there's no need. Are we still sailing back to Road Town tonight?"

Mary Beth shook her head. "The captain changed his mind a while ago. The weather is looking very nasty. We'll probably sail in the morning."

"Where can I find the captain?" For what it was worth, he wanted Pearce to know about Tony Henderson.

"He had some business to finish up with the police in Spanish Town. You know how it's been with this trip—the cruise from hell." She managed a company smile.

Decker studied her for a moment, the guileless brown eyes that seemed to hug everyone she saw.

He thought he'd try something. "Do you know if Justin Grammer's things are still on board?"

She stared wide-eyed. "Yes, I think so."

"Could I see them?"

"I'm not sure. I'd better—"

"I promise I won't remove a thing. I just want his family to know what he left behind."

"Do you know his family?"

"Sort of." It was amazing how easily he could lie now.

Mary Beth bit one of her knuckles and thought for a moment. "The captain would probably freak if he knew, but if you do it quickly, I don't think it could hurt."

"Where can I find his things?"

"Wait here. I'll bring them right up."

She returned in a minute carrying a bright blue garment

bag—cheap plastic you could maybe poke a sharpened pencil through. She laid it on the Formica table.

"Is that everything?" Decker asked.

"Yes, it's all in this one bag. We were going to send it to his family once we reached Antigua."

"Will you watch the door?" He would have asked her to leave, only he didn't want to push his luck.

Decker wasn't sure what he was looking for in the bag. All he wanted was some background, a few more clues into the character of the baffling young man he'd be interviewing later that night. He opened the bottom snap first, unfolded the bag, and unzipped the hanger compartment. It was full of cotton sports shirts, all of them in varying shades of blue and all of them fashionably faded. At the bottom corner of the compartment something shiny caught his eye. He picked it up. It was heavy, about the length and thickness of a carrot, a solid quartz crystal.

"He was pretty serious about the New Age stuff, wasn't he?" Decker said.

Mary Beth was still by the door, watching. "Oh, yes. Crystal therapy, visualization, health foods—all of it. I know, because I have to arrange for people's diets."

Decker flipped the bag over. In the larger side pocket he found underwear, the skimpy bikini kind—all of them blue—and an assortment of blue baggy pants and walking shorts. There were two smaller pockets on the other side. One was stuffed with postcards and books, including a well-thumbed paperback of *Death in Venice* and a tattered, leather-bound New Testament with an inscription inside that said: "To Justin, at 13. Keep God's Word always in your heart. Love, Mimsy."

Mimsy? The rich are different from you and me: They love cutesy nicknames.

He leafed through the book and found passages carefully

underlined here and there in thick ballpoint pen. One in particular caught his eye:

> They woke him and said to him, "Master, do you not care? We are going down!" And he woke up and rebuked the wind and said to the sea "Quiet now! Be calm!" And the wind dropped, and all was calm again. Then he said to them, "Why are you so frightened? How is it you have no faith?"

Crystals and Christ. It could only happen in the nineties.

Decker tried the other pocket and found another well-used paperback—*Healing Yourself: Unleashing the Positive Energy Within.* In the same pocket was a burgundy leather shave kit. He unzipped it, split it open, and found all the usual men's paraphernalia—razor handle, disposable blades, stick deodorant, toothbrush—and a squat plastic bottle of pills. Decker read the prescription label: It had been filled about two weeks ago, at NYU-Cornell Medical Center. "Take four times daily. 100 milligrams. Azidothymidine." It was almost full.

"Ever hear of a drug called..." He looked hard at the word, trying to sound it out syllable by syllable. "A-zi-do-thy-mi-dine?"

"I'm not sure, but it sounds like AZT."

"You mean the drug for AIDS?"

"Uh-huh. They usually give it before the symptoms are full-blown. They say it can add months, even years to the lives of AIDS patients." Mary Beth's mouth dropped when she realized what she was saying. "Those are Justin's?"

Decker nodded, although it made no sense.

He tossed the bottle back into the kit and zipped it. He'd seen enough.

Along Spanish Town beach, the reggae bars were ominously quiet under the darkening sky. Smaller boats were streaming now into the marina, seeking refuge from the wall of clouds moving in from the west. Beyond the harbor, the water was chopping gray and white. Every now and then, a gust of wind would buffet the *Southern Cross,* sounding a low moan through its spars.

Decker sat by himself in a corner of the stern, his mind looping as he tried to sort things out. The AZT explained some parts of the Justin Grammer story, but threw others into mind-boggling confusion. It meant, of course, that Justin had compelling personal as well as political reasons for wanting to bring down Parnell.

But why hadn't he taken the pills with him? That was the question eating at Decker, the one he was most desperate to ask Leslie: Was she lying about Justin's being alive? Was she trying to set him up? But why? And for whom?

He stretched out on the bench and closed his eyes and wondered now if he had been played for a fool. Things had happened too quickly with Leslie, too quickly to seem true even for an ego the size of his own. He was dazzled by her and yet he knew there was something cold and unreachable at her center—perhaps that part of her that had melted in silent tears on his chest.

When he opened his eyes again, he found Ryan sitting at his feet looking glum and bored. He was fingering the buttons on his Nintendo, but the toy wasn't making the familiar electronic bleeps and burps. He turned to Decker, "I heard about the dive. You feel better now?"

"I'm alive. Can't feel any better than that."

Ryan smiled a bit, but then went back to fingering his Nintendo.

"Where's your pal Jenny?" Decker asked. He was glad to have the boy distract him for a while.

"She's packing. Everybody's packing. I can't believe they're kicking us off the ship tomorrow. What a crappy deal." And then more hopefully: "You think they'd let us go snorkeling one last time?"

Decker shook his head. "There's a storm moving in."

Ryan looked without much interest at the horizon. Several giant clouds had broken ahead of the cloud bank, their edges burnished flaming red as the sun slid down behind them.

"I tell you what," Decker said with all the false cheeriness of a parent. "I challenge you to a round of Nintendo."

"Can't. It's busted," Ryan said. "I'm only carrying it around because Mom was going to throw it in the trash."

"What's wrong with it?"

"I don't know. It won't even turn on."

"You check the batteries?"

"They were practically brand new."

Decker remembered something, his brain suddenly turning and clicking like tumblers on a lock. "Did you say Danielle broke that thing?"

"Yeah. She apologized all over the place. She was going to take it back to New York and have it fixed."

"Let me see that for a second."

He reached with his bandaged hands. They were trembling slightly. He checked the back of the plastic casing: four small flathead screws were all that held it together.

"Do you have a dime?"

Ryan stuffed a hand in his shorts. He had a whole pocket full of kid's change. "Yeah. Here." He was curious now. "Think you can fix it?"

"No, but I'm going to look inside."

"Oh."

He pinched the dime between his thumb and the exposed tip of his little finger. The flexing of his hand pained his stitches but the four screws came out easily. Decker laid them on the bench and separated the two plastic halves: the casing was stuffed with wadded bits of newspaper.

"Well, well, what do you know?"

Ryan stared. "Danielle did that?"

Decker plucked away the layer of wadding and there it was—an 8-millimeter videotape, no bigger than his palm.

"Can you find Art Kapinski for me?" Decker asked.

"I think I just saw him in the saloon."

"Tell him to come here quickly and to bring his camcorder."

"Wow. Do you think Danielle was a spy or something?"

"Just bring Art. And wait—one more thing. Don't tell a soul what you've seen. Got that?"

"I'm cool."

Art's cabin was strewn with clothes, mostly his wife's, piled in and around open suitcases. Art moved some things off the lower bunk and invited Decker to sit, then handed him the camcorder. Art showed him how to load the tape.

"What now?" Decker asked.

"Push the rewind first." Decker found the button; the bandages didn't make it any easier. "Now hit play."

Decker's hands were trembling again as he pressed the viewing lens to his eye.

*A cabin interior, dark and grainy, the overhead light cloaked for "atmosphere." A view from the foot of the bunk, circular, fuzzy peephole edges. A voyeur's fantasy: hiding behind a camera, hiding behind—what? A suitcase? Danielle in frame now, standing, lifting off her top. Her breasts bounce just once, stay there, proud. She sits, smiles, turns, settles back on the mattress, knees in air. She wriggles, bottoms slip off, legs splayed—a wispy softness there in the shadowy recesses, like a promise. She flings the bottoms out of frame, motions. Come.*

*An older man now, wavy white hair, enters left, steps out of sad, old-fashioned boxers. Thick as a bear, hairy. In decent shape, considering. Yuks it up as Danielle pushes her head back on the pillow, parts the legs. More shadowy softness. A web.*

*He attends to her, mouth first. Greedy, heroic. A real gentleman. She arches her back, moans, does her best porn star imitation. Oooh, uuunh, aaaaah.*

Enough, Decker decided.

He pulled his eye away, offered the camera to Art.

Art waved his hand. "No, don't think the old ticker could take it."

Decker put his eye to the camera one last time, fumbled for the stop button, but then something unexpected caught his eye.

*The old fart sits on the edge of the bunk, motions to someone off frame. Funny, insistent. Danielle is grinning now, legs still open. Business hours. Parnell gets up, moves out of frame. A young woman mounts the bunk, naked, face turned from the camera. Slow, deliberate, she kneels first, hands splaying the other's knees. And then a slow bending to the task— blunt haircut going down.*

Decker held the camera away, his breath catching, sucked away into the tape's electronic vortex. He could feel the blood pounding through every tortured artery.

"You all right?" Art asked, a voice from another world.

Decker looked at Art, kind, concerned, looked at the floor between his feet. He knew he had to think but he didn't want to. Leslie's sudden appearance in that lurid scene was more than a betrayal, it had undermined his whole reality, pulled out the last bit of earth beneath his feet. Nothing but water now—rising, falling, pulling him under.

"You care to talk about it?" He looked up: Art again. Someone he knew. Thought he knew.

# 11

The rain was dripping from a single point through the thatched roof at Rudy's, big kamikaze drops splattering every second or so on the picnic table where Decker sat waiting, sipping lukewarm coffee. Outside in the thickened darkness the rain was coming down in waves, stirring up bursts of moist, warm air that raced through Rudy's like scattered demons.

It was almost nine. Decker had called Farlidge again just before eight: No word yet on Leslie's status as a PI. Simmons was still working on it, Farlidge said.

"Working on it?" Decker screamed. "All it takes is a goddamned phone call."

Farlidge ignored him. "Are you filing tonight?"

"No, because I'm confused as hell. Listen, I need more help on your end. Find out everything you can about a Tony Henderson, possibly from Dallas. He claims to be a former Navy SEAL. He could be working for the CIA. Do you think somebody there can handle that, or is that too many phone calls?"

"We'll handle it. What about the guy?"

"Just get me the information. I'll file tomorrow."

He hung up, then tried Road Town a second time and managed to reach Baines. Decker asked if he could check on Leslie, and Baines said Givins knew someone with the D.C. police who might help. He agreed to meet Decker at Rudy's at eight-thirty, but that was before the rain started pouring.

In little more than an hour, Decker was meeting Leslie at the La Ti Da. If he had to, he'd face Leslie alone, confront her with the whole thing. He wasn't afraid of her—just shocked, angry, ashamed that he'd been conned. Tony was another matter, though, and every time the suspicion crept into his mind that Leslie and Tony might be working together, he blocked it out, refused to deal with it.

Rudy came out from behind the bar and warmed up his coffee. Decker was the only customer in the place.

"Don't you worry," Rudy said. "De rain, it stop soon. Summer rain always do."

Decker asked if there was a pay phone. Rudy said no, but offered the use of the bar phone.

As soon as Decker got up, a couple of black umbrellas popped in from the rain, and when closed, revealed the two detectives, water running down their gray slickers.

"Sorry, Mr. Decker," Givins said, tapping his wet umbrella against a timber support. "But the voyage from Road Town was quite an adventure."

The two detectives unbuckled their slickers and laid them across an empty picnic table. Then they sat down at Decker's table in their subdued, unhurried way. Both were dressed again in their starched white shirts and dark suits.

Rudy came with the coffee pot and two more mugs, and without being asked, poured the cops coffee. Givins thanked him, then pinched off three packets of sugar from the table basket, and ripped open all three packets into his cup. Baines, the younger one, pushed his cup off to the side and set his black briefcase on the table. The kamikaze raindrops were splattering a few inches to the right of it.

"Did you make the call to Washington?" Decker asked.

Givins nodded.

"What did you find out?"

"There is no one named Leslie Stanton registered as a private investigator in the District of Columbia. Nor, we are told, in the states of Maryland and Virginia."

Decker took a deep breath and, for a panicked moment, felt tears coming on. He squeezed his eyes shut, opened them, and said, "Did you bring the wire?"

"Here." Baines patted the briefcase and smiled.

"What about an eight-millimeter camcorder?"

Baines looked to Givins, who sighed and said, "The department is still waiting to purchase such an item. We have the larger format system."

"Then you'll just have to take my word for what's on the tape."

"There is a shop in St. Thomas, I am told, where we can copy the tape to fit our machine," Givins said. "May I see it?"

"No," Decker said. "Nobody gets this tape until I'm absolutely sure it's in the right hands."

"I take it you lack a certain trust in us, Mr. Decker."

"Right now, I don't trust anyone."

"Yet you seek our assistance—"

"I want you to learn the truth."

"All right, Mr. Decker. We will cooperate fully, at least for this one night."

"What about guns?"

"We prefer not to work with guns," Givins said.

"You're not serious."

Givins nodded.

"Are you crazy? What if Tony Henderson shows up with a gun? How do you plan to deal with that?"

"In our own way, Mr. Decker."

"Terrific."

Givins waited until Baines had pulled out his notebook and said, "So, Mr. Decker, tell us again how you've broken this case 'wide open'—as you put it so forcefully in your message."

Decker told them about his underwater encounter with Tony, about the videotape, and about his upcoming meeting with Leslie. During most of it, Givins seemed unimpressed, his hands locked on the table, his eyelids drooping a little over the bulging eyes while Baines scribbled away. Neither interrupted, until Decker mentioned Ryan's Game Boy.

"Game Boy?" Givins said. He turned to Baines. "Is that similar to a bat boy?"

Decker stifled a smile. "It's a computer game you hold in your hand. They're about the size of a paperback book."

"I see," Givins said. He motioned with his hand. "Continue, please."

Decker finished by suggesting a course of action. He would go wired to his meeting with Leslie as long as Givins and Baines were nearby and ready to assist. When he'd enticed Leslie to say enough to hang herself and the others, the two detectives could move in.

"Can you monitor the conversation?" Decker asked.

Baines patted the briefcase again. "Up to a distance of three thousand meters, depending on obstructions."

Givins stirred a little. "Mr. Decker, there are several troubling points in your statement. First of all, how do you know Miss Stanton is working for Congressman Parnell?"

"I don't. It's just a hunch I have. Why didn't she tell me she was on the tape?"

"Perhaps she is only trying to protect herself," Givins said. "Or perhaps Mr. Grammer."

"I doubt that. In fact, I doubt Justin is even alive." He told them about the AZT prescription and the Bible with the inscription in it. "If he's in hiding, why would he leave those things behind?"

Givins turned to Baines, got some wordless affirmation from his partner, and turned back to Decker. "We're quite prepared to monitor your conversation with Miss Stanton. I warn you, however, that you must not take any violent action against her. This is not to be a personal vendetta."

"Of course not. Nothing personal."

Givins only stared at him, eyelids drooping.

They went by foot to the La Ti Da, Decker under one umbrella, Givins and Baines sharing the other. The rain had stopped by the time they reached the hotel, twenty minutes before the scheduled meeting with Leslie. Decker made a quick check of the courtyard—Leslie had yet to arrive—before all three of them approached the front desk. A muscled young man there in a tank top pursed his lips and rolled his eyes when Givins flashed a badge. He eased up when Givins said he was from the homicide division.

"Oh, good," the clerk said. "As long as you're not from vice."

He was a healthy-looking, clean-cut kid, with a weight-lifter's build and receding short blonde hair. Below the temples, you could see the jaw hinges working underneath the tan. A skull with flesh over it. He spoke with an American accent.

Givins asked if he could use one of the first-floor rooms in the courtyard.

"But of course. Will you be needing extra towels?"

Givins cleared his throat. "The room is for official use only. I ask that you keep our presence here a secret."

The clerk smiled reassuringly. "Discretion is our middle name."

"May we choose any room?"

"Certainly. Right now, they're mostly all open. The rain kept our regulars away, and the late-night crowd won't be here until after midnight."

"May I take a look, please?"

"Help yourself."

Givins and Baines went out together to the courtyard and started pointing and talking. Decker stayed behind in the lobby, fending off smiles from the old men in the lobby and repeated offers of help from the clerk. In a minute or so, the two cops returned.

"We would like the room on the far right, nearest the bar," Givins told the clerk.

The clerk consulted a chart behind the counter. "That would be room number fifteen. Economy class. And you're in luck—a vacancy." He smiled and handed over the keys.

"The rooms on either side, are they occupied?"

The clerk checked his chart again. "No. Nothing until room 10. Our economy class rooms usually don't fill until quite late." The clerk winked.

Givins cleared his throat again. "Very good. Please keep it that way until further notice."

They soon discovered the meaning of "economy class." The room was small, windowless, and sexually Spartan: a sink, some towels, a plastic-covered futon on the floor, a couple of wood benches that could be moved around for God knows what purposes. On a wood shelf above the sink was an industrial-size box of condoms and a posted list of instructions on safe sex under the heading: "How to Love Thy Neighbor." Oddly enough for such a tight space, there were four doors—a back door for discreet exits as well as connecting doors to the other first-floor rooms on either side, evidently for those interested in meeting other "guests" without having to step outdoors.

Decker sat on one of the benches and felt his heart jumping in his chest like a frightened animal as Baines taped two thin strips of canvas up his belly to his chest. At the end of each strip was a microphone head no bigger than a pencil point, wired to a battery pack in his waistbelt. Baines positioned the mikes about eight inches apart on either side of Decker's breastbone.

Decker hadn't thought through his encounter with Leslie until Baines brought out the wire, and now the more he thought about it, the more confused and depressed he felt. If he was right about Leslie's link to Parnell, he could be in serious danger. If wrong, he risked exposing Justin and implicating Leslie for obstruction of justice.

It was a no-win situation, but he had no choice. The videotape alone wouldn't prove that Justin and Danielle had tried to blackmail Parnell, nor would it prove that Parnell had retaliated through Tony with staggering vengeance.

He tried to visualize the meeting. Leslie's deep blue eyes drawing him in. The savvy smile as she scoffed lightheartedly at his accusations. The warm touch of her hand as she tried to reassure him. He was determined not to fall for her tricks again. But at the same time another part of him held on to a kind of twisted hope that told him he was too eager to cast Leslie as a villain. Perhaps his distrust was only a reflection of something deeper: his own self-doubt and the fear that she could never love him.

When Baines finished taping, Decker slipped his T-shirt on and let it hang loose over his shorts. He wanted to hide any sign of the waistbelt and battery pack, even though the latter was no bigger than a cigarette case. Baines had positioned it just above his tailbone.

"Where do you want me to sit?" Decker asked.

"Anywhere on this end of the courtyard," Baines said. "Mind that you don't go pool bathing. You may fire a short."

"What if I sweat?"

Baines grinned. "You are nervous maybe, Mr. Decker?"

"Yes, very maybe."

"The canvas strips absorb the dampness. The wires are insulated."

"Don't forget, we will be listening to every word," Givins said. "In the event of any difficulties, we will make our presence known with utmost speed."

"Armed with what—wet bath towels?"

Givins managed to laugh. "Mr. Decker, you have such a charming sense of humor."

At nine fifty-five, Decker took a seat at one of the small glass-topped tables by the pool. Some of the regulars were trickling in now, most of them solo, waving to friends, congregating around the pool, sitting at the bar. Decker wondered about the little proprieties in such a setting—at what point did you stop the mingling and drift off to one of the 'economy class' rooms?

"Excuse me, but if you've finished your daiquiri, why don't you and I go screw our brains out?"

Or something like that. Who knew.

He sat facing the entrance to the courtyard in case Leslie should pop in and not see him. But that meant he was facing away from the room where Givins and Baines would be monitoring the conversation. If they came running, he would be the last to know.

Decker went down the list of questions he'd scribbled in his notebook. He would play along with her at first, then gradually tighten the screws. He had to sound like a reporter, though, not like someone wearing a police wire—more tough than leading in his questions—or Leslie might simply clam up. It was a fine but critical distinction.

He was worried, too, about his navy blue polo shirt. In the dense humidity after the storm, he was sweating from every pore. If the canvas strips on his chest became soaked, they could bleed through the dark shirt and give him away. He hunched over and set his elbows on the table, keeping his shirt loose over the wires.

At 10:10 P.M., there was still no sign of Leslie, and he feared now she might have gotten wind of Givins and Baines, perhaps through the blonde hunk at the front desk. Adding to his edginess, the men in the courtyard were growing bolder, too, asking Decker if they could join him. He gritted his teeth and said he was being met by friends.

Four minutes later on Decker's wristwatch, Leslie stepped just inside the courtyard in a long, white dress. Alone. She glanced quickly around the pool and, before Decker could catch her, disappeared again into the lobby. He had started after her when she reappeared and spotted him almost instantly. She was smiling as he waved her toward the table.

She walked around the edge of the pool in her no-nonsense way, hips tilted forward, legs moving in brisk, confident strides as the white dress billowed around her tanned knees. She drew stares from some of the men, a mix of curiosity and envy. The dress was loose, sleeveless, scooped at the top—so light and airy it seemed hardly to touch her skin.

"Hello, Rick."

She squeezed his shoulders and kissed him lightly on the cheek. His skin seemed to burn there, as though brushed with acid. He thought of Judas.

"I take it Justin has been delayed," Decker said as they sat down. He tried hard not to sound accusatory.

"He's not coming," Leslie said matter-of-factly. "Parnell might have his people here."

Decker felt his eyes go hot with anger, hurt.

"When do I see him?"

"Soon enough." She smiled. "I'd like to discuss a few ground rules first."

"Me, too."

"Are you all right, Rick?"

"Of course."

"You look ready to bite someone's head off."

"We'll see. Let's hear your ground rules." He kept his eyes open for Tony.

"First of all, I want my name left out of your story—completely," she said.

He nodded. Just then a single trickle of sweat, like the tracing of a fingertip, ran cold down the middle of his back. Somehow he managed not to shiver. He leaned forward, elbows on the table, praying the canvas strips on his chest wouldn't show.

"Secondly, no references to Justin's sexual orientation."

"Impossible. How else do we explain his motive for blackmailing Parnell?"

"Leave it out. His family wants it that way."

"Would they rather have people think it was greed?"

"They'd rather not have people think anything."

"You're being unrealistic."

"I'm looking after my client."

"Good for you, but I've got a bit of news to share." He stared deep into Leslie's eyes, wanting to detect the slightest flinch there, then said it.

"I have the tape."

She was wide-eyed at first, dumbfounded to the point of exaggeration, he thought. Suddenly, she threw her head back and almost shrieked to show her pleasure. "Justin will be thrilled! We'll make copies and go straight to Parnell—"

"No, Leslie," he said, still staring. "I've seen the tape."

She blinked a few times. "Oh." Then she crossed her legs and cracked a smile. The eyes showed neither guilt nor shame, only a kind of weary savvy.

"Did you enjoy it?"

"Sure. I love seeing people used."

She quit smiling.

"Tell me, Leslie. Which do you like better, men or women? Or do you switch on different nights?"

"That's not a fair question, Rick, and you know it."

"Never mind. Forget I even said that. I have far more important matters to discuss. First, I know you're not a private eye, all right? Second, I know damn well you're not working for the Grammers. So let's quit playing bullshit games, okay?"

She stared at him numbly for a moment, then reached out and touched his hand. Tears were beginning to glisten in the corners of her eyes. He thought: the performance of a lifetime.

"I'm sorry it's come to this, Rick. Honestly. I was just trying to help Justin. He's been a dear friend of mine since our days at Yale. He asked me to do those things with Danielle. He wanted something that would really shame Parnell, really scare him. It had to be an all-out orgy or it wouldn't work."

"Justin is dead," Decker said.

"But he isn't," she pleaded. "He's a five-minute drive from here."

"Then bring him here."

"I can't, Rick. You don't know Parnell. He has people everywhere. Listen to me: He is the head of the House Intelligence Committee—do you have any idea who you're dealing with?"

"So you want me to go to Justin."

"Yes—he's waiting. He wants to tell his story. He wants to expose Parnell before he has anyone else murdered."

"Why didn't he take his pills, Leslie?"

The exaggerated double take again, and then: "What pills are you talking about?"

"Justin's pills, Leslie. The ones for treating his AIDS."

She sat back and stared at him evenly. "All right. Justin Grammer is HIV positive. Now go broadcast that in your little newspaper back home. He hasn't suffered enough already, has he?"

"You're evading the point, Leslie. Why didn't he take the damn pills with him?"

She broke into her savvy smile, the one that was supposed to make him feel like a misguided kid. "Justin stopped taking the pills for religious reasons. He was trying to cure himself through faith."

"Oh, come on."

"Why not? Do you think AZT ever cured anyone?"

"It extends life."

"What life? The side effects can be worse than the disease itself."

Their voices were drawing attention now. Decker collected himself. "Why should I believe a word you say?"

"Don't believe me then. Believe Justin. Let's go to him right now, this very second. He's waiting."

"Let him wait. What about the night he disappeared—was he meeting Parnell here?"

"Yes, but Parnell never showed. Justin tried to leave and he was followed. If it hadn't been for the people here . . ."

"They hid him?"

"That first night, and then they found him a place in the mountains."

"Why didn't Danielle go into hiding?"

Leslie threw up her hands. "She was the Maybelline Girl—all that fame and glamour. Maybe she thought no one would touch her. Maybe she bluffed and said she had copies of the tape."

"What about you then? Why aren't you in hiding?"

Leslie closed her eyes and said softly, "Because I work for Parnell."

Decker sat back and took a deep breath. The sweat from the wires was beginning to soak through his shirt but he didn't care anymore. He wanted to yell for the two cops to come running.

"It's not what you think at all," Leslie said. "You *must* talk to Justin. You have to hear the whole story."

She looked across the table, eyes pleading to be trusted, and Decker felt himself falling, spinning downward into their blue depths even as he fought against them.

Instinct told him she was lying, an instinct honed by years of being lied to and used. Skepticism—that was a reporter's only defense. That and keeping your distance, never gravitating to a point of view, never abdicating your right to judge. That way you were always safe, and alone.

Something snapped inside him. A leap of faith?

"How do we get there?" he asked.

"I have a rental car outside."

"Fine, although I still can't think of a single reason why I should trust you."

"You have to, Rick. I'm the only person who can lead you to Justin."

She looked edgy and frightened now, but the set of her jaw, the tension in her brow told him she was hardened in her resolve, ready to accept all risks. But to what end?

There was no other way to find out.

"Let's go," he said.

# 12

In the car, Leslie pulled a black silk scarf from her purse.

"You'll have to be blindfolded," she said.

"You're not serious."

"Justin insists on it."

He looked straight at her, thinking he could stare her down if she were lying, but her eyes never flinched.

"Fine then," he said.

She took the scarf and folded it on her lap and pulled it tight around his eyes. It smelled faintly of her perfume. She tied it with a triple knot.

"All right," he said, "I'm blind."

The small car sputtered and lurched away, and Decker realized with a sudden start that Givins and Baines had no way of following him: They'd ferried over from Road Town. He tried to calm himself. Surely, a couple of detectives could commandeer a car if they had to. But knowing those two, they'd probably thumb a ride.

They sped through the back roads of town—Decker could hear the suction of tires through wet sand—and before long started a winding ascent on a bumpy road: They were heading into the mountains. Decker could smell it, too. The night air rushed in cool and sweet and vibrant with a surfeit of living things, wild and unseen. He could hear the rasping of a million insects and the incessant peeping of tree frogs—like a colony of chicks, as Art had put it—only now they sounded lost and frantic.

Leslie began to speak in hushed tones, mostly about Justin,

about the conditions he was hiding under, how he was looking forward to being free again. The details she supplied, vivid and concrete, gave Decker some comfort: Leslie was either a master storyteller or telling the truth.

She interrupted herself. "By the way, did you bring the tape with you?"

"Why?"

"Justin will ask to see it, I'm sure. You may have to bargain for an interview."

"I'll deal with that when the time comes."

He regretted now not leaving the tape with Givins and Baines. Still, if Leslie or Justin tried to confiscate it, he could lie and say he'd made copies. Lying came easily to him now, just as trust came hard.

The car slowed, went left, and suddenly they were going downhill, chattering over bumps and depressions, crunching over gravel—a driveway, no doubt.

"Is this it?"

"Almost."

The car leveled off and they were gliding over grass now; he could hear it brushing against the tire walls. The brakes squeaked a little as they came to a stop.

"Can I take this damned thing off now?" He reached for the knot behind his head.

"I'll get it."

When his eyes were freed, he was staring into the side of what looked like an old stucco barn. The headlights made two big yellow circles on the moldy white paint. The building stood in a small clearing, nestled into the side of a hill. There was an open door on the first level, down some stone steps. The gravel driveway continued uphill to a wide double door, apparently for storing trucks or tractors.

"So how does Justin like life on the farm?"

"It's not a farm. You're looking at one of the oldest rum distilleries in the Caribbean."

To their right, just inside the peripheral glare of the headlights, lay an old well: a circle of flat stones covered by a metal grate. No bucket, no pump. Decker wondered how they retrieved the water. Siphons?

"Is the place still in operation?"

"Has been for two hundred years. They make the best rum around. The real thing."

"No doubt."

Leslie turned off the engine but left the keys in the ignition and the lights on. Decker let her get out first, then slipped the tape out of his pocket and dropped it underneath his seat. Just in case.

Leslie went back to the trunk of the beat-up Vega and pulled out a blocklike heavy-duty flashlight, the kind fishermen use. She returned to the front of the car where Decker was waiting and aimed the light at the barn's open lower door. It looked as dark as a coal bin inside: one more blind entry to the unknown.

"After you," he said.

He followed her down the stone steps and into the distillery, her long white dress floating ghostlike into the blackened space.

The dirt floor was moist and springy to the step, the air cool and damp and cloyingly sweet with the smell of . . . what? rotting sugarcane? As Leslie poked the light around, Decker caught snatches of the room's contents: open barrels filled with dark, bubbling liquid; bags of sugar piled high against a wall; empty bottles strewn across the floor. They sidestepped a huge wooden bucket and, next to it, a putt-putt engine belted to some rollers. It looked like an old-fashioned washing machine.

Leslie fixed her light on a set of rickety open stairs at the back of the room. It led to an open second floor where everything seemed darker still.

She shouted, "Justin! We're here!"

Sharp as a handclap, something shot from the rafters and circled overhead in the gloom. Decker covered his head.

"Barn owl," Leslie said calmly. "Come on. He's up this way."

She had started for the stairs, Decker close behind, when a hammering sound broke out—a slow, restless thumping in the dark. It seemed to be coming from the floorboards upstairs.

Decker stopped; he'd reached his limit. "What the hell's up there?"

"Mules, Rick. It's where they stable the mules. Don't be such a nervous wreck."

"I thought this was a distillery, not a farm."

"They use mules to haul the sugarcane, okay?"

He followed her up the stairs, the dizzying heat and smell of rum mash growing stronger with each ascending step.

Upstairs, they were greeted by goats, four of them, their eyes lit up like yellow marbles. They bleated and moved off in a pack to a corner as Leslie passed through. She trained her flashlight on three open stalls against the far wall. The mules there stirred and clomped as Leslie approached, their big rounded flanks shifting, black tails flitting. They seemed agitated, Decker thought.

"Justin?" Leslie called out, softly this time.

She headed for the middle stall, in a hurry now, and squeezed past the mule.

"Oh God, no! It can't be!" Her voice was pure anguish.

Decker tried to follow but the mule shifted and pinned him against the stall with its hard, matted flank. He shoved the animal with both bandaged hands and worked his way in.

"No, no, no!"

Leslie was on her knees, sobbing and rocking, a man's body spread before her in the hay. He was lying on his back, perhaps asleep. Decker couldn't see the face, but he could see the blue blanket wrapped tightly around the torso and legs, the white feet sticking out, long and tapered, Goya-like.

He pressed Leslie's flashlight between his hands and shone it on the man's face. It was the same face he'd seen staring back at him dozens of times from the photo in his notebook—the eyes haunted and visionary, as though they had seen this future, this end point in time, from the very beginning.

Only one difference now: On Justin's forehead, just above the left temple, was a small clean hole, blackened and puckered around the edges. The blood there was clotted but still bright red.

Decker shivered in the close heat.

He turned and pointed the flashlight around the barn: nothing but goats, hay, the chaff of sugarcane. But the darkness seemed to brood as though the barn had a consciousness of its own.

Leslie was still on her knees, silent in her grief, clutching her face between her hands. Decker tucked the flashlight under his arm and put his hand on her shoulder.

"We'd better go," he said.

She shrugged his hand away and stood, the mule braying at her sudden movement.

"Are you satisfied now?" she said. "You have your story now. It's right there, dead on the ground."

"I didn't kill him, Leslie."

"Yes you did! You and your damned interview."

She pushed him aside and squeezed past the mule and out of the stall. In the darkened loft, she stopped and took a deep breath and sobbed. Decker came up behind her, a hot white softness in the dark. He wanted to touch her, hold her, but he could feel the heat of her anger.

"I still don't get it," he said. He set down the flashlight and let the darkness envelop them.

"No, you wouldn't. Can't you see I was followed this evening? I led them straight to Justin—all because of your damned interview."

"But Tony must have been miles away."

"You think it's just Tony?" She laughed. "Stuart has people all over these islands. He buys people, uses them, spits them out."

"Including you," Decker said.

"Yes, me, too," she said. "I worked for the bastard. Long enough to learn to hate him."

"Then it was you who set him up."

"Who else could have gotten him down here? I arranged the whole thing, just the way I arranged all his little liaisons."

"And you did it for Justin?"

"Why does it matter? It's over now. Dead and finished."

"Because I want the whole story, Leslie. All of it, dammit. From the beginning."

"The *whole* story." Her voice was thick with contempt. "What the hell do you know about the *whole* story? You can't possibly know until you've lived it."

"Then tell me. Tell me what I don't know."

"All right." She took a deep breath and seemed to draw the darkness around her like a shield. "You don't know what it's like to be abandoned, cast off by your family, by all the people you thought were friends. Or what it's like to see the fear in a nurse's eyes because she has to touch you, or wash you, or stick a needle in your arm. Or worst of all, what it's like to die by inches, day by day, minute by minute. Imagine your muscles, your guts, even your brain, rotting away into something that was never you, couldn't *possibly* be you. It's like watching yourself in the grave, only you're alive and aware of everything that's going on. *That's* what you don't know."

He couldn't see her face but he could hear her breath catching.

"I'm sorry, Leslie. If you lost someone to AIDS—"

"Yes, I've lost someone. I've lost lots and lots of someones. Because that someone, someday, will be me."

He heard what she had said, but he wasn't certain, wasn't willing to be certain. He almost said, "What do you mean?" but in the moment before he said it, he already knew. He reached for her but she pushed him away.

"Don't!" she snapped. "Don't try to prove anything."

He locked his arms around her anyway and she began flailing, small fists beating on his sides and back, but he held on and wouldn't let go. In a while, she stopped and started crying and he rocked her in his arms, a small, quivering child. They stood there rocking in the dark for a long while, listening to the dry buzzing of the flies, until the goats turned curious and gathered round, nuzzling and sniffing at their legs.

Outside, they made their way across the tall, wet grass to the car. Leslie checked the backseat with the flashlight. It was empty. They got into the car.

Leslie settled into the driver's seat.

"Damn!" she screamed. She pounded the steering wheel. "Damn, damn, damn!"

"Now what?"

"The keys are gone." Her voice was shaky. "I left them in the ignition, now they're gone."

"Are you sure?" His heart squeezed in his chest.

"Yes, I'm sure."

The trees and vines around them seemed to press in closer, full of moving shadows. Decker felt his hands throbbing again beneath the bandages.

"We'll walk," he said, trying to sound calm.

He reached under the seat for the tape, then thought better of it and left it there. He could always come back later.

He got out of the car and, with his first step, tripped and fell, his knees and elbows going hard to the ground. He lay there in the wet grass thinking, you clumsy idiot. Get a grip. Take control. He tried to raise himself to his knees, but a lightning blow to his back flattened him again. A steady pressure on his spine kept him there, cutting him in half just above the battery pack for the wire.

"Where's the tape?"

A light swirled in the corner of his eye. He heard the snick of an automatic, then Leslie screaming from somewhere, nowhere, "You bastard! You said there'd be no more killing!"

"Get back in the vehicle—now!" It was Tony's voice, insistent, but no louder than it needed to be.

"Dammit, you promised. You killed Justin, you bastard!" Decker heard the car door slam.

Tony reached down and jammed the gun to Decker's temple and said, "Don't move." He stuffed his hand into the back pocket of Decker's shorts, pulled the flap out, then dug with his fingertips along the outsides of his thighs. Decker's face was pinned to the ground, the grass there squirming with small life, when Tony found the battery pack.

"You're wired," Tony said, stunned into a normal tone of voice. He yanked the flimsy belt and tossed it. The pressure on Decker's skull never let up.

"Who wired you, asshole? Who the hell are you working for?"

"What wire?"

A blow to his back took his breath away. He gulped for air, felt the rage rush to his brain, the blood tingle in his scalp.

"Get up," Tony said. "On your knees." There was a stinging kick to his ribs this time. "Hands behind your head."

Decker rolled over, got to his knees, arched his back against the pain.

Tony blinded him with the flashlight. "One more time, where's the tape?"

"The tape's gone, Tony. It's on the way to Cincinnati. I mailed it this afternoon." He said it with such vehemence he almost believed it himself.

"Not possible. The post office has been under surveillance for the past seventy-two hours."

"Who's doing all this scut work, Tony? The CIA? The DEA? Parnell must be awfully important to you boys."

Tony rested the tip of the gun barrel on Decker's nose. Orange-yellow tracers from the flashlight swirled in the backs of his eyes, like Fourth of July sparklers.

"You can talk now, or you can talk to a specialist later. Believe me, you're better off talking to me."

"I hid it."

"Where?"

"I can show you."

"Just say where, goddammit."

"Why should I? The cops are on their way."

"Is that who wired you? The BVI boys?"

"They know I'm here."

Tony laughed. "You seriously think I'm afraid of a couple of nigger cops?"

Tony backed away a foot or two and shouted to Leslie inside the car. "Search the vehicle."

"Don't be an idiot," Decker yelled to her. "He'll kill us both."

The snap-kick to his stomach sent the air out of him like a punch on a paper bag. Decker doubled over, guts twisting, the hot rage inside looking for a way out.

"Move it, Leslie! We don't have all night."

He battled a long, long moment of despair, his chest an aching vacuum, his nose buried in the wet, defeated earth. But when he at last undoubled, his lungs filling in a deep rush, he saw his opportunity: Tony was looking in the car window, supervising Leslie's search.

Decker forced himself to one knee, shaking, hands braced to the ground like a sprinter. But when he tried to spring he couldn't move. His legs were numb, dead, all the rage bottled up there, weighing him down. He heard himself groan—the half-stifled scream of someone trapped in a nightmare—and yet in that horrible moment, the car door flung open and sent Tony reeling backward, delivered by an act of providence.

Decker caught him from behind and they tumbled over the slick grass. It seemed like child's horseplay until Tony, by some calculated move, ended on top and straddled Decker's chest.

Tony tried to bring the gun barrel down. Decker blocked it with both hands and the tip exploded in a rocket of light, sparks stinging like pinpricks across his forehead.

Decker was certain he'd been shot, some part of his brain matter carved out, but it didn't matter because his bandaged hands were pressed around the barrel of the gun and Tony was grunting, swearing, straining to bring it down.

In seconds, the battle was lost, the cold barrel against his nose, the smell of burnt powder up his nostrils like the Fourth of July.

Roll, he thought, you've got to roll *now* when he heard the loud, hollow cracking sound above his face.

Tony's head jerked upward as though grabbed by the hair. But then he slumped forward again, his torso a collapsing wall.

Decker lifted his hands to catch the falling weight, then heaved him aside.

Where Tony had been stood Leslie, legs akimbo in her white dress, slapping the big flashlight in her palm.

They found jumper cables in the back of the Vega and used the cord to bind Tony's hands and feet. Tony was unconscious but alive, a gash above his right ear—far worse than the powder burn on Decker's forehead. Unconscious, Tony was all legs and arms, unhinged and heavy, like a giant windup toy. Stuart Parnell's windup toy.

They found the car keys in Tony's pocket, then dragged his body across the grass and, with one quick heave, dropped him into the trunk of the car. They folded his legs in the fetal position to make him fit. Leslie slammed the trunk and said, "There, dammit! Enjoy the ride."

They sat against the trunk and caught their breath in the damp mountain air.

"Tell me something," Decker said. "How did you get so chummy with Tony?"

"I had to. It was the only way to protect Justin."

"You knew all along that Tony killed Danielle. Why didn't you do something about it?"

"I *didn't* know—not until he tried to drown you. When we got back to the ship, I thought I could make a deal. I told Tony I could deliver the tape if he would stop the killing. I told him Stuart would vouch for me."

"So much for deals." He was thinking, too, of Leslie's promise to share information. "And you think Tony followed you up here this evening."

"Or someone tipped him off. They have informants all over the island by now."

He touched her cool, bare shoulder. "I haven't thanked you, have I?"

"For what?"

"I was nearly decapitated back there."

She hugged him, a big friendly hug, head against his chest, but not like before in the cabin. He touched her cheek, damp from exertion, and smelled the perfumed heat of her hair.

"Let's get out of here," she said, slipping away. "I need a long, cool drink and a shower."

He took her by the hand. "Listen, I have to know one more thing," he said. "You can refuse—"

"I won't," she said, and leaned back against the trunk.

"You don't know the question."

"But I know what you're thinking. It's what everybody thinks at some point: How did a nice professional girl—an aide to a congressman—happen to be HIV positive? What heinous, unnatural act did she commit?"

"I wouldn't have put it that way."

"But that's what you're thinking, isn't it?"

"You don't have to answer."

"I want to, only to get it behind us. Okay?"

"Fine."

"I contracted it the way most people do, because I trusted someone. He was an administrator for the National Endowment for the Arts. We had a two-week fling about four years ago and then he dumped me. I had no idea I was HIV positive until his doctor called about eight months ago and told me I should get tested."

"I'm sorry."

"Yeah, I'm sorry, too. For me and for two million other people in this country. But I feel healthy, strong. At least for now. And I only get teary every once in a while, as you've already seen. If you're worried about our little encounter, don't. I was extremely careful. And, if you didn't already know, a woman is eight times more likely to contract the virus from an infected man than vice versa. Now let's go."

He tugged her by the hand. "Our little encounter? Is that what it was?"

"Yes."

"Then why should it have happened at all?"

"Because I felt moved to do so, and you certainly didn't mind."

"What if I wanted to make it something more?"

He took her arm between his bandage and thumb and tried to pull her close.

"Don't." She pushed at his hand. He let go.

Maybe she was right. Maybe he didn't have the guts now, but he told her anyway: "Then don't say you're being abandoned."

"I know what I'm doing."

She brushed past him and around to the driver's side and into the car. He settled into the passenger side and took some deep breaths, the drowning feeling pressing at his chest again. There was a moment of silence as they both listened to their own breathing. Outside, just above the endless drone of all that invisible crawling life, another sound—the mechanical whine of a truck in low gear, straining up the mountain road.

"Oh, God," she said. "Parnell must have called out the army."

Decker laughed. He hoped it was only Givins and Baines, but he didn't dare tell Leslie about the wire. It felt now like a betrayal.

"He could have, believe me," Leslie said. She started up the car. It promptly stalled.

"Here," she said, handing Decker Tony's gun. "Be prepared to use it."

"How?"

"I don't know. Figure it out."

She stomped the gas pedal and ground the ignition while he held the gun in his bandaged hand. There was no way he could get his finger on the trigger. He considered removing the bandages but his grip was probably useless anyway. So he stuck the gun between the brake handle and his seat, barrel pointed down, then reached under his cushion and pulled out the tape.

At last the car started, the whole frame shuddering. Leslie gave it gas and put out her hand. "I'll take that."

"Sorry, it's not yours."

"Yes it is. It's my ass showing on that tape. Hand it over, bub."

"It will be state's evidence soon enough."

"No, it won't. It's bad enough *you* saw the tape."

"Will you use it to convict Parnell?"

"Don't be ridiculous. No one's going to *convict* Parnell. I intend to use that tape to do exactly what Justin and I had planned to do all along—scare the hell out of Stuart Parnell. I'll make him back down on the AIDS bill, and I'll make him leave me the hell alone."

The truck was drawing nearer. Down the hill, fractured bits of headlight strobed through the trees and vines.

"You're not thinking, Leslie. Parnell is finished. Zilch. A nobody. With this tape, we can nail Parnell without even going to court. Every TV tabloid show and news station in America will be dying for footage. Christ, they'll make two-hour primetime specials out of this thing."

"Rick, it's my privacy and my life. Give it to me."

She reached over and picked up the gun.

"Oh, come off it, Leslie."

"I'll shoot, Rick. I don't give a damn about your story."

She leveled the gun at his chest. He heard the determination in her hard breathing. "I'll do it, Rick. I've come too far to stop now."

"Listen to me," he said. "It's not just for me. It's for Justin, for you—for everyone. We can't let Parnell get away with this."

"He *will* get away. And my only protection is that tape."

"You can't run for the rest of your life, Leslie."

"How much life do I have left?"

She meant to be flip, but her voice quavered on the last few words. The sound of it bit into his heart.

"Is it what you really want?" he said.

He knew then that nothing, not even Parnell's hide, was worth adding to her pain.

She lowered the gun and sobbed, "Yes."

He handed her the tape. "I wish you all the luck in the world."

He stepped out of the car and closed the door. There was an endless series of things now he wished he could undo.

"Aren't you coming?" she said.

The time had come to tell her. "There's no place to run, Leslie. They know everything. I've been wired the entire time."

"You shit! I don't believe this. Whose wire?"

"Givins and Baines."

"How could you?" She threw up her hands. "I can't believe this."

They both saw the headlights appear at the far end of the driveway, a good hundred yards away. The lights were bouncing slowly up the narrow gravel road.

"I'll send you a postcard," Leslie shouted.

She rammed the gearshift into reverse like pulling a trigger and the car spun backward in the wet grass. She stopped, rammed it into first, and started fishtailing around the periphery of the open field looking for a way out. There was none, only a green wall of trees and shrubs and tangled vines.

The truck, an old Chevy with a wooden flatbed in the back, swerved left at the end of the drive and skidded to a stop on the gravel, blocking any chance for an exit. The driver's door popped open and a black man jumped out. He immediately took cover behind the front hood.

Leslie picked up speed as she swung the Vega around and veered back toward the truck. It was clear where she was heading: a cluster of bushes between the left fender of the truck and the driveway. She intended to plow through.

Her headlights caught Baines as he raised his gun onto the hood. It was a long shiny Smith & Wesson, something right out of a cowboy matinee.

Decker ran screaming, hands in the air. "Don't shoot!"

Baines jumped from view a fraction of a second before the Vega smashed through. The car's front end nosed in the air and landed on gravel, but the rear snagged in the bushes, the back wheels throwing up branches and leaves like a weed eater. The engine growled, gasped, and died.

Decker could hear Leslie shrieking inside the car. He ran faster, but before he could reach the car, Givins stepped out of the truck and blocked the way.

"She's fine," he said. "Just a bit upset with herself." He was unruffled in his starched shirt and black tie.

Decker stood behind the Vega. He could see Leslie pounding her fists against the steering wheel. The smell of defeat—burnt oil, burnt rubber—clung to the damp air.

Baines reappeared from the bushes and went around to the front of the car and stood in the headlights. He steadied the big gun in both hands, aiming through the windshield.

"Don't shoot her!" Decker shouted. Givins was still blocking his way. "She's OK! Do you hear me?"

"Let us handle this, please," Givins said. He had a flashlight in his hand. "Is she armed?"

"There's a gun in the car. I don't think she'll use it."

"I suggest you stay clear, Mr. Decker."

"There's no reason to shoot her. She didn't kill anyone."

Decker tried to control his panic as Givins approached the driver's door. Maybe Leslie was right. Maybe the whole island was working for Parnell.

Givins stopped just short of the door. He flashed the light inside.

"Remove yourself from the car. Hands on your head, please."

Leslie broke out laughing, high-pitched and hysterical.

"Dammit, Leslie!" Decker shouted. "Don't be stupid!"

Givins repeated the order, less politely this time. Baines cocked the hammer on the big Smith & Wesson.

Decker wanted to leap onto the car. "Leslie, goddammit!"

She laughed again and shouted through her window, "I can't! The door's stuck!"

Baines tightened his grip on the gun.

"Then please exit from the passenger side," Givins said.

Decker held his breath as Leslie reached over, her head disappearing behind the passenger seat. The door popped open. She moved slowly over the emergency brake to the passenger seat, all the while Baines tracking the movement of her head. She gripped the top of the open door, the Vega rocking a little on its nest of limbs and leaves, and pulled herself out.

When she stood and shut the door, Decker drew a deep breath, thinking it was all over except the handcuffs and the tears.

Baines was moving in closer, his face impassive and calm, when Leslie suddenly screamed and fell.

Baines fired. It was like a cannon shot in the dense night air, rolling thunder through the hills.

Time stopped and gravity seemed to disappear as Decker scrambled over the trunk and over the roof of the car. He leaped onto the driveway, landing on his hands and feet, and found Leslie already kneeling there, laughing. Lying in front of her like a broken necklace was a red-and-black snake, shiny as vinyl in the side glare from the headlights. The bullet had cut it neatly in two.

"Coral snake," Baines said, lowering his big gun. "Quite poisonous."

Givins came around to the front of the car in his own good time. "Well done, Sgt. Baines," he said. "I see you've been practicing."

"Yes, sir. Mostly for sport."

Decker helped Leslie to her feet but Givins stepped in and separated the two and handed Leslie over to Baines.

Givins eased Decker aside. "You needn't worry, Mr. Decker. We have most everything on tape."

"Then what the hell took you so long?"

"We were detained while making arrangements to borrow this exquisite vehicle," he said, pointing to the truck. "Fortunately, it came equipped with a large gun."

"Why didn't you call in the Spanish Town unit?"

"No one in. They were dispatched to Dead Chest, I am told. A matter of a stolen boat."

"Tony?"

"Possibly."

Leslie was leaning against the side of the truck while

Baines frisked her respectfully at arm's length. Decker wondered if he would find the tape.

"I'd like to contact a lawyer," Leslie said. "Do you allow that in this country?"

Givins was the one who answered. "You may—in due time. Lansforth, escort her to the back of the truck."

Baines gently turned her around. He pulled a pair of worn brass handcuffs from a back pocket and had her hold out her hands.

"You're not charging her?" Decker said.

Givins nodded. "Attempted assault on an officer of the peace. Complicity in extortion and blackmail."

"She saved my life," Decker said. "She had nothing to do with the murders."

"Yes, we know. It came through on the wire."

"Then why take her in?"

"In part because that is the law. In part for her own good. As you know, Mr. Parnell is a very powerful man."

Baines took Leslie by the arm and brought her over to where Givins and Decker were standing, just in front of the Vega's headlights. He stopped her several feet away.

"She wants a private word with Mr. Decker," he said.

"I see no problem with that," Givins said, and turned to Decker.

Baines backed away a little as Decker approached. Leslie smiled coquettishly, the old flirt again, her blue eyes dazed and shining in the headlights.

"Closer," she said, as though it were a game of trust me.

He reached out and hugged her, bending at the waist to make room for her cuffed hands. She slid her glossy cheek along his and whispered in his ear, "The tape is under the seat, darlin'."

When they separated, she smiled, a peaceful look that said not to worry, and then Baines led her away to the back of the truck. He watched her go, her dignity somehow still intact in the careful way she held her hands, fingers laced, elbows tight to her sides. He thought it an outrage that she should be treated like a common criminal.

Givins laid a hand on Decker's shoulder. "And where might our primary suspect be?"

He was forced to think a moment, having completely forgotten Tony. "Hold on," he said. "I'll need the keys."

Here was his chance, he thought. He went around to the Vega's passenger door and crawled into the front seat on his hands and knees. He found the tape with his first swipe under the driver's side, pinched it between his thumb and bandage, and discreetly stuffed it in his pocket. Then he snagged the keys from the ignition and hopped out.

"He's in the trunk," he said. He handed Givins the keys.

With Decker following, Givins squeezed through the bushes back to the trunk and opened it.

Tony was still motionless.

Givins placed his fingertips along Tony's neck. "He's alive."

"What a shame," Decker said.

They lifted Tony out of the trunk and dragged him by the legs and arms to the back of the truck. With Baines's help, they heaved him onto the makeshift wooden truckbed.

Leslie was already there, sitting lotus-style behind the cab, her head bent in exhaustion. Baines helped position the body crosswise between himself and Leslie, then settled back against the side gate with the Smith & Wesson in his hand.

"What about Justin?" Decker asked.

"We can return in the morning. I'm certain he has no travel plans for tonight."

Givins opened the driver's side of the truck cab. "After you, Mr. Decker."

Decker climbed in and slid over the sticky vinyl to the passenger seat. The cab was filled with a pungent blend of odors—gasoline, manure, ancient mold, and sweat.

Givins started the truck and whipped it around in the grass, grazing the old stone well with his right tire. At the end of the driveway, he took a right down the mountain road. Looking over the left fender, thousands of feet below, they could both see Spanish Town—a thin necklace of twinkling lights along the bay.

Decker's chest was still pounding with excitement, exhaustion, a tinge of disbelief. It was finished. The tape was in his pocket, the puzzle solved. All that was left was nailing Parnell.

"What might be your plans now, Mr. Decker?"

Givins was bouncing in his seat, both hands steady on the wheel. In his white shirt and black tie, he could have been a farmer on his way to a Saturday night revival.

"I write my story, sleep, go back to Cincinnati."

Givins was silent a moment, considering. "You are not afraid, then, of Congressman Parnell."

"No. Not once my story's in print."

"Ah, yes. So you think the pen is mightier than the sword."

"Sometimes. It depends on how sharp the pen is."

"And perhaps how damning the videotape."

Givins turned and grinned and Decker's heart sank to his seat, thinking he would demand the tape.

But Givins only laughed a little and turned his eyes back to the road.

# 13

As big and macho as its name, the ferry *Bomba Charger* was plowing the sea waves at breakneck speed when it looped wide to the north for the entry into Road Town harbor. It was the third ferry of the morning from St. Thomas, via Virgin Gorda, on schedule for a 10:00 A.M. arrival and jammed with islanders dressed in their colorful finest for a Saturday of shopping. On it, too, were the far less festive passengers of the *Southern Cross*, all of whom had spent the night scattered in hotels in Spanish Town—paid for out of their own pockets—after Captain Pearce had put them off the ship. All in all, it had been a fitting end, Decker thought, for a cruise that had never quite lived up to its billing. Still, no one could complain about the weather that morning: It was one more perfect day of fragrant breezes and rapturous sunshine.

Decker was among the *Southern Cross* refugees soaking up their last bit of sunshine on the ferry's upper deck.

For him, the cruise had been both a dream and a cathartic nightmare. Janet was far from his thoughts now, as far as if she occupied some distant land he had inhabited long ago and to which he would never return. He basked now in that sad, wistful feeling—touched with expectation—of one journey in his life coming to an end and a new one about to begin. Back home, far from these steaming islands and burning sun, the chilled clarity of fall was already on its way. He looked forward to that, but he would also miss the islands, the dazzling sun and sea and fragrant air, and Leslie, who would be alloyed to all those things in his memory, infusing them forever with mystery, allure, danger, tragedy.

Decker felt surprisingly alert considering he'd stayed up most of the night. Givins had dropped him off at the La Ti Da, where he checked into one of the plush second-story suites, ordered coffee and croissants, then cleaned up his sutured, throbbing hands and got down to writing. It felt good—shamefully so—to pull together all the horrific pieces of the last few days and put them down in words and make them mean something, anything.

When he finished the piece, sometime around 4:00 A.M., he couldn't sleep. He lay in bed, lights on, thinking carefully about what he should do with the tape. It no longer made sense to carry it with him, especially if Parnell's people were still on the island. He needed to mail it, ship it somehow, but the Spanish Town post office was no doubt crawling with surveillance. The clerks might be intercepting packages, too, anything addressed to the States.

He had an idea. It was 5:00 A.M. He found his submarine adventure novel and, using the pocket knife he kept in his shaving kit, carved a rectangular block from the inside pages. He dropped the tape inside, wrapped the book in part of an old shopping bag he found in the closet trash, and headed downstairs to the reception desk.

The night desk clerk was an older man, gentle looking, with hair and mustache dyed back to the approximate chestnut color of his youth. Decker slipped him one of the hundred-dollar bills he kept tucked away in his wallet for bribing emergencies, then wrote down the address of Fred Gomez, an old Columbia buddy of his who was now a Paris correspondent for a business magazine. Decker promised to send the clerk another hundred once the package arrived.

"Really?" the man said, a twinkle in his hazel eyes. "Well,

I'm not that expensive. Just send me a note and let me know how you're doing, okay?"

Just before 8:00 A.M., Decker put the finishing touches on his story—scribbled out in longhand on a legal pad, and slopped here and there with coffee—and phoned the metro desk. Far-lidge, that suck-up, was already in his office.

"Decker, if you ever hang up on me again like you—"

"Shut up, Ron, and take some dictation."

Farlidge grumbled, but once he'd heard the first sentence of the story, grew quiet, then increasingly excited, interrupting Decker several times with shouts of "Un-fucking-believable!"

When Decker had finished, Farlidge said, "I'll call Sally Beth immediately, and we'll start putting together a page one centerpiece."

"What do you think of the lead, Ron?"

"Inspired. Let's keep it the way it is."

Decker had been unable to resist a bit of tabloid sensation-alism:

SPANISH TOWN, *Virgin Gorda*—Blue had been his favorite color in life, and so in death it was no surprise to find Justin Grammer swaddled in blankets of blue.

Grammer's body was discovered early this morning in a mountain stable near this small Caribbean resort town. There was a single bullet wound in his forehead.

The disappearance and death of Grammer, 22, the eldest son of one of Cincinnati's wealthiest and oldest families, is a story of adultery, blackmail, murder, and political intrigue. It's a disturbing and treacherous tale that reaches from the gay bathhouses of the Caribbean to the marbled halls of Congress.

Authorities have so far arrested one man in connection with Grammer's death—Tony Henderson, age unknown, who claims to be a Dallas engineer and former Navy SEALs com-mando. Police here have yet to confirm his identity.

Expected to testify against him is Leslie Stanton, 29, a top
aide to powerful U.S. Rep. L. Stuart Parnell (D-S.C.), who
herself has been implicated in a plot to blackmail Parnell . . .

The story went on to detail the blackmail scheme, the lurid sex
tape, and the death of Danielle Evans, whom Decker called a
"top fashion model" for want of a less tabloidlike label. He kept
Ellen out of the piece altogether, still uncertain as to how much
she knew of the scheme and when. He would try to reach her
by phone in New York once he returned to the States. He
prayed she'd made it safely.

Decker demanded and won a sidebar to the main story
detailing the congressional bill Justin had died trying to sabotage
and, after some loud wrangling with Farlidge, got a promise that
Simmons, the paper's Washington correspondent, would write
it that morning.

"You were right. It's got everything," Farlidge told him on
the phone. "And we scooped the whole country on it. Now tell
me sending you on that cruise wasn't a brilliant idea."

"Muchos kudos, Ron. But try to remember two people are
very dead."

"They'd be dead anyway."

"Don't be so sure."

Decker still felt the sting of Leslie's accusation—that Tony
would have never found Justin had Decker not been so insistent
about an interview. Maybe. But he kept telling himself that if he
hadn't intervened, hadn't found the tape, Tony would have
killed them all—not just Danielle and Justin but Leslie and
Ellen as well.

Decker's biggest frustration was not being able to name
Parnell as the prime culprit, although the story dropped more
than a few hints in that direction. After a quick phone conference
with the managing editor, Farlidge decided against directly

accusing Parnell, since it was only the word of Leslie—who was charged with blackmail—against Parnell's. Farlidge argued that the links between Parnell and Tony would come out during the trial anyway. In the end, Decker didn't care: He had the tape, which was more than enough to sink Parnell and launch a major congressional investigation.

"What about pictures?" Farlidge said.

"What do you mean pictures? Rebo's gone."

"Negatory. He refused to leave. He thought you might need help."

"Where the hell is he?"

"A place called the Sand Man Hotel. Somewhere in Road Town. Tell him we need pictures of the distillery."

"Ron, I'm not sure I can even find it again."

"You'll have to."

"No, Ron. My plane leaves in four hours. I plan to be on it and out of here."

"You realize this is insubordination."

"Add it to my file."

"Forget it," he said, sounding indifferent now. "I'll see if AP can do it." Then his voice became a leer. "By the way, are you premiering that tape when you get back?"

"No one sees the tape except me and the proper authorities."

"Oh, come on."

"There's no 'come on' about it, Ron. If you guys need to see some skin, go hit the nudie bars in Kentucky."

Dealing with Farlidge was child's play compared to Decker's next call that morning, the one he'd been dreading since the night before. He took a deep breath and punched the numbers for the Grammer estate in Indian Hill. A man who sounded suspiciously like a cop answered the phone. Decker identified himself and asked for Felix Grammer.

"He's not in."

"I've got important information about his son."

"What's the name again?"

"Rick Decker. With the *Eagle.*"

"Why is there so much static on this line?"

Decker spoke more loudly. "I'm calling from the Virgin Islands. I have urgent information about Mr. Grammer's son."

"Why don't you tell me and I'll tell Mr. Grammer."

"Because it's private, that's why. Who are you?"

"Never mind who I am. I know who you are. You're one more scum of a reporter trying to weasel an interview."

"Listen, asshole. In about three hours, the *Eagle* will hit the streets with a front page story detailing exactly what has happened to Justin Grammer. Now if that's how his father gets the news, I'm holding you personally responsible for his reaction. Now what's *your* name?"

There was a moment of silence at the other end, the sound, perhaps, of stifled rage being weighed against a weekly paycheck. Then, in a subdued tone, the man said: "I'll see if I can locate him."

"Make it quick."

A few seconds later, an older man answered the phone in a deep, refined voice that sounded as if it had never been raised, had never needed to be.

"This is Felix Grammer. May I help you?"

Decker identified himself for the third time and said he had bad news about Justin. "The worst, I'm afraid, sir—your son is dead."

There was silence at the other end, but this time the motivation was harder to guess. When he spoke again, Felix Grammer sounded irritated and somewhat skeptical: "Why haven't the police notified me?"

"They will. I just wanted to warn you that the *Eagle* will be running a story this afternoon. I'm afraid your son was murdered."

Decker expected a sob, a gasp, an expression of outrage, anything, but all the old man said was, "Tell me, do you plan to dredge up past details of my son's life?"

"You mean the fact that he was gay?"

Again, an icy silence. Decker went on: "I'm afraid I'll have to. It was partly your son's devotion to gay rights that led to his being murdered."

"I see." The voice was dry, impersonal. "So you're saying my son deserved to be murdered."

"Not at all. But he took a big chance with some very powerful people, and he paid the price for it."

"Tell me," the voice said confidentially, "who is your editor?"

Decker wasn't intimidated. No one, not even Felix Grammer, was big enough to kill the story of Justin Grammer and Stuart Parnell. It was bigger than all of them.

"Ron Farlidge. You want his number?"

"That won't be necessary." Without a thank you or an angry word, Grammer simply hung up—probably, Decker thought, the way he'd hung up on his son all his life.

The passengers from the *Southern Cross* were scattered around the ferry's open deck. Art and his wife were sitting together at the very back, wanting, it seemed, to be left alone. Art had told Decker earlier that he hated saying good-bye. "There were too many men in the war I never saw again. Good men like you."

Lyle was at the front, sitting on a bench behind the pilot house, his feet perched on his big hard-shell suitcase and his hands massaging the back of his neck and skull. Lyle was easy to read: He was hung over.

Off to Decker's left, Ryan was standing at the port rail with

Jenny, holding her hand as though it were some precious object quite separate from Jenny. As the ferry cut across the open harbor, headed for the pier and the inevitable parting, the two were whispering, no doubt exchanging all the innocent young lies of summer's end, about writing and visiting and never forgetting.

Maureen and Connie were sitting together one row of seats ahead of Decker and off to his right. Maureen was holding her face and hair up to the wind and sun, trying, it seemed, to capture some final essence of the Caribbean, while daughter Connie was staring at the deck in a deep funk. Every now and then she would steal a backward glance at the open sea, a mix of longing and contempt on her young face that only a teenager could muster.

With the ferry nearly on top of the pier, the pilot waited until the last safe instant to throttle the engines. The big boat nosed down into the water, drifted for a second or two, then suddenly bumped and chattered as the propellers were thrown into reverse. The ferry sidled up to the pier like a waterborne bronco, bucking, pivoting, thudding against the buffers.

Hundreds of islanders jostled on the pier, a carpet of brightly colored clothing and black, shining faces, eager to board for the return trip. Among them, Decker spotted a tall, immovable object—thick arms folded below his chest, thick legs planted like tree trunks on the pier.

While the ferry was still maneuvering into place, Decker went downstairs and squeezed ahead through the other passengers. He was one of the first to hit the pier when the boarding gates opened. Rebo was there to greet him with a handshake and a clamped hand that nearly paralyzed his shoulder. He was dressed in the bright, cool cottons of the islands—red and yellow shirt, white shorts—and a pair of black leather sandals.

"Man, do you have any idea how hard I've been tryin' to reach you?"

Decker scoped his new outfit. "You mean, when you weren't too busy shopping?"

Rebo jabbed his arm. "Seriously, man. I took the ferry out to Spanish Town yesterday, hung out all afternoon at Rudy's. Then somebody tells me the ship is sailin' back to Road Town, so I head back here, only the damn ship never comes. I feel like a captain's widow."

"You're forgiven."

"I talked to Farlidge this morning. I guess I missed all the fun."

"Far more than you can imagine."

They went back along the pier to where the suitcases were being unloaded and started the anxious search and wait for their luggage. Rebo was especially concerned about what was left of his camera equipment. It wasn't long before he spotted a young deckhand holding a steel suitcase above his head, about to heave it toward the other luggage stacked like cordwood in the middle of the pier. Rebo snatched it out of his hands so quickly the boy thought he'd been mugged.

Decker had just found his green duffel bag when Maureen came up and pecked him softly on the cheek. "Thanks," she said, backing away again. She nodded toward Ryan, who was pulling down a massive suitcase from the top of the luggage pile. "You can't imagine what a difference you've made," she said.

"He's a great kid."

"Isn't he, though?" She was beaming. "You'll have to come visit us in Seattle sometime. We have lots of room."

"I'll try. You know how those things go."

"Say you'll come anyway. Ryan would love it, and so would I."

Decker was saved from a direct lie when Ryan and Connie came over dragging the last of their things. Connie stood off by herself looking impatient and embarrassed while Ryan stepped up and shook hands with Rebo and Decker and started talking to everyone at once. "Hey, maybe we could all do this again next year. I mean, on a different ship. Jenny said she and her mom go every year."

"Honey, Rick may have other plans by next year."

Decker smiled. "It might be nice to see the islands under more relaxed conditions."

"Promise?" Ryan said.

"We'll see."

Connie started to whine: "Mo-o-m, we'll miss the plane." Ryan tugged his mother's arm: "Dibs on the window seat, okay?"

Decker and Rebo helped them load their bags onto a dolly and then watched as the family headed down the pier to a line of waiting taxis. Ryan turned once and gave the high sign. Decker ached a little in the sudden knowing he would never see him again, or Leslie, or Ellen, or any of the people he'd come to know on the cruise. It felt like the last day of summer camp.

"Come on," Rebo said. "Let's grab our stuff and get the hell out. My wife is waitin' at home for her propers."

They dragged their things to the narrow street at the end of the pier and started competing with a dozen other passengers for a taxi. The air there was stifling, the sea breezes of their voyage gone.

"Listen," Decker said to Rebo. "You go on to the airport. I'll meet you there." He couldn't leave the islands without a final word with Leslie.

"No way, pal. We leave together or we don't leave at all. I'm not traipsing all over these damn islands trying to find you if you don't show up."

"I'll be at Road Town prison."

"As if I didn't know."

"I'll only be a minute."

"How do you know you won't run into one of Parnell's flunkies? And all for some damn woman who can't keep her ass out of trouble."

"She saved my life, Rebo."

"All right, fine, dammit. If you have to go, then let's go together and be done with it."

"I knew you'd see it my way."

Rebo grunted.

Out of nowhere, an old brown Corolla with darkly tinted windows squeezed through the traffic and pulled to a quick stop by the curb where they waited. Reggae thumped and skittled from the car's dark insides, rattling all the doors.

The passenger door swung open and a deep voice shouted over the music, "Airport?"

Decker shouted back. "No, Road Town prison."

"Hop in, mon!"

The driver was a total surprise: He looked like a punked-out suburban white kid—black hair buzzed, Ray•Bans on, gold studs dotting his right ear like so many upholstery tacks.

"Is this a cab?" Decker asked.

The driver pointed to his meter.

"Just get in," Rebo said impatiently, tossing their things in the backseat. Then he got a glimpse of the driver. "Oh, shit. Swing low sweet chariot."

"Any port in a storm," Decker said.

Rebo piled in the backseat, Decker in front. A deodorizer hung from the rearview mirror. The car smelled like a freshly cleaned urinal.

The driver turned down the music, pulled down the Ray•Bans. "Long time, no see, mon."

Decker felt a jolt as he connected with a pair of deep blue eyes. A second later, he burst into laughter.

"Look at you!" he said. "What in the hell—? Wait a minute. Did you make bail?"

"Bail, shmail. Hang on to your seat belts."

Leslie zoomed off into the crowded street honking at hapless pedestrians and bikers. She seemed born to the profession.

"I'm driving you guys to the other side of the island. There'll be a boat waiting there to take you to St. Thomas. From there, you can fly straight to Miami."

"What about our reservations?" Decker said. "We were supposed to fly to San Juan this afternoon."

"Take it from me, you don't want to be anywhere near San Juan. Parnell has his people there ready to strip-search both of you. If they don't find the tape, they'll plant drugs in your luggage and you'll be in deep doodoo with the DEA by the time you arrive in Miami."

"Terrific. Now how the hell do you know all this, and what are you doing out of jail?"

Before she could answer, Decker slammed his hands against the dash as the car screeched to a halt. There was a truck stopped in the road just a few yards ahead, loaded with a mountain of mango crates, part of which had toppled and lay smashed and scattered on the road. Oncoming traffic streamed around the mess while Leslie pounded the horn.

Decker glanced behind the car, fearing it might be a setup or a squeeze play, but there were only taxis and bicycles as far as the eye could see.

Leslie settled down enough to resume the conversation. "Let's say I 'escaped' last night," she said, "with a little help from our friends, Givins and Baines."

"You bribed them."

"You don't give them any credit, Rick."

"*I* don't."

"They know they can't fight Parnell in court. Too many people above them on the take. But they don't have any love for Stu, either, believe me. They've seen to it personally that Rebo, you, and I come out okay."

Finally, in a cloud of diesel smoke, the truck lumbered off to the right side of the road. Leslie zigzagged through the fallen crates and zoomed up the empty lane.

Within minutes they were on the outskirts of town, where the run-down shops and motels disappeared and the bright green hills began, trembling in the late morning heat. The road forked: left to go inland, right to follow the oceanfront. Leslie veered right.

"What about Tony?" Decker asked.

Leslie took a deep breath. There was something amused and bloodless in her smile. "Tony was shot this morning in the act of fleeing," she said.

"Jesus. Killed?"

"Very. One of the guards at the detention center filled me in before I left. Apparently somebody slipped Tony a gun. It was loaded with blanks."

"Givins?"

"It could have been anybody. Maybe Parnell. Nobody wanted Tony to talk."

Decker had no sympathy for the man, but the cold-bloodedness of the scheme nearly made him shiver. "This thing is out of control, isn't it?"

"Welcome to Washington politics."

"That's all the more reason we should nail Parnell."

"We?" Leslie said.

"Aren't you coming with us?"

She shook her head. "I've done a lot of thinking about my future—limited as it might be. I want to start a new life here."

They were out of town and in the clear now, cruising along a paved two-lane coastal road. The smooth ride seemed a luxury. On their right, waves slapped and foamed over the rocky berm. To their left, the island greenery climbed straight up the hillside and into the blue.

"They'll find you, Leslie. Why don't you come back to the States and help us get Parnell. You can dicker with the feds and never spend an hour in jail."

"No way. I've had it up to here with lawyers and lobbyists and that whole sleazy scene. I'm spending time down here. Givins says he can help me find work on one of the chartered yachts. They never spend more than two nights in any one place, and as long as they pay their dock fees, nobody ever bothers them. I could certainly find that an attractive life-style for a while."

"And when you get sick?"

"Then I get sick. Who knows? I may have another five, seven years before that happens. At least here I'll be under far less strain."

They rounded a sharp curve to their left—the southeastern tip of Tortola. Leslie slowed down a tick or two. "There's your boat," she said.

A quarter mile ahead, anchored a safe distance from the rocks, a shining white Catalina bobbed in the morning sun.

Leslie crossed the center line and pulled left off the road, stopping along a narrow sandy strip at the foot of the hill. They could smell the spray coming off the rocks on the other side of the road—the fecund, feminine smell of the sea.

"The pilot's name is Dickson," she said. "He'll take good care of you."

"I don't know how to thank you," Decker said. He heard Rebo groan in the back seat.

"You don't have to," Leslie said. "Just come look me up in a couple of years."

"How do I find you?"

"Ask Givins. He'll know."

"Come on," Rebo said, opening the back door. "I'm not getting stuck on this island for the rest of my life." He stepped outside and began pulling out their things.

Leslie turned to Decker, a rueful but determined look in her eyes, then bent forward and kissed him lightly on the cheek. "Good-bye," she said softly. "I won't forget you."

Decker clenched his hand behind her head and gave her a kiss to remember. Her eyes were still closed when he moved to the door. "You'll be seeing me again," he said.

"You'd better not be lying. I had enough of that in Washington."

"Take care, darlin'," he said, teasing.

"You, too, bub. It's a dangerous world out there."

The blue eyes gave him one last shining look as he closed the door.

Leslie peeled out of the sand and swerved on to the road. In a few seconds, the little Corolla disappeared around the bend, the dying sound suddenly cut off by the hillside, and all that was left was the shimmering illusion of the sea and the foaming of the rocks, calling them home.